the ~~Marie~~ ve

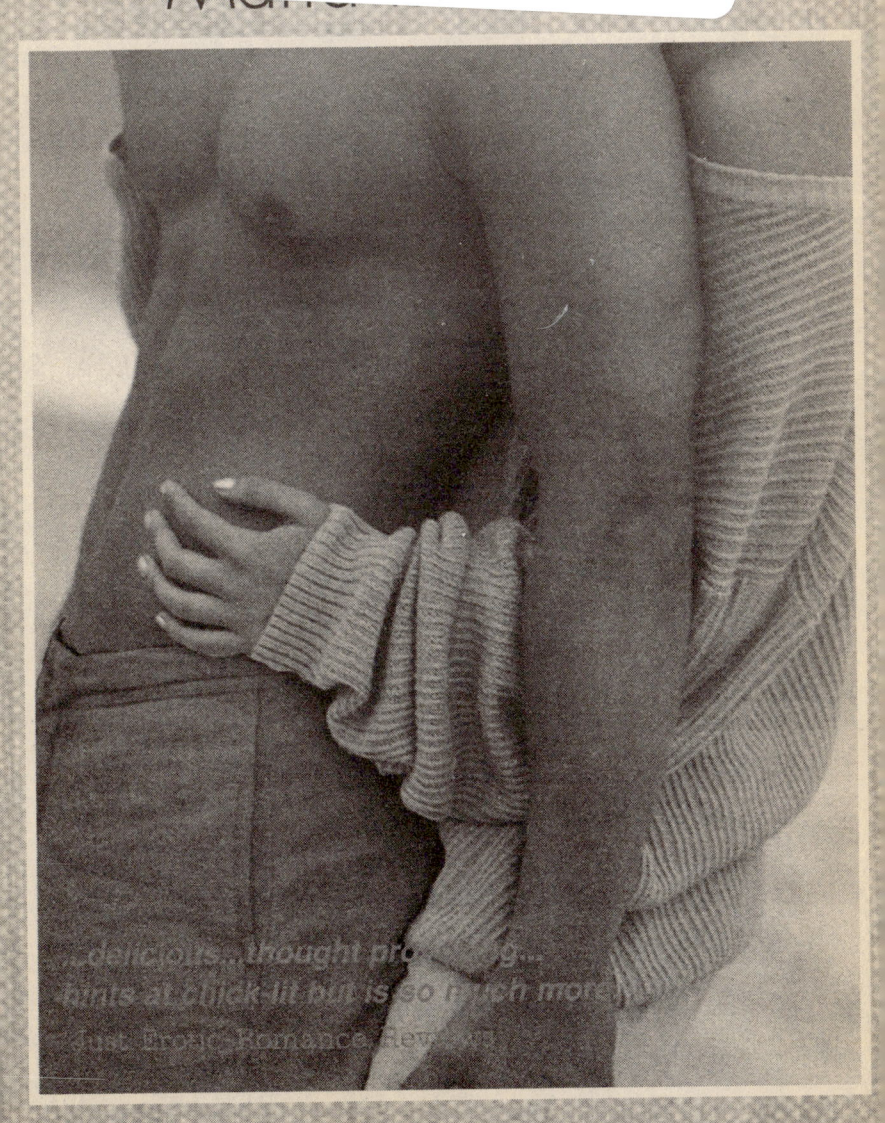

...delicious...thought pro...ng...
hints at chick-lit but is so much more...
Just Erotic Romance Reviews

an erotic romance

THE FABRIC OF LOVE
Copyright ©2004 by Magic Carpet Books, Inc.
All Rights Reserved

No part of this book may be reproduced,
stored in a retrieval system, or transmitted in any form,
by any means, including mechanical, electronic,
photocopying, recording or otherwise, without
prior written permission from the publisher and author.

First Magic Carpet Books, Inc. edition September 2004

Published in 2004

Manufactured in the United States of America
Published by Magic Carpet Books, Inc.

Magic Carpet Books, Inc.
PO Box 473
New Milford, CT 06776

Library of Congress Cataloging in Publication Date

The Fabric of Love By Maria Isabel Pita

ISBN# 09755331-3-4

Book Design: P. Ruggieri

THE FABRIC OF LOVE

Maria Isabel Pita

DEDICATION

*For Stinger, the man I love.
Thank you for always believing in me, and for giving me more
than I can ever express no matter how many books I write.*

*And for Merlin, who always keeps me company
while I write by passionately chewing his bone or sleeping
and dreaming curled up at my feet.*

AUTHOR'S NOTE

Last night the full moon felt like a spotlight shining in my brain and pulling on the wet strings of all my veins as if my mortal flesh is some kind of corset relentlessly being tightened by myriad efforts at self-improvement, so I can look and be my absolute best for that elusive man – that dream I had – of a life-long soul-mate.

I couldn't sleep. According to the flaming red numbers on my digital clock, I lay awake from about 2:29 to some time after 4:00 thinking and thinking; weaving thought after thought without coming to any wearable conclusions. Then I must have fallen asleep at last because I had a nightmare that the man I loved no longer loved me. He was featureless – his face was composed of all the photographs of us being happy together – and I was so furious and grief-stricken that I clawed viciously into these falsely idyllic images with my fingernails. He smiled placidly, maddeningly, and said, 'These things happen.' It was a profound relief to wake up again to the moon's unblinking glare like a divine hand shining a flashlight into the cobwebs of my thought processes as I thankfully remembered true love isn't a dream. The net of circumstances fashioning my life had indeed finally captured my heart's desire. Part of me still couldn't quite believe it (hence the nightmares) but it was true, and I smiled contentedly as I gazed at his naked body lying beside mine, long and sleek and relaxed as a big cat's on our moonlit bed.

Every day we spend together, all the words we say to each other, every thought, every feeling we share, every experience, every hope, every sadness, every dream is part of the fabric of our love, of our life which has become magically one. Sometimes the emotional fabric of our relationship is as mysteriously stimulating as black leather; often it's as cozy and comfortable as a cotton throw on a cold winter night; and always it makes even the roughest circumstances feel smooth as satin, rich as velvet and warm as silk-lined wool. Whatever the emotional fabric of our love, I know in my soul that it's woven with an unbreakable and somehow eternal thread. Maybe one day I'll learn how to sew a dress, but for now I'll stick to what I do best and tell the story of how two other lovers met…

PROLOGUE

"And as she worked, gazing at times out on the snow, she pricked her finger, and there fell from it three drops of blood on the snow... Not very long after she had a daughter, with skin as white as snow, lips as red as blood, and hair as black as ebony..."

Once upon a time – right now, actually – there lives a beautiful young woman named Mira. Her last name doesn't matter, but if you must know it's Rosemond, inherited from her father like half the genes in her pool, although 'microcosmic sea' would be a better analogy for the depth of thoughts and feelings composing her unique personality. Nevertheless, it was the sensual hum of 'Mm' and the buzzing energy of 'ee' and the profoundly joyful sigh of 'ra!' that greeted her when she entered the world, cradling her soul in consonants and vowels forming a special sound to make her feel at home in her individual mystery. You might argue that children's names are picked at random, but it can also be said there is no such thing as coincidence, and in Mira's case the name given her at birth truly suited her. In Spanish 'mira' means 'look' and look she did from day one, avidly studying her surroundings from the moment her eyes opened, and it wasn't long before she was curiously touching and assessing the shape and texture of everything she could get her pudgy (and already passionately possessive) little hands on. Her parents fondly brag to friends that their daughter was born an Interior Designer. From a very early age, Mira frowned severely, scrunching her face up in warning that a fit of outraged howling was imminent, if whatever they hung up over her crib didn't please her. Plastic toys and mobiles painted in garish primary colors were at once banished from her bedroom, and silvery, lavender-colored wallpaper glimmering with hints of forest green in the sunlight soothingly surrounded her as she was growing up, having immediately replaced a terrifying décor of painted teddy bears and other zoologically unrealistic nightmares.

Mira grew up a child of the four seasons – fall, winter, spring and summer were all clearly defined in her psyche. If she had any complaint it was that it didn't snow quite enough to get her out of school. The white-washed dullness of public school classrooms was an affront to her senses, including her sixth sense – from a very early age she sensed that learning about the world was supposed to be a lot more fun and entertaining in the sense of involving her whole being, which consisted of her feelings and imagination as well as her fact-filled brain. Fortunately, the world outside was glorious, and when the weather was nice she liked taking her Barbie's camping down by the creek. She loved seeing their colorfully made-up and perpetually smiling faces contrasted against dark, hard, threatening rocks. It was unbelievably exciting to Mira that her surrogate selves actually got wet, and that there was real danger of them being carried away by the current, the dirt tainting their pure, plastic skins making it look vulnerably alive. She almost ecstatically enjoyed exposing her sensual dolls to the elements. She loved seeing the sun shining on the different colors of their hair, and the water lapping around their stiffly swimming arms and legs. Her own large, living hands were in control of their fate, holding and maneuvering their bodies the way the laws of the physical world she was learning about in science class surrounded her. This childish perception eventually led her to conclude a part of her was a vast, immortal awareness expressing Itself through the laws of manifestation – an eternal consciousness enjoying endless experiences of Itself through the dolls of its incarnations. But at the time she was still much too young to entertain such profound metaphysical thoughts. She simply relished the feel of the cool, rushing water contrasting with the warm caress of sunlight on her skin, and the dark thrill she experienced as she subjected her numerous pretend bodies to the sucking depth of the mud between the slick rocks on which they perched as lovely as mermaids. Her mind had not yet so defined it, but in her soul she knew all the world's elements were there for her soul to be creative with. Even before she could express the concept, she knew her spirit was immutable in essence no matter what happened to the forms through which it adventured and however much it loved them. That's not to say she wouldn't have been seriously upset if she had lost any of her dolls in the creek because in a sense they *were* her. Her Barbie's were still the only way she was able express the invisible, yet all-consuming intensity of her feelings, symbolized by the water threatening to carry her heroines away and by the dark mud sucking on their daintily arched feet, which were designed to wear only sexy high-heels.

History was Mira's favorite subject; she read about it voraciously, lying awake well into the night, fascinated by the different styles of life people had enjoyed throughout the ages – different clothes and food and homes and ways of expressing their thoughts and feelings. She was horrified to learn about the Oriental custom of binding women's feet, blithely unaware that the dolls she played with were having a similarly binding and shaping effect on how she perceived herself. She clearly remembers the first time she watched the Miss Universe pageant with her father. She enjoyed the spectacle of living dolls clad in the magnificently colorful costumes of their native cultures, until it dawned on her that they were competing against *her* too, which seriously offended her. No one had asked *her* to be in the pageant. The only thing that assuaged her wounded pride was the knowledge she was still too young for other people to see the woman who looked back at her from the mirror through her glowing, honey-colored eyes. So she grudgingly forgave the world its blindness even as she ran upstairs to the bathroom to gaze at herself, thinking, *I'm more beautiful than any of them...* Mira didn't realize it at the time, of course, but it was her soul talking. Even when pimples bloomed like poisonous red flowers across her face, and braces imprisoned her smile behind iron fences, she never lost sight of who she really was deep down or gave up hope that her flesh-and-blood would eventually catch up.

It amused her doting father to no end that Mira, at the tender age of six, declared herself more beautiful than the reigning Miss Universe. He smiled. 'Whatever you say, dear.'

'Or at least I will be when I grow up!' she insisted fervently.

'Mira, my love, there's more to beauty than meets the eye. Remember, beauty is not just skin deep.'

Subconsciously, she pondered her father's words for years, because it was the eyes that beheld beauty, she knew, yet she also sensed there was a deeper part of her that responded to it. And this reasoning led her to conclude so-called good taste has invisibly deep roots like the big oak tree in the front yard. It was this tree that first aroused in her an appreciation for clean and hard but also organically supple lines. Yet serious as this impressive life form was, she sensed it enjoyed being decorated by the elements. It looked absolutely splendid in the fall – a living palette of red and gold and oranges she struggled to capture on paper with her crayons. Then in the heart of winter the ancient oak was either hauntingly naked, its dark, open arms reaching for the heavens, or it was cloaked in snow and making her feel as if the silence around it was communicating a mysterious secret to her straining senses. For her the spirit of the tree was best revealed in the bold black-and-white lines with which it impressed itself on her vision after a snowstorm, much more so than during its lush abandon in the spring, when it was just another guest at the wild party nature threw every year at the same time.

Mira was the apple of her parents' eyes, and if as she grew older some of the things she said caused a shocked retort to stick in their throats, they only loved her all the more for it. A mild couple, they never rocked anyone's boat, including their own, so perhaps that was why they so enjoyed the heady wind of their daughter's exuberant imagination. Mira transformed the sedate sheet of their marriage bed into a sail swollen with promise as from the moment she was born it seemed she directed the course of all their lives.

Like any healthy girl, Mira had friends while she was growing up, but none of them could match her intense creative energy, and one fine summer evening she walked out on her best friend. She had gone over to Anna's house to spend the night, and eagerly began suggesting fascinating games they could play, beginning with Barbie's in the den using all the paper tombstones she had made for the graveyard and all the individual portraits of each doll she had drawn to hang inside the haunted Mansion.

'No,' Anna said placidly.

'Okay, how about Arabian Nights?' Mira went on, undaunted. 'We could set up your dad's camping tent in the back yard and pretend we've been captured and are being held prisoner in an oasis by handsome-'

'No,' I don't feel like it.

'Okay, then how about Mission Impossible? I brought my tape recorder to record the mission.'

'No.'

'Well then how about Go-Go Dancers? We can stand on chairs in the basement and pretend that upstairs is the hotel where we go-'

'No, I'd rather just watch TV, okay?'

'What?!' TV, her perennial enemy swallowing all her wonderfully exciting ideas and reducing her best friend to a zombie staring glassy-eyed at the screen. She left in a rage, infinitely proud of herself as she stomped the three blocks home. It caused quite a scandal, Anna's mother calling Mira's mother to find out what had happened, and Rose tactfully trying to explain to her that Mira had concluded her friend's inertia was dangerous to her health.

It was especially wonderful for Mira when she could manage to organize a war in her neighborhood. She divided all the kids up into two armies, always making sure to make the best looking boys her enemies so she could enjoy being shot by them. And the most fun part of the game for her was spreading herself out as seductively as possible on the grass to experience their reaction to the sight of her lovely, vulnerable body as they ran by. Unfortunately, they usually reacted with indifference, but the rare joy of having one of them bend down and mourn her loss, then perhaps risk his life to remove her from the battlefield and give her a proper burial, was worth all the usual frustration. And after a while, she automatically came alive again, which set her to thinking that the dead must feel similarly neglected if their living relatives cease to pay any attention to them just because they happen to be dead. They're just in a different stage of the game, that's all, and after a while they'll be reborn again as naturally as she got up from the battlefield of her yard and ran back into the fray. That's how it seemed to her, anyway, which may explain why she was never able to find any truly interesting playmates.

To her mother's carefully concealed chagrin, Mira pointedly ignored any baby dolls unsuspecting relatives chose to give her for Christmas or her birthday. She made it quite clear from the time she was very young that she had no intention of growing up and becoming a mother just to watch someone else grow up and become a mother to watch someone else grow up and become a mother in an endless vicious cycle. She planned to live her life to the fullest even when she still didn't have a clue what that meant. Rose didn't know how to embroider (she had a hard time just sewing the buttons back on her husband's dress shirts) so it wasn't likely she had pricked her finger while she was pregnant with Mira and wished for a baby with lips as red as blood, skin as white as snow and hair as black as ebony, but that's what she got anyway. Mira's coloring was a mystery – her mother's hair was blonde and her father's was light-brown – as though some anonymous relative from generations past had sought to be reborn through her. Mira secretly believed she wasn't related to anyone except herself, really.

Does anyone ever really enjoy being a teenager? It was hell giving up her Barbie's, but her body increasingly demanded to be the star of the show, no longer tolerating symbolic understudies. This terrible transition between the beautiful freedom of her imagination, and the struggle to embody it so she could make all her dreams come true in reality, is one Mira (like many other one-time adolescents) prefers to forget. Ever since she could remember she was grateful her parents had not condemned her to an all-girl school, for as she told her best friend in third grade, 'I would die if I couldn't be around boys all day.' Mira was also grateful she was only forced to attend Catholic school for two years before graduating to the licentious freedom of High School, although in many ways she enjoyed her uniformed stint in St. Leo's. All the classes went to church every Friday morning, a ritual that united her religious sensibilities with those of her heart and body – she loved glancing at the boys and seeing them glance at her while they did enigmatically attractive things like kneel and pray and take communion. For her there was no sight more devastating on the planet than seeing the boy she had a crush on wearing an immaculate white shirt and black tie sinking to his knees after receiving the Body of Christ in his mischievously smiling mouth. *Oh, God, I love him!* she thought. *I love him! I love him! I want him, please, God, I want him so much!* Some of her conversations with Jesus weren't exactly eloquent. And this delicious smoldering attraction to the opposite sex had been fanned by her hormones to a painfully raging fire by the time she turned fifteen. Even though she couldn't resist exploring the bases, she never went all the way, stubbornly saving herself for her soul mate. However, when the man of her dreams still hadn't shown up by the time she turned nineteen, Mira at last surrendered the ruby-red jewel of her virginity, which really wasn't worth anything in the 20th Century anyway.

CHAPTER ONE

"How can a silly beast give one any rational advice?"

Mira very reluctantly opens her eyes. Big glowing irises the color of newborn spring leaves gaze back at her intently. 'Merr,' says Stormy, and butts his soft gray forehead against hers.

In all her twenty-seven years, Mira has never known such an affectionate cat. If her friendly feline doesn't realize that his weight on her chest is making it difficult for her to catch her breath, and if he's infinitely ignorant of the fact that he murdered a beautiful dream, the loving 'good morning' he always gives her more than makes up for his innocent transgressions.

'Stormy!' she gasps, lifting the padded pressure points of his paws off her chest and diaphragm. 'You're such a silly, stupid cat!' she coos.

A rumbling purr courses through his languid silver-gray body

The Fabric of Love

hanging over her like a storm cloud.

'Mami was having the best dream you silly, stupid pussy!'

'Purr... purr... purr...' The tone of her voice translates the insults into loving compliments inside his blessedly small brain.

Mira sets him down on the lavender sheet beside her, but he promptly leaps off the bed, his mission to awaken her accomplished. He will be off in search of his black sister; they cannot long be parted. Sekhmet – named after the ancient Egyptian goddess of strength and aggression – would never dream of saying good morning, and if she did consider it her greeting would undoubtedly take the form of a calculated swipe of her sharp claws.

Mira lingers languidly on her feather mattress. One of the many virtues of being self-employed is that she sets her own schedule. She scarcely remembers the last time she was forced to get up at the crack of dawn, which always made her feel there was a fatal crack in her psyche through which her soul was seeping away and leaving her with an empty, existential anxiety only the sunrise cured her of. Having spent most of her life (ever since she learned how to read) devouring books, Mira is aware of the ancient Celtic obsession with thresholds and crossover moments. In her opinion, rising before the sun places you in one of those powerfully vulnerable moments when the line between dimensions vanishes and the darkness outside is indistinguishable from the darkness within, in which the cold fear of death can be soothed only by the sun's rebirth.

Throwing her arms luxuriously over her head she stretches the rocky path of her spine against the thousands of feathers cushioning her skeleton, wrapped in silky-smooth flesh like a haunting present from her eternal spirit to her sensual soul... One of the few drawbacks of being self-employed is the temptation to indulge in poetic metaphysics in order to prolong the effort of dragging her body out of bed and starting a day she knows will not be half as stimulating as her sleeping and waking dreams. She always sleeps naked, loving the soft caress of Egyptian cotton sheets against her skin, and as she flings them off another temptation to linger on her cloud of feathers presents itself in the form of her very desirable body.

The sight of her firm, round breasts with their long, thick nipples never fails to excite her. She loves how small and tight and flushed with color her aureoles become when they're aroused, and it doesn't take much to raise erotically charged goose bumps on her bosom's rosy buds, sending her nipples thrusting up and out like hungry stamens. She usually can't resist cradling her soft tits in her hands, and squeezing them appreciatively. What she needs is the tip of a handsome man's tongue flicking across her tense peaks as lightly and swiftly as a hummingbird's wings awakening the sweet warm nectar between her thighs, the achingly tight bud of her pussy protected by thick and tender petals. It has been so long since she allowed a man to penetrate her, that the mere thought of her labial lips blooming open around a hard cock causes her sleepy clitoris to peer excitedly out from its fleshy hood. Knowing this almost painfully thick, long dick is only a figment of her imagination doesn't stop Mira's juices from flowing as she imagines it slowly filling her... and when this legendary erection begins thrusting, ramming violently into her, she gratefully surrenders to the invasion setting her on fire... deep moats and castles under violent siege fill her mind as she crushes her body's magically sensitive seed beneath two fingertips. She rubs herself furiously, igniting a beautiful conflagration in the nerve-endings piled so thickly beneath her clit a timeless blaze dedicated to the goddess of pleasure soon rages in her pelvis as she climaxes...

Afterwards, there's no excuse left for not getting out of bed and abandoning the mattress she knows is stuffed mainly with the small black feathers of anonymous winged creatures, because every now and then one of them stabs her painfully in the middle of the night by way of revenge.

* * *

Mira owns several lovely hand-painted teapots, but they serve primarily as decoration in her kitchen as every morning she simply fills a mug with water and micro-waves it for a minute before adding her Organic Earl Grey teabag and a little of her favorite soy milk creamer. Usually by now she has already gone for a jog through the neighborhood and dressed for the day, but on this particular morning she is in the grip of an irresistible ennui. If she had a morning meeting scheduled with a client she would fight the mild depression fogging her positive energy by applying a light layer of make-up to her face – seductively blending black eyeliner with the shadow of sadness in her dark-gold eyes – and by dressing professionally, but also with an eye to looking sexy; no boring corporate suits for her, thank you. She got her fill of polyester-cotton blends working for a large interior decorating firm that hired her fresh from college, principally for her looks, although she hadn't realized that at the time. The ink on her degree had barely dried before she found herself questioning her choice of profession. Selecting the right table and chairs for corporate boardrooms from a list of pre-approved suppliers was not her idea of being creative. She felt like a cog in a machine that would run more smoothly without her; her imagination kept having the disruptive effect of a mote of dust on a programmed computer chip. The CEO's of banks, chemical companies, and other multi-million dollar corporations failed to appreciate the colorful, life-affirming changes she suggested they make to their abstract decorating schemes. She lasted thirteen months at her first job because she was beautiful enough to express her unorthodox concepts to men who enjoyed watching her talk without listening to what she said, the Memo on their desk already having determined the acceptable look of their new offices. Mira's role was to be decorative and to stroke their egos while making sure the right tables, chairs and abstract paintings were delivered.

The view outside the many windows of her small house blatantly defies her dark mood. Another glorious May day has dawned in northern Virginia. Maybe how unconsciously happy and fulfilled nature is in the spring is what's getting on her nerves and making her profoundly jealous. For Mira it's easier to be alone in the winter with the passionately warm flames of a fire keeping her company, her body hidden beneath cozy sweaters and black house pants not constantly taunting her with the knowledge that her youth and beauty are flowing by unappreciated; unpenetrated. But whether she likes it or not, it's springtime now and she keeps her windows open night and day to catch the cool breeze and to avoid awakening her central air conditioner – the evil Freon-eating dragon living in her utility room breathing out poisonous fumes. Her open-window policy has her parents seriously concerned about her safety, but she enjoys the deeply soothing and strangely stimulating sound of leaves rustling in the wind too much to worry. Dad leant her half the money she needed to buy these three acres of tree-filled land, and her 'doll's house' as he fondly nicknamed it is the best thing that has happened to her in her adult life so far. At least she isn't condemned to an apartment's cage, where she might or might not be allowed a single pet. Her two beloved cats, and all the life growing around her, help keep her soul company while she waits...

Still wearing her violet silk robe – a skimpy affair from *Victoria's Secret*, her favorite multi-billion dollar corporation – Mira sips her hot tea as she unlocks the kitchen door and steps out into nature's delightful rush hour. Three stone bird baths and six wooden feeders hanging from the strong branches of several oaks and maples make her yard a favorite pit stop for countless birds, and many of them even seem to call it home. A double flash of red in the corner of her eye signals the flight of two cardinals from one spot in the treetops to another, and she takes another sip of tea pondering the mystery of birds' flight patterns. How do they determine where they soar to next with such energetic purpose? The branches of trees all look pretty much the same to her, and yet these light feathered beings always seem to know exactly which one they want to land on next.

Caffeine's chemical coach urging her brain cells to wake up and begin exercising themselves again, Mira wishes all the possible courses her life might take were as visible as a tree's branches, and that in one of them she could spot what her soul longs for, her heart soaring on the wings of relief and joy as she flies straight into his arms...

She sighs and walks barefoot towards her garage, enjoying the slightly rough texture of the cool gray stones in such contrast to her warm and tender flesh... flesh that has not been caressed by a man's hands in how long? She has lost count of the months and suspects enough have passed to make a whole year, a long time, and yet apparently not enough time for her loveless curse to end, because the divine blessing of true love still remains only the dream of a girl raised on fairytales. After she had her pussy pricked by more rejected suitors than she can count, she became totally disenchanted with the so-called dating scene and unofficially swore a vow of celibacy akin to sleeping away her youth and beauty waiting for her soul-mate. Yet are these tales of 'once upon a time' that always end 'happily ever after' in true love as bad for a woman's soul as eating fast-food is for the body? Certainly feminists want her to think so, but Mira loves her red leather-bound book of *Grimm's Fairytales* rather like a good Christian loves his bible. In her opinion, it is utterly simplistic to consider fairytales part of society's millenniums' old attempt to suppress the independent spirit in women. Anyone with half a brain not lobotomized by excessive social consciousness can see that fairytales are metaphysical equations involving the opposing yet complimentary forces of man and woman, fire and water, sun and moon, nature and spirit, matter and energy popularly referred to as ying and yang, a concept she knows a good deal about as a casual practitioner of *Feng Shui*. Mira suspects that a prince and princess living happily ever after is an esoteric way to describe a person initiated into the mystery of his or her existence who is at one with the forces shaping all of life. And this is pretty much how she feels about true love… she and her other half will come together as one fulfilled whole that will be infinitely wiser and more beautiful and creative than they can ever be apart…

'Meow!' Sekhmet's preemptory tone rouses Mira from her Grim reverie as she fishes a key out of the pocket of her thigh-length robe to open the garage door.

'Good morning, my lady.' She smiles affectionately at Stormy's sister where she sits in the grass in the regal pose of her ancient Egyptian namesake, her lovely face held perfectly straight over her long legs, her slender haunches sleek black pyramids behind her.

Sekhmet's yellow eyes glare up at her with an expression that clearly tells Mira she has just exceeded the level of clueless stupidity her haughty feline expects from people.

'What?' Mira snaps, arrested by the glassy stare that invariably makes her feel like Sekhmet's pet human.

The black cat does not deign to reply but simply sits there, her whole body strangely taut and transfixed with purpose, as if she is trying to communicate something vitally important...

Mira gasps.

The sound of glass shattering against stone harmonizes with the chirping of birds.

She dropped her cup of tea only half drunk at her feet. She is accustomed to Sekhmet occasionally bringing home a boyfriend or two, but this time she has wandered as far as the zoo and scored the supreme catch of a big black panther... then her vision shifts into focus and she sees a man kneeling in the grass wearing skin-tight black leather pants. The instant her brain registers his true form he seems to suddenly appear before her and she cannot for the life of her understand how she failed to perceive his presence before. He is wearing an equally tight long-sleeved black leather shirt and black boots. Sekhmet rubs against them passionately, purring wantonly and further astonishing her owner, who has never seen her display such affection for anyone except her brother.

'I'm sorry,' the man speaks in a deep, quiet voice as he rises, 'I didn't mean to frighten you.'

Mira just stares at him as he walks towards her. Her heart is still pounding between her breasts from the shock, which won't seem to comfortably ebb as the sight of him rushes into her visual cortexes like a high tide filling all the sad, empty spaces inside her.

Following him, Sekhmet sniffs disdainfully at the spilled tea.

'Stay back, sweetheart,' the stranger urges gently, genuflecting before Mira's bare feet, and the cat and the woman both watch him intently as he picks up the pieces of broken glass and collects them in his other hand. Mira thinks of saying, 'You don't have to do that' but the polite words can't seem to get past all the emotions in her throat. Her view of his broad shoulders in slick, gleaming black is having a vertiginous effect on her ability to think straight, as though she is falling into a black hole that suddenly, impossibly, formed in the middle of her backyard. His hair is cut short and the same shining black as his clothes, as is the goatee framing his smile when he glances up at her... a smile that dims significantly as his eyes fall back down to her naked thighs...

She lifts one foot to step instinctively away from his open appraisal of her naked flesh, but he suddenly grasps her ankle. 'Don't move,' he commands his fingers warm and hard against her skin. 'You'll cut yourself,' he explains, releasing her leg to snatch up the offending shard of glass. 'There, I think that's all of them.' He straightens up.

'Thank you,' she declares stupidly, since it is his fault she dropped the cup and broke it in the first place.

'My pleasure...?' He arches a questioning black eyebrow above eyes the same color as the stones beneath her feet.

She breathes her name, 'Mira!'

'Phillip.' He holds the palm filled with broken glass up between them.

She wonders if he is offering the broken fragments to her, but then her brain shifts into rational gear. 'My trashcan is over there,' she says, and watches, focusing on his tight ass and long legs, as he strides over to the grey metal canister concealed behind a trellis gloriously overgrown with a wisteria vine in full bloom. He lifts the lid, and deposits the shards in the empty bin with a musical clangor mysteriously echoed by all her nerve-endings as he approaches her again.

She is torn between clutching her robe tightly closed over her breasts and making sure her thighs aren't too exposed. Okay, so *Victoria's Secret* doesn't make the most practical garments on earth; the slippery silk seems designed to fall open in all the right, or under certain circumstances all the wrong, places. And there is another way she feels compelled to defend herself. 'Why are you in my yard?' she demands mildly, because another part of her really can't resent such a striking intrusion. 'And why are you dressed like that at nine-thirty in the morning?'

'Please forgive me.' He picks Sekhmet up by the scruff of the neck like a kitten and cradles her slender buttocks in his other hand. 'Your lovely animal here tempted me into taking a short cut home this morning, and I dared to assume if I had her permission it would be all right with her owner as well.' His ink-black goatee makes his grin seem bright as the crescent moon causing serious tidal waves in her heart. *Feng Shui* understands that the moon affects the human body, which is made primarily of water, but nowhere in any of her textbooks on the ancient art of controlling the flow of energy has she ever read about the possible effects of a handsome stranger dressed entirely in black cutting through her yard.

'You know, it's much better to meander than to cut a path straight as an arrow,' she informs him, vaguely aware she is rambling inanely, because her pulse is telling her quite clearly the energy this man has brought into her garden is not negative. The sun could not be shining more brightly, yet Sekhmet is filling the atmosphere with a thunderous contentment, and Mira realizes with a start that this is the first time she has ever seen her proud cat so unselfconsciously relaxed.

'So, should I consider your land off limits in the future?' he asks, his carnivorously civilized white teeth no longer visible, but the ghost of a smile lingers in the dimples defining the corners of his slender mouth.

'Um, I didn't say that,' she stammers, mentally cursing herself for her submissive response even as the look in his eyes thrills her. She has never seen such irises... like the stones beneath her feet at different times of the year they look at once shockingly cold and painfully hot to the touch of her soul staring deeply into them, unable to look away. 'Where do you live?' she demands a bit breathlessly.

He pretends to glance over his shoulder. 'Oh, just across the way.'

'Just across the way where?'

He smiles. 'You know, over the river and through the woods...'

'Those directions lead to grandma's house,' she retorts, but can't resist returning his smile. 'You look more like the wolf.'

'I was on my way home from work.' At last he deigns to at least partially explain his intensely sexy attire.

Her mind races trying to come up with professions which require a man to wear skin-tight black leather, and suddenly a fear sharp and cold as a knife stabbing her in the gut wrenches the dreaded question from her like a cry of pain before she can stop it. 'You're gay?!'

His laughter feels like church bells ringing and announcing the end of the plague. 'No,' he says firmly, setting Sekhmet gently down at his feet, 'but I certainly appreciate your fervent curiosity.'

Abruptly, he reaches for her right hand where it is clenched over her heart holding her robe modestly closed, and this time she doesn't step back away from him. As she returns his penetrating regard, the thought crosses her mind that she didn't get out of bed after all; that she is still lying on her feather mattress wrapped in lavender sheets, dreaming. On the other hand her vision is strikingly clear and telling her that even his hand is attractive, with long, strong, fingers that are neither too masculine or too effeminate, his fingernails neatly trimmed but not obviously manicured. Maybe she notices these details to distract herself from the fact that she is letting a complete stranger grasp her hand and wrench it gently free of her robe, which faints dangerously open. Glancing down at her chest, Mira becomes self-consciously aware of her hard nipples impressing themselves on the fine fabric.

'Relax,' he whispers. A soft smile never leaves his mouth, as if he is privy to an infinite number of profoundly amusing secrets. He gently pries open her fingers, clenched into a fist around a key that has left an imprint on the map of her palm intersecting with all her life-lines. She gazes at the living bas relief in her skin as he unlocks the garage door for her.

'I owe you a cup of tea, Mira.' He slips the key back into the pocket of her robe with a swift, light caress she can neither take offense to or appreciate.

The knowledge that he is about to be on his way is intolerable. Outwardly, he will only be a minor disruption to her morning, but in truth his slender black form has already had the devastating effect of a tornado on her thoughts and feelings, which she knows will keep revolving obsessively around him. 'You can cut through my yard any time,' she says fervently, and is rewarded by the sight of his smile fully reaching his eyes for the first time.

'Thank you, Mira, you have a beautiful garden. But if I may observe, although I have absolutely no complaints about your attire, you hardly look dressed to drive anywhere.' He glances at the screen door leading into her kitchen. 'And didn't I see a car parked out front?'

She is overjoyed to realize he is fishing; he wants to know if that was her car he saw in the driveway or if she has someone – a man – in the house with her. For half a heartbeat she considers keeping him in suspense, but it's not in her nature. 'I use my garage for storage,' she explains.

'So, you're not one of those women who judges a man by his vehicle?'

He seems to be teasing her, his smile blooming briefly into a grin again, yet looking at it feels strangely like studying a flower up close while behind it she never ceases to be aware of the storm-grey, threatening horizon of his eyes. Yet the quality of his stare is not threatening in the sense that it frightens her; it is threatening in an exciting way, like lightening striking so close to home all the lights go out and force her to light candles, that kind of threat. 'Well, I wouldn't say that, exactly... Phillip.' She tastes his name on her tongue and feels warm all over for an instant as if she just downed a shot of hard liquor. 'I admit I often judge a man by his vehicle, the fleshly kind, the one with four wheels isn't that important.'

'Then what do you keep in your garage, Mira? You don't strike me as a pack-rat.' He glances at the garage door. 'Is it full of gardening tools and boxes of old clothes and books? Yet you're also not exactly dressed for gardening right now, are you. And if you only use the place for storage, what was it you so desperately needed to get at nine-thirty in the morning before you'd even finished your cup of tea?'

She likes the way his mind works too much to be offended by his intrusiveness, because obviously none of this is any of his business. But of course nothing is really obvious except how attracted she is to him, which places the conversation under the jurisdiction of entirely different laws than those which operate in normal polite society. 'Well, as a matter-of-fact, Phillip, in the Chinese horoscope I am a Rat.'

He crosses his arms over his chest. 'And I'm a Dragon.' He is at least six-feet-two inches tall, which combined with his attire makes his imperious stance quite effective.

She opens the garage door. 'This is my treasure room,' she confesses proudly, switching on the overhead light and stepping into the cool, temperature-controlled space. She hears the sound of his boots following her inside and triumph, pure and absolute, fills her to the very roots of her being for a timeless moment.

CHAPTER TWO

"That is a wonderful animal, with most singular ideas."

The stranger's high-pitched melodic whistle threads itself through the room like an audible lasso as he takes in the contents of her garage. 'Oh, Mira, Mira,' he says quietly.

'I'm an Interior Designer,' she says as if it explains everything.

'Does that mean if I hire you to do my place I can buy anything I want from your collection here?'

'No, this is all mine!' She knows she sounds like a selfish little girl defending her enormous toy box, but she doesn't care, and the nipples practically poking through her robe certainly don't look childish; they belong to the full breasts of a grown woman who loves all the objects surrounding her as dearly as children who are a part of her and enrich her life in different ways. Not wanting to continue prudishly holding onto her robe, she slips her hands into the pockets and says a silent prayer for it to stay modestly closed. But apparently the only word her guardian angel hears is 'closed' because right on cue Phillip closes the garage door behind him. The lock falling into place only makes a small harmless clicking sound, but it has an explosive effect on her psyche. Suddenly, she is seeing a whole different world as her handsome, charming neighbor is transformed into a threatening stranger inexplicably clad in sadistic black leather on a sunny weekday morning in rural Virginia, and she is trapped inside her garage with him. More than one of her ex-lovers warned her she was entirely too sweet and trusting for her own good, but she supposes it is entirely too late to heed this warning now. Only the fact that he doesn't approach her in a threatening way, but instead walks over to another side of the garage, diffuses her anxiety somewhat.

'Exquisite!' he exclaims beneath his breath, reverently caressing a few inches of the hand-woven tapestry covering half the western wall of her treasure room. 'Where did you find this?'

'At an antique flea market, of course.'

'And here I thought flea markets were just full of junk.'

'Well, mainly they are,' she agrees, 'but they're like thrift stores – you never know what treasure you might just find that was meant just for you to find and no one else. The thing is, people can be so stupid, they don't even realize what they have.'

'I won't ask you what you paid for this, Mira, because that's rude,' he speaks with his back still to her as he studies the pagan hunting scene depicted by the multi-colored threads, 'but what you're telling me is that you essentially robbed this masterpiece from its unsuspecting previous owner?'

'I didn't rob it, I paid for everything in here! If they were too stupid to realize how much their possessions were worth, that's not my problem, and I see no reason why I should have enlightened them, especially since they were getting rid of these beautiful objects in the first place, which means they didn't really love and appreciate them-'

'Like you do.'

'Like I do,' she echoes, edging back towards the door as he turns towards her again. Then the next second she is ashamed of her cowardly and suspicious brain when he changes course to admire the ivory-skinned doll perched on top of a pile of small Oriental rugs that in turn rest on an antique dresser. 'She looks like you, Mira,' he comments, stroking the doll's long raven hair, and then he runs the ball of his thumb along her pouting red mouth in a light, sensual caress that parts Mira's own lips as her breath catches watching him. 'You have excellent taste, my beautiful neighbor.'

The compliment literally makes her feel weak in the knees, which in turn forces her to question her disrespect for clichés, because obviously some of them obey real physiological facts she is amazingly finding herself the victim of on this dream-like morning. 'You still haven't mentioned what you do for a living, Phillip.' The question is an effort to root herself in reality and to assuage her reason, which keeps insisting she is a fool to be alone with a total stranger who could easily overpower her physically.

'I'm a Master,' he replies, casually moving on to another aesthetic object in her collection that catches his eye.

She laughs, but hardly because she thinks his response is funny; it is the only way to vent the rush of emotions inside her. 'You're a Master,' she repeats in the hope he will elaborate on his unusual and intriguing profession, but all he says is 'That's right' as he admires her small painting of a handsome Native American Indian man. She tries another approach, 'Do you dominate men or women?'

'I told you, Mira, I'm not gay.'

'I never thought you were... I mean, it's just that when you said...'

'No need to explain.' He turns to face her again, and this time walks straight towards her.

The garage door is right behind her, she can easily turn and run, but instead she doesn't move a muscle as he comes and stands a mere hand's breadth away from her.

'You have some beautiful things here,' he says quietly, 'but you're the real treasure, Mira.'

'Thank you,' she whispers.

'My pleasure.' He caresses her hair just as he did the doll's raven locks. 'I love your hair. Most women cut it stylishly short these days, unfortunately.' He also traces the shape of her lower lip with the ball of his thumb, and it stuns her how hard it is to resist the impulse to take it in her mouth and suck on it like a baby at last offered a bottle containing the mysterious formulae of all she desires...

'Do you get paid to beat women?' she asks faintly, and he completely takes her breath away with his reply.

'Sometimes.' He pauses as if aware she needs time to remember how to breathe. 'But usually it's much more complex and subtle than that, as I'm sure you can imagine.'

'Can I? I'm not... I'm not sure I can.'

'And I'm sure you can,' he insists, no trace of a smile softening the firmness of his mouth. 'For instance, I think that if I tell you to untie the sash holding your robe closed, you'll obey me, Mira.'

'Oh, right!' She laughs, and once again takes a step back away from him, but for some reason only one step, not the three or four steps that will actually get her to the garage door and freedom. She reasons he can easily stop her if he wants to, yet she knows this is just a flimsy excuse concocted by the Catholic school girl inside her seeking to defend her virtue. The naked truth is she has absolutely no desire to escape his penetrating stare.

'Untie your sash, Mira,' he commands in a soothing, almost gentle tone. 'Trust me, I won't hurt you.'

'Isn't that what they all say?' she demands.

'Maybe, but you know I'm telling the truth.'

'How can I possibly know anything about you when we just met?' She is desperately buying herself some time before succumbing to the inevitable. Yet why it should be so inevitable she has no idea since most women in her situation would undoubtedly make a run for it and call 911.

'A man and a woman can know the most important things about each other the instant their eyes meet if they're really looking and listening with their souls, Mira.'

It is the incredible fact that he reasonably acknowledges the existence of her soul as no other man has done that undoes the sash of her robe as her fingers do exactly what he said they would and obey him.

He wrests the sash out of her hand.

Only her tense nipples keep the silk cloth from fainting open and exposing her. Mira considers certain types of clothing constrictive. She would never consider owning a pair of tight jeans, the only pants in her wardrobe are comfortable cotton leggings; she only tolerates cotton bikini underwear because occasionally they make sense and are necessary; and the countless sexy lace panties she owns are primarily designed to be ripped off. Beneath the robe she is completely naked.

'Are you seeing someone?' he demands quietly, wrapping the ends of the sash once around both his hands and stretching it taut.

She stands motionless as a statue, as if emulating a work of art will transform what is happening into something less shamefully sinful; as if it will protect her from the hot touch of his eyes as she pretends he is only objectively admiring her figure. 'No, I'm not,' she answers just as softly, as if they both know a loud, normal-sounding voice will break the spell she is in, a spell that is allowing the inconceivable to take place.

'You shave your pussy for your own pleasure?'

The undisguised admiration in his voice relaxes her a vital degree. 'Yes, it feels nicer that way...' Nothing like this has ever happened to her before, yet it feels strangely familiar, and as he steps behind her, the violet sash looking almost sacredly beautiful against his pitch-black leather, she remembers... it's like being in confessional and speaking about her most intimate transgressions to a nameless man just because he calls himself a priest. 'What are you doing?' she gasps, but the question is rhetorical since he is obviously tying her wrists behind her back.

'Everything you want me to.'

'But... but I don't want you to do anything,' she lies.

'I'm betting you were raised a Catholic.'

'How did you know that?' His powers of perception please her, and mysteriously make her feel less guilty about what is happening by confirming her instincts that she is surrendering to a man who appears to be worthy of having both her body and soul in his hands.

He steps around in front of her again. Her eyes are wide and trusting and only a little afraid as she gazes up at his face fully acknowledging that what he said was true – the wordless script of his features told her profoundly important things about him the second she saw him. What is transpiring now is her response to this knowledge by her intuitive self, which always works much faster than her reason, anchored as it is in the highly conflicted society that programmed it.

'You're so beautiful!' he whispers almost angrily, and the passionate compliment deepens the thrill of his hands slipping into her robe. Her chest heaves beneath a flood of feelings as he cups her naked breasts in his hands. 'Do you trust me?' he asks, looking down into her cleavage as he squeezes her soft mounds and grazes their exquisitely sensitive peaks with the balls of his thumb.

'Yes and I have no idea why!' she confesses all in one breath.

'I work three nights a week at a BDSM club in D.C. It's a private venue; you won't have heard of it.' He squeezes her bosom appraisingly. 'I dominate successful business women and even a few politicians, women with power who are otherwise in complete control of their lives.'

Mira senses he is telling her more about himself and his exotic profession to help her relax, and she finds what he is saying so fascinating she can almost forget to be afraid. His fingers kneading her tits might as well be directly massaging her brain as the deep pleasure makes her feel thoughtlessly warm all over. 'These women willingly submit to you?' she asks, part of her jealously resenting she isn't the first one to fall under his assertive spell.

'They become my slaves, Mira.'

She gasps, 'Your slaves?!' as he pinches both her nipples between his thumb and forefinger, and suddenly she is sure she is dreaming as she watches the tip of his tongue flicking swiftly and lightly, like a hummingbird's wings, against one of her breast's rosy buds. She moans with a satisfaction that goes much deeper than the mere physical sensation, because it was this very tongue she saw in her imagination as she was masturbating in bed this morning; it looks exactly like the image she had in her mind of a man's tongue as she stroked herself. And if his tongue lives up to the fantasy concocted by her brain, it seems very promising that his penis, and its skill, won't disappoint her either. The mere thought of being so fulfilled so soon – when she thought she would be celibate for many more months to come – makes her pussy juice with longing to be opened up by a big, hard cock. When he transfers the attention of his agile tongue to her other jealous nipple, she becomes fully conscious of her hands tied behind her back and the fact that she has no power to control his actions, yet the heat of desire is melting the coldness of fear and replacing it with an entirely different tension. Her cunt is tightening with anticipation not trepidation, and suddenly the only thing she is afraid of is that he won't actually fuck her. Then in the next heartbeat she can't believe she so desperately wants a man who just admitted to being a kinky gigolo, and her offended pride stiffens her back... or maybe it's just that she wants to push her breast deeper into his mouth.

'Mm!' He sucks furiously on her nipple.

His fingers digging almost painfully into her tender tits squeezes the question out of her, 'Do you sleep with all your slaves, Phillip?'

He glances up at her face, amusement flashing in his grey eyes like distant lightning. 'I always sleep alone, Mira.'

'I mean... do you fuck them?' She resents that he forces her to say the word.

'Rarely.' He straightens up. 'Only if I'm seriously inspired.' He slips his hands out of her robe. 'When I am inspired, it's always free of charge, and right now, Mira, I'm immensely inspired. Can you handle it?'

'Yes...'

He yanks her robe open, fully exposing her breasts and belly and the tender mound of her freshly shaved pussy. She knows from looking at herself in the mirror that there is an almost heart-shaped gap where the top of her thighs open up and merge with the tender bulge of her pudenda, which makes her think of a dolphin's smiling face.

He steps back to admire the view, and how hard his mouth suddenly looks tells her more clearly than words how beautiful she is. Everything about him suddenly seems harder, the look in his eyes especially, and there is a distinct bulge in his tight pants that wasn't there before. She holds her head high, proud of her body and of the obvious effect it is having on him. He tied her wrists against the center of her back, thrusting her breasts forward, which in turn arches her spine and pushes her buttocks out in a way that makes her feel dangerously vulnerable. If it wasn't for her robe covering the cheeks of her ass, all her orifices would be exposed to him.

'You're lucky I had a long night, Mira, otherwise you'd be in serious trouble right now, but never fear,' he unzips his leather pants, 'you'll still get as much as you're ready for.' His cock springs out towards her fully erect, and if it does not possess the damaging dimensions of her imagination, it is still more than big enough to safely satisfy the profound cravings of her flesh. 'Do you like chocolate?' He pulls a condom out of his back pocket.

'I love chocolate...'

'Good, because I'm going to treat you to a nice big chocolate cone this morning for breakfast. On your knees, sweetheart.'

She sinks to her knees on the garage floor with more gratitude and hopeful reverence than she ever felt at church. The cement is unyieldingly hard against her skeleton, but she doesn't care. All she cares about is proving to him, showing him, what a good cocksucker she is so he'll want to come back to her, and next time they can forgo the chocolate latex frosting.

He threads his fingers firmly through her hair. 'I'm going to fuck your mouth like a cunt, Mira,' he warns, yet just as in Stormy's brain insults are transformed into compliments by the tone of her voice, Phillip's threat feels like a wonderful promise to the blood pounding through her heart as she prepares to take his chokingly large penis into her mouth. 'I'm going to fuck your beautiful face,

Mira, because you're so fucking beautiful!'

He penetrates her mouth slowly at first, giving her orifice time to adjust to his dimensions; letting her tongue and teeth get a feel for what they're dealing with, giving her time to make her mouth an utterly smooth, yielding hole. With her wrists tied behind her back and his hands gripping her skull, all she has to do is tolerate the strain on her legs, keep her mouth wide open, and relax the muscles of her throat, the hardest task of all, because even though he starts with slow, half strokes, his head is soon grazing the back of her throat... and then more boldly caressing it, filling the darkly sensitive entrance to her neck. She closes her eyes and concentrates on not gagging as his hips pick up speed. The condom really does taste like dark-chocolate, and despite how completely fulfilled she is in a physical sense, the chemical flavor leaves her feeling strangely empty; mysteriously hungry for the unique taste of his semen, and, eventually, for the heady rush of his cum drenching her tongue. Naturally, she has given blow-jobs before, but no man has ever used her mouth so roughly. She discovers just what it feels like to really have her mouth fucked as hard as a pussy. There is no physical pleasure in it for her whatsoever, only effort, but for some reason she loves every breathless second.

He slides his full length in and out between the devoted ring of her lips faster and harder, and then he keeps her face pressed firmly against him, making it even harder for her to breathe as he moves her skull very subtly back and forth, caressing his head with the infinitely sensitive flesh of her neck. Mira has never been deep-throated before, not like this, and she imagines there is something to be said for his skill that she somehow resists the urge to gag around him; nevertheless, it's a huge relief when he slips out of her and she is able to take a deep, shuddering breath, her cheeks flushed with pride at her skill as much as from the strain.

'Very good, Mira.' He releases his cruel grip on the roots of her hair and strokes it gently with both hands. 'But you didn't expect me to come like that, did you?'

She hears herself whine softly, 'My knees hurt.' Suddenly, she is confused and a little frightened again, unable to rationalize why she so enjoyed his oral selfishness.

'I know they do,' he says mildly. 'Would you like to stand up or lie down?'

For some reason being given a choice when it is turning her on so much to feel helpless makes her want to cry. 'Please!' she whispers, casting a pleading glance up into his unreadable eyes.

'Please what?' He strokes her hair again soothingly, smoothing it back away from her face as if his caress will help untangle her thoughts.

'Please!' she repeats, a sob catching in her throat.

'You want me to fuck you, is that it?'

She closes her eyes in mingled relief and shame at the idea of having to beg him to fuck her. Isn't she beautiful enough that he can't resist her?

'On your feet!' he commands, and yanks her up himself before she has a chance to obey.

She doesn't know whether to be relieved or disappointed as he quickly frees her wrists. Then excitement overwhelms all other emotions as he pulls her robe off.

'God, you're magnificent,' he says through clenched teeth as he leads her by the hand over to where her doll is sitting, innocently observing the erotic proceedings. He grips her waist to lift her onto the dresser, and clutches the bottom of her thighs just above her knees to hold her legs open around him. She is torn between the vision of his erection poised at the entrance to her flesh and the proximity of his face, the magnetic pull of his hard mouth parting her own lips in a silent plea for a kiss. Yet there is something intensely arousing about the fact that he is about to thrust his cock into her cunt before their tongues have even politely touched. She wraps her arms around his neck, and the sweet sensation of her labia blooming open around the thick head of his penis makes her moan in anticipation of the rest of him completely filling her.

'It's been such a long time,' she tells him, not because she wants him to be gentle but because she wants him to look forward to the tight fit he can expect from her pussy.

'It was worth the wait,' he says, and penetrates her both with his eyes and his hard-on.

She cries out as she feels her tight cleft clinging to his rigid length like a silk glove shaping all her innermost contours to his, and she wonders how she could possibly have survived for so long without experiencing this glorious fullness in her pelvis. He lodges his penis deep in her vagina, and then holds perfectly still.

'Oh, God, please...' She presses her hot vulva against the cool leather enclosing his scrotum, clinging to his shoulders as her hips writhe desperately around his cock planted deep inside her. It is absolute torture how patiently he waits to begin stabbing her into a higher form of life in which their bodies will beat together like a single heart... 'Oh, God, fuck me,' she begs, 'please! I can't bear it!'

His tongue thrusts between her lips as he pulls his erection almost all the way out of her, threatening her with its loss for a terrible second before he rams it back in.

Mira is only vaguely aware of her cries filling the garage like an intangible but priceless treasure, her nerve-ends close to short-circuiting with pleasure from the combined motion of his tongue in her mouth and his penis in her pussy, both of them thrusting and dipping and swirling and opening her up until she feels ecstatically bottomless. He fucks her with such force the black leather sheathing his naked flesh begins to feel like much more than just a sexy outfit, and there is another benefit to it as well... with only his driving erection rising out of the zippered crotch her clitoris comes into direct contact with the small metal tongue, and its cold, hard licks merging with the sensation of his head kissing her cervix is stimulating the very real possibility of an orgasm inside her.

'Come for me, Mira...'

'Oh, yes, I want to... I want to...'

'Then do it. I can feel your pussy tightening, you're almost there... come for me!'

Her brain doesn't think it's possible, usually she can only climax by touching herself, and she is astonished when her body quickly succeeds in obeying him.

'Oh, yes, yes...' She hears him whisper as she comes around him, her sweet hot juices wasted on latex and leather as she breathlessly buries her face in the hard space of his chest.

Once her pussy stops pulsing around his dick, he pulls out of her. 'Come here.' Her legs unsteady beneath her, he leads her to a faded gold antique chaise lounge. He doesn't need to tell her what to do; she reclines gratefully across it, bending her arms over her head as she absorbs the magnificent sight of his fully erect cock free of the condom. Dazed and relaxed as she is by her powerful orgasm, she still does not fail to notice and appreciate that he discards the semen-filled plastic carefully at his feet, making sure not to let it touch any of her beloved antiques.

'I'm going to come all over your beautiful breasts, Mira. Play with them for me.'

It is her pleasure to oblige. She is so aroused, her nipples look carved out of rosy marble in the soft golden light designed to show off all her precious possessions. She watches the slick, pumping violence of his fist in wide-eyed fascination. She has never seen anything so arousing as this man stroking his erection in front of her.

'What are you saving all these treasures for?' he asks abruptly, the almost indiscernible breathlessness in his voice the only sign he is close to coming. 'Not enough room for them in your doll's house?'

'Oh, my God, how did you know that's what I call it?'

'Because it's small and you're a doll, Mira.'

She would laugh if it wasn't for his intensely serious expression, to which she responds instead by arching her back and thrusting her breasts up towards him. She moans in the grip of an indefinably pure sensual pleasure as his cum begins raining down on the soft hills of her bosom, vanishing like snow into warm ground against her skin. He flings his head back as he ejaculates and her breath catches in sympathy watching him force every last drop of pleasure from his erection, which shows absolutely no sign of diminishing, and the staying power of his hard-on has her pussy juicing in selfish admiration.

'Jesus,' he whispers, and this slight crack in his masterful aura makes him look even sexier to her as she sits up, compelled by years of hygienic indoctrination to find something to clean herself off with. 'Oh, no you don't, you're leaving my cum all over your breasts,' he says as if reading her mind, or perhaps just her eyes, which she has been told are very expressive. 'You're not showering until my sperm has completely dried on your skin.' He smiles as he reaches for both her hands and draws her up into his arms. He kisses her forehead, and it feels as though he is rewarding her for not letting her cowardly reason ruin what just happened between them. Then he takes her hand again and leads her towards the door. She stops with the intention of picking up her robe, but he says, 'No, I want to see you walking naked through your garden.'

Stepping outside ahead of him, Mira feels transformed from the woman she was only just a little while ago, sipping her cup of tea in the grip of a mild depression, into a wildly sensual nymph who, for once, spent the morning the way it should be spent, fucking shamelessly.

Stormy and Sekhmet are sprawled directly in her path on the gray stones leading to the kitchen door in what she thinks of as their ancient Egyptian brother and sister pose – various limbs entwined with their regal heads together. For once Sekhmet is gazing up at Mira with a mild, almost approving expression.

She crouches down to pet them as always the urge to do so proving irresistible. 'This is Stormy, Sekhmet's sister,' she tells Phillip, smiling at him over her shoulder.

There is no one there.

CHAPTER THREE

"Even if the world is coming to an end, I must go out for a little relief."

Mira unlocks the door and walks into another empty space. She is concentrating on her work as never before, the only way she can keep at least a small part of her brain from thinking about Phillip night and day; he has even penetrated her dreams, usually an inviolate space where she can always count on finding solace from any problems and disappointments besetting her. For hours after he vanished, she had refrained from showering, very glad for the sensation of his cum drying on her skin that proved he had been real and not just an intensely vivid figment of her overactive imagination.

At the moment, Mira is glad her sandals make an efficient clicking sound on the hard-wood floor, helping to keep her focused on the objective physical reality surrounding her that is her responsibility to bring to life. Usually stepping into a virgin space she knows is all hers to decorate is exciting, but on this gloomy morning the blank white walls depress her like the sight of bleached bones in the desert of her loneliness. The sharp corners of the empty rooms feel like knife cuts to her soul, and naked windows looking out on a gray sky evoke dead, unblinking eyes from which color and hope have been forever leached.

Mira knows she is deliberately stoking her dark mood with these melancholy mental images, but she cannot resist indulging herself while she does a slow walk-through of the Arlington condo she has been hired to decorate, and which undoubtedly cost its new owner a small fortune. At least he had enough good taste to choose a place with natural wood floors instead of carpeting the sophisticated dimension of crown molding a lovely island kitchen with real granite countertops and stainless steel appliances suited to a masculine owner; ceramic tiled bathrooms (linoleum floors and wall-to-wall carpeting are on the top of Mira's undesirable list) and best of all, a gas fireplace big enough to warm all the rooms in winter without having to resort to the flesh drying misery of central heating. Also an added bonus is a tiny balcony opening up off the living room, although why anyone would want to sit out there just looking at other tall, architecturally uninspired buildings while listening to the traffic on Fairfax Drive is beyond her comprehension. When she steps out onto her porch she is surrounded by nature, but she supposes that at night so high up the glowing red-and-gold flow of traffic below, and lights coming on in the neighboring buildings, will be lovely in the sense that luminosity is aesthetic to the human psyche's innate need for life and warmth and the sense of hope they provide. Nevertheless, she much prefers living on ground level surrounded by trees, whose company she generally prefers to that of people.

Her slow, brooding walk-through of the condominium completed, she has no excuse not to get to work. She sets her heavy purse down next to the front door and fishes her electronic tape measure from its malleable black leather depths. Her purse proves some of the new theories in physics about space folding to create other dimensions, because it usually takes her a small eternity to find anything in it.

She is willing to bet a considerable chunk of her fee that, as a general rule, architects who design million-dollar condos are not Chinese. Everywhere the laws of *Feng Shui* are so blatantly violated the architects were either in gleeful league with the forces of evil or had no idea what they were doing. Sometimes she feels as much like a spiritual fire-fighter in charge of damage control than an Interior Designer. The first problem she makes a note of concerning Ian McFarland's new home is the fact that his front door is directly across from the elevator shaft. Whenever he lets himself in and out, a stream of unfiltered, and potentially hostile energy will flood his living space while at the same time any positive energy accumulated inside rushes out. She will have to soften the entrance into the living room from the small foyer with a curtain that will serve as an energy dam to keep the home's positive *chi* inside and help block any negative *chi* pouring in from a hallway traveled by countless strangers, each one a unique universe of energy.

Fortunately Ian (who called her last week after being referred to her by one of her satisfied former clients) sounded ideally submissive to her designer's will. She only spoke to him for a few minutes, but she sensed he was wealthy and wise enough (in that order) to agree with most, if not everything, she might suggest for his new living space, which will, of course, make her job a lot easier. It is also much more fun for her when she is given the freedom and the power to exercise her talent and imagination without too many restrictions. She loves a client with a big budget, no doubt about it, and yet working for people with financial constraints affords her a different kind of challenge she also enjoys, being a firm believer in the magic of thrift stores and antique flea markets, where treasures can be found that don't cost an arm-and-a-leg. (If this saying was literally true, Ian McFarland, like many of her former clients, would be crippled for life.)

Mira begins her measurements with the living room. Its best feature are the three six-foot-high windows to the west of the gas fireplace; however, at a certain time of day they will let in too much light, making the room hot and uncomfortable during the warmer months of the year. Brief as her conversation with Ian was, she hung up feeling quite positive about her new client's amiable and open disposition. He won't consider his manhood threatened by the feminine detail of curtains supplementing more masculine blinds.

The kitchen won't require much work on her part since all the appliances are in place. She suspects the architect did not choose to position the stove away from the refrigerator because it is good chi to keep these opposing forces apart, nor did he or she give a thought to whether or not the stove was placed against the wall on the other side of which the occupant will be sleeping. She makes a mental note to position Ian's bed away from the spot on the wall where the stove sits so the active energy of heat will not disturb his sleep.

She will have to decide, after she actually meets him in person, whether or not she should share her thoughts on *Feng Shui* with him. She has learned from experience that human beings can be strange creatures. If when she is determining the placing of individual pieces of furniture in each room she happens to mention, for example, that the foot of the bed cannot be directly facing the bedroom door because that's known as the 'death position' she can never be sure how a client will react. Once a woman was so disturbed by the image that she promptly fired Mira, as if getting rid of the source of the thought would dispel the fear it consequently haunted her with. That, of course, was an extreme case; most people are not quite so melodramatic. Nevertheless, she has learned that discussing a home's *chi* can make its owner uncomfortable, as if she is trying to see through their clothing by talking about something as mysteriously intimate as the direction and flow of their personal energy. Some people become almost embarrassed, as though she is casually stripping their clothes off to comment on the positive and negative way the skin flows over their bones and helps shape who they are and how they feel. Of course, other people merely smile condescendingly at the concept that an invisible energy has the power to affect their emotions and circumstances, although, fortunately, most of her clients possess at least a modicum of imagination.

Feng Shui means 'wind water' which she thinks is a lovely way to describe the flow of thoughts and feelings, at once spiritually abstract and sensually incarnate, that compose her unique personality. Nevertheless, it is sometimes best not to tell the people she is working for why she makes the decorating decisions she does, why she wants the desk in that particular corner of the study or why the walls should be the colors she selects, etc. With knowledge comes responsibility, and many people don't really seem to desire conscious control over the powerful energy of their feelings. They don't want to think they might be at least partially responsible when bad things happen to them; taking perverse comfort in believing everything is random chance and they are only hapless victims. Mira finds such profound spiritual laziness appalling, and such clients make it hard for her to be inspired about her work knowing it will only be appreciated on the most superficial level, at

The Fabric of Love

best. But a job is a job, and she is lucky to have one she enjoys so much most of the time, a job that enables her to be creative and to shop for a living. What more can a girl ask for?

Usually the first items on her shopping list, especially when she is working on a condominium and not a house, are plants, and lots of them. In her opinion, if you can't be around trees – prized for their power to block negative *chi* and attract good luck by providing fresh oxygen, making it easier and more pleasant to breathe and therefore to live – then you must absolutely possess as many indoor plants as possible.

Mira thanks all the Powers-that-Be for her electronic tape measure, which makes the task of recording a living space's dimensions much easier. Apart from the fact that she cannot understand why anyone would buy an apartment when they could afford a house, by the time she finishes her measurements she has concluded that her new client is a lucky man. There is only one serious structural poison arrow to deal with in his new home – the front door directly facing the elevator. Apart from that, especially since she will be supplying all his furnishing and lighting needs, the *chi* should flow quite nicely for Ian. Especially beneficial are the north and south facing windows that will let a breeze in from both directions. Although the quality of the air might be dubious, a slightly tainted wind is better than no wind at all.

The *Feng Shui* issues momentarily settled to her satisfaction (and she in no way pretends to be anything other than an inspired amateur, not actually having a degree in the ancient art form) Mira glances at her watch, and with the choreographed precision she is increasingly coming to expect from life, she hears the front door open behind her. Ian is right on time for their lunch appointment, where they will discuss in detail what he imagines his new home looking and feeling like, i.e. where she will seek to seduce him into believing that his heart's decorating desires are flatteringly synonymous with her own excellent professional tastes.

'Hello,' she says brightly, turning to face her new client, and a fist of *chi* hits her straight in the womb as she watches him step into the empty room. Ian McFarland is a strikingly attractive man, and it is immediately apparent that he has splendid taste in clothes. One look at him tells Mira designing his living space is going to be an exciting challenge the pleasure of which might, hopefully, eventually, enable her to forget the man in black leather who cut through her yard and her life with such devastating consequences to her peace of mind. Before Phillip, she was contentedly, positively, waiting for her soul-mate. Now, even though she feels she has met him at last, she still doesn't know where he is and can't find him. Approximately seventy-three hours ago he ejaculated all over her naked breasts and she has not seen or heard from him since.

* * *

Mira has never managed to develop a taste for the business lunch. Apart from the fact that she prefers not to eat too much during the day to keep her energy level up, she doesn't like mixing business with pleasure. It's not because she is afraid her business will suffer, but because she resents wasting even a few minutes of her miraculous incarnation, and discussing a financial arrangement with a total stranger feels like deliberately stirring chalk into her food. She loves eating too much to relish having her attention distracted from the pleasure of its consumption, except by someone she is actually attracted to, in which case the conversation provides an additional stimulating spice to the dining experience. During business lunches, she is careful to order only a soup or a salad or a vegetarian sandwich – as much as her sensitive system can handle in tandem with the vital tension of getting to know new clients and what they desire. Maybe it's because she doesn't really care about their feelings and yet is forced to swallow and digest an entire open buffet of their thoughts and opinions that her dessert often consists of four citrus-flavored Tums.

Decorating your home is a very exciting task, and Mira doesn't blame her clients for being eagerly and anxiously talkative. She responds with a calm smiling assurance she wears like a mask to soothe their flighty energy like a bird's ruffled feathers as their untrained imaginations soar from one stylistic branch to another. While she pretends to be casually enjoying her soup she is intently absorbing her clients' personality and mentally designing their new nest in the hope that she can lure them into it with a minimum of effort, although usually she has to cast a complex net of designer terms over an erratic flock of ideas that would never succeed in settling down to a livable aesthetic without her firm guidance. Mixing bad taste with her meals is another reason she dislikes business lunches. The mere mention of leopard skin bedspreads, bear rugs and glass coffee tables ruins her appetite.

Lunch with Ian McFarland is one of those blessed exceptions to the rule deepening Mira's belief that there is no such thing as coincidence only choreography if you keep your positive outlook in shape and follow the subliminal music of your intuition. To avoid the often hellish traffic on Route 666 (as her environmental consciousness likes to think of it) she took the train into Ballston, secure in the knowledge that her new client would drive them anywhere she desired for lunch. She gleaned this much just from the quality of Ian's voice when they spoke on the phone, and the moment her eyes met his, her instincts were confirmed. First she assured herself he was indeed hers for the rest of the afternoon; that he wouldn't have to run back to the office for a last minute meeting. Thank God he wasn't a doctor, and not only was he not on call, he said, his cell phone was turned off. The hasty note scribbled in her Day Calendar in a skeletal scrawl – *Take I.M. shopping after lunch* – promised to flesh itself out into a highly enjoyable afternoon... an active, busy afternoon that would keep her brain cells occupied, diverting their obsessive focus from... but she doesn't even want to say his name in her head!

Much as Mira enjoys specialty shops and antique markets, she never minds a quick trip to *Crate & Barrel* with new clients – the ideal generic place to start out as she gets a feel for their tastes, or lack thereof, not to mention a feel for how much they're actually willing to spend as opposed to how much they say they are. With that plan in mind, she has Ian drive them to *Café Deluxe* in Tyson's Corner, also a good place to enjoy one of her favorite light lunches – a roasted vegetable sandwich with Goat Cheese on toasted whole-grain bread. Yet much as she intends to keep busy and stop thinking about Phillip, details seem to keep cropping up everywhere that remind her of him, for example Ian's stunning black Ferrari. Okay, so it doesn't really matter to her what kind of car a man drives, but it certainly doesn't hurt either when his vehicle feels like an extension of her sensuality as they fly down the highway together at the speed of daydreams all promising to become very pleasantly real in the form of the driver behind the wheel.

Mira and Ian don't talk much during the drive to *Café Deluxe*, but it isn't because they don't feel comfortable, on the contrary; they keep casting smiling glances at each other amidst sporadic light conversation secure in the knowledge that they're already in a relationship. He is a wealthy, successful man, and she is his talented (high-priced) Interior Designer. The fact that they are both attractive, young and single gives their professional relationship potentially exhilarating dimensions. For years he will have to live with the furniture she helps him choose and how she arranges it for him, traditionally the role of a girl-friend or a wife... and with this thought the watch-dog of her reason reminds her with an annoyingly trite bark that just because he isn't wearing a wedding ring doesn't mean he's not attached.

'You come highly recommended,' he says abruptly, keeping his eyes on the road. They are a remarkably vivid green that remind her of Stormy's eyes mysteriously deepened by the shadow of a soul perceiving itself in the reflective surfaces.

She smiles. 'I'm glad to hear it.' She likes compliments as much any girl.

'How long have you been in the business?'

'About six years now, but only four-and-a-half working on my own.' She tells him about the decorating firm that hired her right after college, and it's a good sign that he doesn't appear to question her reason for leaving and adventuring out on her own at the risk of losing a cushy annual salary in order to fully exercise her creativity. Perhaps it is only her own stubborn hopefulness, but she gets the feeling he understands where she's coming from, and his mild expression (at least what she can see of it in profile as he drives) hovers encouragingly between serious attentiveness and smiling relaxation without obviously approving or disapproving of anything she says. Living in D.C., it makes her wonder if he is some sort of diplomat, but she concludes that he is much too at ease in his own skin to be a government employee. At least that's her opinion and she has been wrong before, but not often.

'So, may I ask what you do for a living that you can afford my services, Ian?'

He laughs. It is the first time she hears his deep, almost silent chuckle, and it makes her feel good all over, like a big cat purring just for her.

'You may.'

She waits, but the only response she gets is an adorable dimple carving a hole almost as deep as her curiosity into his visible cheek. 'Well?' she demands.

'I'm Regional Director for the Salvation Army.'

'Get *out* of here!' Now it is her turn to laugh, in amazement. She is delighted to have her powers of perception excelled, a rare enough event to excite her with the sense that the world is a much more wonderfully complex place than she can imagine. 'That's the last thing I would have guessed,' she declares, her sharp surprise feeling rather like a cosmic spank she finds at once stimulating and reassuring.

'I know,' he says simply, 'and I know what you're thinking.'

'What?' She holds her breath, turned on by having her perceptions penetrated by a man skilful enough to do so.

'You're thinking that I didn't exactly find the suit I'm wearing in the bargain bin of one of our local thrift stores.'

'Well, yes…'

'I was born with a comfortable Trust Fund I've since invested in the Stock Market,' he confesses, 'which supplements my modest salary, but I feel I know you well enough already, Mira, to guess that you can appreciate it's the satisfaction I get from my work that's important.'

'It's much easier to feel that way when you have a lot of money in the bank,' she points out with uncharacteristic cynicism.

He takes his eyes off the road to look directly into hers for an instant. 'Yes, it is,' he admits.

'I'm sorry!' she apologizes fervently, 'I didn't mean to imply that I don't believe you, because I do, and I feel the same way about my work… although obviously I'm not helping people the way you are…'

'There's no need for you to explain, Mira, you make a valid point.'

'You must have women swooning at your feet,' she teases, subconsciously defending herself from his charm by divorcing herself from the rest of woman kind. 'A selfless philanthropist and a successful player all rolled up into one sexy package. How can any girl resist you?'

'They can't,' he concedes mildly, but he takes the right turn into the *Crate & Barrel* parking lot with such speed she has to cling to the seat to keep from falling into his lap.

CHAPTER FOUR

"And in the despair of her heart she jumped down into the well the same way the spindle had gone. After that she knew nothing; and when she came to herself she was in a beautiful garden, and the sun was shining on the flowers that grew around her."

The gloomy clouds have parted, the sun has come out, and it is now one of those glorious Virginia days that people who live in other states can only dream of. The sky is a vibrant blue softened here and there by fluffy white clouds like cotton balls from the Goddess' cosmetic jar. A cool breeze, with just the slightest edge of a chill to it, gently caresses goose bumps across her skin so she can better appreciate the warmth of the sun penetrating it. There is no humidity to speak of, making the air so crisp that colors and shapes cut into her vision with a sense of significance transcending mere aesthetics. And everywhere birdsong punctuates these sweet, illusive instants of inspiration when pleasure in the physical world and a belief in life's divine soul come joyfully together inside her. This sensual communication with nature is still wonderfully possible in Fairfax County where Mira grew up, one of the richest counties in the nation, and to her its wealth is indeed summed up in green – the green of leaves, leaves belonging to the big old trees that are still there, protected, not plowed down as they are elsewhere with a murderous lack of respect for life and the environment.

As they stand before the café's hostess and her pulpit – red crosses bloodying the seating chart of hedonistic parishioners come to worship the delicious mystery of taste buds and a digestive track – Ian asks Mira where she would like to sit, and she requests a table out on the balcony. They are led to a choice spot next to the open glass doors leading in and out of the restaurant, protected from the sun by the edge of the one of the large red-orange umbrellas. The round café-style table is delightfully intimate because it is Ian sitting across from her. If she was with a normal client she would have requested a big booth with plenty of personal space.

Their waiter brings them two menus and walks leisurely away again with their drink order. She already knows what she wants, but she pretends to peruse the selection because it affords her a good opportunity to surreptitiously study her client while he is engrossed in the task of making his choice. Usually such fair skin on a man doesn't appeal to her, and she wonders why now confronted with such a fine specimen of the type. Perhaps it is because she likes a touch of forcefulness (okay, yes, masterfulness) in a man, the arousing illusion of which would be harder to maintain if she could tell what he was feeling, and Ian possesses the kind of skin that blushes easily; she would be too easily able to gauge his emotional reactions. Yet looking at him now, she can't help but think this is a misguided assumption on her part, and that she has very foolishly been limiting her love-life to more olive-skinned partners. She has also never been attracted to a man with red hair, yet perhaps it is time to reprogram her erotic software with some new sensual input.

He looks up from his menu and catches her staring at him. Inside, Parisian cabaret-style posters decorate the walls of the restaurant in primary reds and yellows on a black background depicting long defunct actors and exotic liquors, and in an ad for the mystical drink, Absinth, the bottle is the same almost unreal green color as his eyes.

'What were you thinking just now?' he asks, smiling as though whatever she says will please him.

'I was just wondering what it would be like to drink Absinth,' she lies truthfully by only sharing a portion of her thoughts with him. She sets her menu down, and he immediately places his on top of hers. 'Not that I'm into drugs or anything.'

He stands up, and for a terrifying moment he seems to be walking out on her, but he merely shrugs off his jacket, and then drapes it over the back of his chair before resuming his seat, and it is enough time for her to be very pleased with what she sees. His shoulders are not as broad as... never mind, they're broad enough, and he possesses that wonderfully lean build that actually looks good in a white dress shirt stuffed into silky slacks held up by a brown leather belt. His suit isn't exactly olive-green, it's more like the color of leaves deep in a forest on an overcast day, a soft, muted green at once soothing and stimulating to her vision draped on the haunting branches of his skeleton... and his tie is almost the same greenish-violet as the wallpaper of her childhood bedroom...

The waiter returns with their drinks – bottled water for Mira, ice tea for Ian – and to take their orders.

'The Roasted Vegetable Sandwich is delicious here,' she tells her handsome new client, but he opts for the Turkey Club instead, and then they're alone again. Even here on the balcony of a restaurant overlooking a busy street she can rest her eyes on trees every now and then as they converse. She can almost distinctly feel his interest and curiosity taking strong, deep root in her, and in response she finds herself blooming trustingly in his company. She finds herself opening up to him, talking to him about everything and nothing, as they say, and the time goes by quickly. Then suddenly they hit a snag in the conversation, and the fantasies she was weaving about their future together snap free of the metaphorical loom to whip her heart painfully. They are discussing the layout of his new condo, and for some reason she happens to mention that she has the perfect corner set aside for his wine rack.

'I won't need a wine rack,' he says firmly, and abruptly drains his glass.

She sits in silence attempting to absorb this statement, but being an avid disciple of Dionysus, she clings stubbornly to the lost promise of their perfect compatibility for a few more desperate seconds.

'I haven't had a drink in over five years,' he adds, studying the check the waiter placed on the table between them as intently as a fragment of the Kabala containing vital esoteric information. He slips a platinum Master Card into the appropriate slot in the black leather folder, and slides it half over the edge of the table. 'I'm an alcoholic.'

* * *

Ian graciously drops her off at the Vienna metro station where she left her car. The chemistry between them fizzled out before it even had a chance to overflow the test tube. All that's left is the professional shell of their relationship. She will do a fabulous (even if not a passionately inspired) job on his living space, and he will fill her checking account with a nice big fee for her services, and that's it. Nothing was said about his revelation, and for about half a second that split her personal universe painfully in half, she actually considered becoming intimately involved with him anyway and forsaking her devotion to Dionysus. After all, her potential soul-mate was more important than a glass of wine... more important than all the warming, inspiring, relaxing, food-enhancing glasses of a divine beverage as old as civilization she would be giving up for the rest of her life... No. She couldn't do it. Her soul-mate couldn't possibly be a recovering alcoholic. Her guardian angel often appears to have a sense of humor, but it has never been so cruel.

As the waiter returned to collect their payment, Mira had time to rise from the ashes of the possible burning love between her and this red-headed man that had fired her imagination. 'Oh, well, that's all right,' she said lightly, 'there are plenty of other things we can put in that corner besides a wine rack... it was just a thought...'

His strained smile made her think of a pink Band-Aid uselessly placed over a fatal wound. For a second she felt horrible, guilty and afraid that she was making a big mistake. How could she possibly judge such a kind, intelligent and attractive man by the fact that he would never be able to share a glass of wine with her by the fireplace? One minute they were talking as happily as birds chirping at the beginning of spring, the next it was the dead of winter and all the lovely fantasies swirling around in her head had fallen like dead leaves buried beneath a sudden frosty silence. But Mira has always dared to be selfish in order to remain true to herself. Even as Ian rose, and graciously helped pull her chair out for her, she decided there was no reason for her to give up something she desired simply because, for whatever reason, he hadn't possessed sufficient self-control over his own appetites.

'I'll be out of town for the next couple of weeks,' he says as she steps gracefully out of his Ferrari. 'I'll call you as soon as I get back.' He smiles just as he did when they first met in his empty condo, and she sincerely appreciates the clean slate he is handing her.

'I'll look forward to it, Ian,' she replies, but once inside the comfortably familiar interior of her old candy-apple-red Camaro (a gift from dad for her high school graduation) she heaves a deep sigh and rests her head back against the bone-colored leather, closing her eyes and regrouping her energies for a minute before switching on the ignition. She has to face it – part of her is relieved Ian is no longer a candidate for her life-long affections. She is relieved because it means she can stop pretending not to think about Phillip. She is relieved because it means her intuition about the mysterious stranger in black leather might be more than just her imagination. She is relieved because she doesn't have to stop thinking about him anymore, which is hopeless. He is *all* she has really been able to think about since they met.

She turns on the engine, and drives gratefully home to Falls Church following a series of back streets to avoid the beginnings of rush-hour traffic on the more major roads.

An old white pick-up truck is parked in her driveway filled with a motley assortment of gardening utensils so old and well-used they look more like archaeological relics themselves than tools used to dig. She smiles. Ramon is here, although she has secretly nicknamed him Ra after the ancient Egyptian sun god. She glances at her watch. He will just be finishing up, making his seemingly effortless magical touches to her lush and extensive garden. She gets out of the car and walks around the side of the house in search of him. Ra likes to work wearing only skimpy cut-off shorts that conceal the bare essentials required by modern social conventions, another reason she gave him an ancient Egyptian name, because his work shorts are so ancient, loose and frayed at the edges they very much resemble a loin cloth from a distance. And the Pharaohnic look is delightfully complete whenever he wraps an old white T-shirt or towel around his head to keep sweat from dripping into his eyes. Unfortunately, it's not hot enough for that in May, but she still pauses to enjoy the picture of his lean brown body bent over one of her white stone vases as he tends the sublime explosion of violet petunias overflowing its borders.

'*Hola*, Ramon!' If she calls him Ra she will have to launch into a historical explanation that could take a very long time since she suspects his brain is not much bigger than her two cats' combined.

He looks up, and his smile of pure, unfeigned pleasure in her presence never fails to flatter her.

'*Hola*, Mira. *Como estás?*' He walks towards her in his usual slow, unhurried way, and as he approaches her, she admires his broad shoulders, hard pecs and ribbed abs with the same superficial pleasure she sucks on a Hershey's Chocolate Kiss.

'*Bien, gracias. Agua?*' she asks quickly, because engaging in conversation with Ra is like deliberately wading through quicksand; his thought processes aren't the fastest in the land.

'*Sí, porfavor, gracias.*'

'With lots of ice!' she adds cheerfully to cover up the fact that she is bee-lining it for the kitchen door, only there is something blocking her way inside. She stops and stares at the obstacle, unable to make sense of it as her pulse accelerates from the effort. She feels Ra step up behind her, and then walk past her to pick up the object of her contemplation – one of her empty half-gallon low-fat milk cartons with the top cut off to accommodate a bouquet of violet roses just beginning to bloom. He smiles at her again and stands there holding the impromptu vase as reverently motionless as a living relic from purer centuries visiting a temple to make an offering. And apparently Mira is the very reluctant goddess. She loves what Ra does for her garden, she has no desire to let him go, but if he begins exhibiting a more than extremely casual personal interest in her the sacrificial axe will have to fall...

He looks down at the house keys in her hand, glances at the lock on the kitchen door, and then looks back at her face, the glint of a question sparking in the dark depths of his eyes.

She realizes he is waiting for her to open the door so he can carry the roses inside for her. 'Ramon, you shouldn't have...'

His brow furrows slightly as he translates her words into Spanish in his mind, followed by the much longer process of trying to figure out exactly what they mean. The revelation of comprehension is beautiful to behold as his eyes ignite like hot coals and he grins at her, displaying all his perfect white teeth. 'Ah, no!' he says, laughing and shaking his head. *'Estavan aquí cuando llege.'* He glances down at the step leading up into the house, gesturing with his free hand. 'Here... found I.' Next he indicates her recycle bin and caresses the carton. 'I put in water so would not die.'

'You found these roses on my doorstep?' she cries, the concrete step leading up into her kitchen suddenly looking as beautifully significant as an altar.

'*Sí*, someone left for you.' He reaches between the thorny stems and extracts a small white card.

She takes it from him and turns it over, her heart in her throat. She is reminded of the large, beautifully ornate capital letters that begin each chapter in her book of fairytales. There is no name on the card, merely the exquisite calligraphy of the letter $\mathcal{P}$.

'Phillip!' she breathes.

* * *

The big, black, beautiful *P* with its elaborately curled ends has Mira riding a wave of euphoria all evening. There can be no doubt that the dozen violet roses are from Phillip, and the first thing she does before she gets Ra the glass of ice-water she promised him is rescue the beautiful blooms from the milk carton. She arranges them in a vase made of tiny multi-colored pieces of glass and places them in the center of her little living room just as all her thoughts center around the man who gave them to her. She is at once supremely happy and bitterly disappointed. Phillip was here, he came to see her again and she missed him, a terrible fact that takes the form of a physical tightness in her chest that is almost painful. Ra is standing in her kitchen, patient as the life-sized statue of an ancient Egyptian worker. She is sorry he found the roses before she did, but she is grateful he saved them from wilting.

'*Agua o cerveza?*' she asks brightly.

He smiles as though catching a glimpse of paradise.

She returns his smile, and offers him one of the bottles of *Sam Adams* that has been sitting on the bottom shelf in the back of her refrigerator for so long they date back to the Boston Tea Party in her personal history. She never drinks beer, and has no idea why she bought that six-pack in the first place. Some man she dated briefly probably left it there, and now she's glad he did because it enables her to offer her messenger of happiness a small reward. Ra heads back outside with his beer to finish what he was doing before he goes, and at last she is alone with her joy. The relaxing sensuality of solitude is deepened by the promise of highly desirable company in the future… and by the slapping sound of the cat flap rocking gently back and forth as Stormy slinks inside. 'Merr!' he exclaims in mingled pleasure and protest that she is finally home after being gone for so long.

'Stormy, baby, come here, sweetie!' He is a more than willing victim of her rapture as she cradles him like a baby against her chest. His eyes narrow into ecstatic slits, and the vibration of his purr feels like a warm, relaxing massage to her soul.

The cat flap rattles again and Sekhmet makes a loud, yowling entrance. She pointedly dips her face into her empty food bowl, and then glares up at the spectacle her silly brother and their pet human are making of each other.

Mira laughs and sets the limp gray rag of Stormy down beside his contrastingly tense sister. 'You're in luck tonight, Sekhmety-poo, because mommy's in a very good mood!'

'Mreow!' Translated, 'Don't you ever dare call me that again!' and 'Yeow!' clearly says, 'Bring my food out now! Why are you keeping me waiting?'

Stormy contently licks one of his paws, and then rests his head on Mira's sandaled feet. His roughly soft cheek doesn't graze her toes in the possessive act of scenting her and claiming her as his territory; it simply rests there for a long moment in a beautiful gesture of affection that takes her breath away with love and respect for this creature born on her doorstep three years ago. Once their mother – an all-black stray who has haunted the neighborhood for over a decade – finished nursing them, and was sure Mira would take care of them, she vanished and was never seen again, but she could not have left her children in a better home. Mira regularly drives all the way to *Webber's Pet Supermarket* to buy the healthiest, most nutritious cat food money can buy, and occasionally she supplements their gourmet diet with cans of Salmon, Tuna and Crab meat. Tonight definitely qualifies as a special occasion, and whenever she celebrates so do her pussies.

As she pours herself a glass of chardonnay (figuratively shuddering at the mere thought of giving up this ritual of a relaxing glass of wine in the evenings after a long hard day) Stormy and Sekhmet dig away at the tender pink meat of an Alaskan Salmon. Their bowls are on opposite sides of the kitchen. When they were kittens, Sekhmet would quickly devour her food, and then promptly begin devouring her brother's portion. She eats more slowly now, but she is still in the bad habit of stealing from her mild-mannered sibling, who steps meekly aside and begins licking his paws. Mira never ceases to be amazed at Stormy's gentle selflessness, and she keeps a watchful eye out for him, making sure he doesn't fall victim to his sister's greed as she leans against the counter sipping her wine and unwinding from the stress of three long days trying not to think about Phillip. Now at last she allows the memory and feel of him to fill her whole being with a deep, wonderfully promising warmth as the fruit of the vine branches through her veins and relaxes her into daring to feel nothing but hopeful...

All waves crash, some dashing themselves passionately against rocky shores while others gently surrender to the soft caress of white sand on a paradisiacal island. When Mira's euphoric wave inevitably begins to ebb, she finds herself in a place she has never been before – in an exotic world ripe with dangerously sinister terms like Master and slave, dominance and submission... suddenly she is afraid and in need of another glass of chardonnay.

She takes her wine into the living room, kicks off her high-heeled sandals, and curls her legs beneath her on the black leather sofa in front of the violet roses – his second gift. His first gift was the powerful climax he gave her, and it seems she hasn't been able to think straight since then. The unexpected, violent pleasure she gladly suffered that morning was like the shipwreck of all the normal, comfortable beliefs about love and sex she was sailing through life in. Now she finds herself curiously dazed and wandering a timeless realm deliberately left off all conventional maps as though it is located where dragons once dwelled at the ends of a flat world.

Dreaming of the man who calls himself a Master in a sexual and psychological subculture she knows next to nothing about, hints of oak and tropical fruit awash on her tongue as she sips her wine's liquid sunshine, Mira is possessed by the image of a proper young English woman – her white shirt and long skirt torn and soiled – stranded on a beach surrounded by a wild jungle, and she is destined to fall in love with a handsome barbarian king despite his humiliating harem and his fierce, arrogant ways. And Ian McFarland is the captain of the ship that fatally crashed into rocks and drowned, leaving her to fend for herself... leaving her alone with Richard, a man she knows essentially nothing about except that he frightens her a little... and turns her on a lot. Stormy leaps onto the sofa, and she gladly lets him curl up on her lap. 'How can I possibly get involved with a man who spends at least three nights a week with other women?' she asks him, and he stops purring abruptly, picking up on her distress. 'Yet he says he rarely sleeps with them, and if we become involved *rarely* will have to become *never* and carved in stone forever!' He begins purring again furiously. Not knowing when she will see him again is torture, and yet it also turns her on in a perverse way; the fact that he might show up at any second keeps her in a heightened state of arousal. 'Stormy, I have to get up, baby,' she tells him reluctantly, and he jumps off her lap obligingly. The pussy between her thighs is silently but inexorably demanding her attention.

In her bedroom, Mira flings off her dress, which leaves only the black lace panties she chose to wear this morning for luck. She slips the delicate fabric slowly down her legs, the shimmering pearly drop of sweet-smelling juice crowning the cotton crotch testifying to how wet she has become thinking of Master Phillip. This is the first time she actually dares call him that in her mind, and a thrill of trepidation only stokes the warmth between her thighs. Now that she is free to think of him, she wonders exactly what he does when he dominates women. She sincerely hopes flavored condoms are not involved!

The few sex toys she possesses are housed in a red velvet box, and now she pulls out her favorite dildo – a firm but tender white cock with life-like ribbing, a realistic curve and a pronounced head rising from the shaft. At last she can admit to herself how erotically charged her body has been since a man she didn't know commanded her to open her robe for him. But as she lies back across the bed, it doesn't feel right to believe she didn't know him. Even though they had only just met, he still felt mysteriously familiar to her in a way she can't rationally express but which is nevertheless unquestionable.

The cool and lifeless plastic is no substitute for a warm, living erection, but her pussy is crying to be filled, and this thick pacifier is better than nothing at the moment. The dildo may possess a life-like appearance, but it in no way feels like a real penis. The experience of Phillip's hard-on opening her up was effortlessly pleasurable; her innermost flesh embraced him lovingly, gratefully. Not so with the dildo. Her tight hole resists the invasion of the plastic organ, refusing to bloom naturally open around it. She has to gently and very slowly force the surrogate penis into her vagina. She lodges it halfway up inside her with one hand, rubbing her clit with the other, and soon the rubber cock is able to slide all the way into her juicing slot. Only the red cap (which she has never unscrewed to insert batteries to active the vibrating mechanism which only annoys her) is visible between her labial lips at the heart of her vulva. Her eyes are open, but she is not seeing the blank white ceiling... she is seeing a tall, broad-shouldered figure dressed all in black standing before her pumping his glorious erection... she climaxes immediately, almost too quickly, and the relief is only briefly physical, the rest of her is more turned on than ever.

Anxious to avoid the mild depression using a dildo tends to fill her with, Mira quickly rinses it clean and places it back in the red velvet box. She then rescues her remaining half glass of chardonnay and takes it into the bathroom, intent on the simple pleasure of a long hot shower to slough off the day's disappointments, and to baptize a fresh new self ready for everything.

CHAPTER FIVE

The magical staff used by magicians may have been camouflaged as a broom in the Middle Ages to hide it from agents of the Inquisition, hence the legend of witches flying across the moon on a broom...

In the middle of the night a storm rolls in. A flash of lightning illuminates Mira's full-length mirror and transforms it into the silver sheet of a moonlit lake from which Richard emerges, his black leather outfit gleaming wetly; clinging tightly to his body as he steps into her bedroom from another dimension, using the mirror's wooden frame like a doorway. In the impenetrable darkness that follows, Mira tells herself it was only her dream-drenched brain imagining what her eyes just saw as the pounding of her heart merges with the rumble of thunder outside. It seems a flash of her own subconscious brilliance when lightning strikes again and reveals the impossible truth of her vision. She sits up in bed with a cry, clutching the violet sheet to her breasts as Stormy and Sekhmet greet the man in black like their long lost big brother, purring joyfully around his boots.

'Oh, my God!' she whispers, thrilled to the bone by this casual display of unfathomable powers proving what she has always believed – that life possesses much more interesting sensual dimensions than her frigid reason can even conceive of...

There is a crashing rumble directly outside the window as a divine flash captures the shape of everything inside the bedroom while leaching it of all living color. Her senses are thrown into a confused panic as a forceful gust of wind snatches the sheet away from her naked body. Her scream is drowned out by another earth-shattering boom that sounds just like one of the old oak trees outside collapsing across her roof.

'Don't be afraid,' a man's voice whispers, carrying effortlessly over the storm's audio and visual chaos. 'It's all *us*, Mira, can't you feel it?'

At once she remembers, and it is with the bittersweet sense of falling back in time that she falls back across her violet bed sheets in Phillip's arms...

And suddenly wakes up alone in the dark to the ringing of her cell phone on the nightstand, its preemptory electronic bid for attention rising above the sound of wind-lashed rain beating against the window panes. She cries out in pain as Sekhmet leaps onto her legs and sinks the claws of her front paws into her thighs through the bed sheet. Stormy is right behind his sister, but he prefers the safety of Mira's chest where he perches Sphinx-like, staring earnestly into her eyes to let her know he wants her to exert a calming influence over the atmosphere.

'Mreow!' Sekhmet is more skeptical about Mira's powers and digs her claws into her skin again in furious denial that she is afraid.

She gently flings Sekhmet to the foot of the bed and cradles Stormy in one arm as she reaches anxiously for her cell phone. Her red digital clock brands 2:09 a.m. into her brain, signaling either a crank call or a life-threatening emergency on the other end of the virtual line. The few seconds it takes her to reach the phone feel like a much longer amount of time as her mind races… there aren't even any actual phone wires stretching like haunting black veins between her house and her parents' home; their voices have to journey up into space, all the warmth and meaning behind them disembodied for infinitesimal seconds before being bounced back by a satellite to enter a body again through the vehicle of the ears, just one miraculous sensory control in the complex adventure of physical incarnation…

She thanks God for the luminous violet display that enables her to find the 'Answer' button in the dark as she registers with relief that the number calling her is not familiar. 'Hello?' she says breathlessly.

'Don't be afraid,' a man's voice says quietly.

She sets Stormy down on the floor and gets out of bed, needing a solid surface beneath her to convince herself she isn't still dreaming.

'I hope you don't mind I looked up your number.'

'Of course I don't mind.' Her cellular is both her home and her work number; she got rid of her landline ages ago.

'Are you alone?'

'Well, not exactly…' She glances down at Stormy and Sekhmet circling her ankles, their ears thrown back anxiously. 'And if Sekhmet keeps sinking her claws into me, I'll need to call 911 and get some handsome paramedics over here.'

The effect his laughter has on her is in no way diminished by the fact that it has to travel up into space and then back down through the atmosphere again; it still makes her feel weak and warm all over.

'I just find it hard to believe a woman as beautiful as you isn't taken.'

'Oh, I've been taken alright, the only problem is no one's been able to hold me.' She is amazed at the light-hearted banter she is managing, and wonders if it's a symptom of sensual disorientation caused in part by being awakened in the middle of the night during a thunder storm that penetrated her dreams along with the man calling her, and in part by a relief so deep she feels herself falling and falling, waiting for him to catch her in his arms and hold her forever... but unfortunately it's only his disembodied voice flowing through her blood like the warm, spiced wine they used to drink in Medieval times she has always been meaning to try.

'That's going to change, Mira.'

Once again her feminine brain translates his sexy threat into a sublime promise as she doesn't so much sit as collapse onto the edge of her bed. 'It already has changed,' she confesses to this black leather-wearing priest speaking to her through the passionate veil of the storm. 'You're all I've been able to think about for the last three days, Phillip. Why did you just vanish like that?'

'You just answered your own question.'

She feels hurt by the way he deliberately tormented her, and then reluctantly remembers what he calls himself – a Master – and that his profession (or isn't it more like a lifestyle?) occasionally involves beating women, and apparently not just literally, because for almost ninety hours (even while she was asleep, it seems) the thought of him, the memory of him, the longing to see him again has whipped her soul even as she struggled to resist the thought of him; as she struggled to escape her painful obsession with him while at the same time dreading a return to her former freedom in which he did not exist, an existential pain far worse than the suffering of wondering if she would ever see him again. 'You didn't have to disappear for me to keep thinking about you, Phillip.'

'I know I didn't.'

She can't help it, she respects him for not indulging her, either with an explanation or with a justification for his actions. 'I guess you're not at work tonight,' she observes as neutrally as she can manage.

'I told you, Mira, I only work three nights a week.'

Considering what his work consists of (the excruciating details of which she has yet to try and picture) 'only' seems a rather unsuitable qualifier, but she keeps her catty claws sheathed, not wanting to frighten him away with a jealousy she has no right to feel yet. Or does she? 'Do you cut through lots of other women's yards?' she demands mildly.

His laughter is the best answer he can give her. It's the same way he laughed when she asked him if he was gay. 'No, that's the first time a pussy's ever tempted me into trespassing like that.'

Now it's her turn to laugh. 'I'm so glad she did, but then I don't believe in coincidence.'

'What do you believe in?'

'I believe in choreography, Phillip.'

'Mm, and judging by our first *pas de deux* together, the universe is more inspired than I ever dared hope.' He speaks so quietly her ears have a hard time capturing his voice over the sound of the rain beating against the window panes, but her heart hears him loud and clear. 'And if our first dance together is any indication, you don't have a problem with me leading, do you?'

No, I love it, she thinks, but is not ready to admit it yet. 'I don't know what you mean ...'

'Yes, you do.'

She wonders if she only imagined the slight note of disappointment in his voice that sears her soul like acid.

'I'll use an analogy I imagine you can relate to, Mira. Think of Ice Dancers... when the man throws his partner up in the air, she has to trust him to catch her and not let her fall. When he sends her into a spinning death spiral, it's a combination of her own submissive grace and his skill and strength that keep her safe and make the dance between them truly beautiful. Do you understand?'

She has never understood the dual nature of her heartbeat until now – hope and dread, excitement and fear – they are who she is and there is no distinguishing between them, until she makes the conscious choice to do so and whispers, 'I think so...'

'Good, then I'll be in touch again soon. Be ready.'

'When...?' But there is only empty space paradoxically ringing in her ears. She holds the phone away from her face, and sees the words printed in indelible black *Call Ended*. Thunder rumbles, farther away now, but her cats still leap shrilly onto the bed beside her. 'Oh, God, what am I getting myself into?' she asks them.

Stormy purrs, Sekhmet yowls, and somehow their reply is just how she feels inside. Despite what she must admit is a rather stimulating anxiety akin to stage fright before a major performance (she was in the Drama department all through high school and college) she is happier and more thrilled to be alive than she can remember being in all her adult life. She worries it's too soon to feel this way about a total stranger, but he ceased to be that the instant he penetrated her, and it's too late to go back now. What he made her feel is part of her forever, and yet only the beginning of a relationship that promises to challenge and fulfill her as she has never been challenged and fulfilled before.

* * *

'Mira, why don't you ever call?'

Oh, Christ, this is the last thing she needs – to talk to her mother the morning after the night she agreed to become a man's sex slave. She didn't actually say so, but it was clearly implied when she essentially agreed to do whatever he said. 'Hi, mom, I'm sorry, it's just that I've been so busy lately.'

'Well...' A deep sigh. 'I suppose that's a good thing.'

'Yes, it definitely is, it means I won't ever have to ask you and dad for money again.'

'Oh, Mira, dear, you know we don't mind-'

'No, but I do. I actually have money saved and business is great.'

'I'm so happy to hear that, dear.'

'You don't *sound* happy.'

'It's just that we never see you...'

'Mom, that's not true.' At least not from what Mira admits is her own decidedly selfish perspective. She hasn't had her cup of tea yet this morning, and this phone conversation with her mother is making the one she had last night with a man feel increasingly like a dream as thunder rumbled and lightning flashed outside indistinguishable from her tumultuous emotions.

She remains on the phone chatting with her mother with only a fraction of her mind engaged in the conversation as she microwaves water for tea, and slips some high fiber whole wheat bread slices into her toaster. She is not yet awake enough to juggle her anxious anticipation concerning the intense sexual relationship she is embarking upon, with her sweet and comfortable love for her parents and the guilt she feels at not spending enough time with them. Rose's affectionately worried and needy voice makes Mira feel as if she is standing on a wharf about to deliberately board the ship flying a black flag painted with a white skull and crossbones while her parents watch, incredulous and horrified, as their innocent little girl willingly sells herself into slavery...

The microwave bell chimes just as Rose asks with a similarly high-pitched indignation, 'Have you even heard a word I said, Mira?'

'Mom, I have to go now, I'm meeting with a client this morning,' she lies. 'But I'll call you later, I promise. I love you. And tell dad I love him, too, and that I'll come over for dinner again soon.'

'You promise?'

'I promise.'

'We love you too, dear, take care... and keep your windows closed at night, please!'

'Uh-huh. Bye.' She gently tosses the phone down on a black potholder. She wonders vaguely what it would be like to leave the house and be unreachable by anyone, interacting only with people she actually meets in the flesh. Her cell phone's technological butler is always with her, announcing in clear black letters or numbers who is seeking an audience with her. More often than not she sends everyone to the Drawing Room of her voicemail to await her pleasure. Phillip's number is stored in memory under Received Calls, yet these coordinates to his soul are absolutely useless to her because she would never dream of calling him. He said he would be in touch again soon. All she can do is wait.

As her tea steeps and she is spreading organic strawberry jam over the hot slices of bread, it dawns on Mira – with a sense of wonder much sharper than the butter knife – that her attitude has always been naturally submissive. The man makes the first move, and keeps making them while she either submits to his attentions or rejects them.

'I'll be in touch again soon...' The memory of his sexy, threatening, promising, everything-she-could-ever-have-hoped-for-in-a-man's-voice, is affecting her appetite. Suddenly she isn't interested in breakfast, but she makes herself eat, and drink her tea knowing caffeine withdrawal and hunger pangs will interfere with the smooth flow of her creative energies. She needs to enter the measurements of Ian's condo into her computer; the monthly bills are due to be paid; she should renew her ad in a local paper, and make an appointment for Stormy and Sekhmet at the Vet for their annual shots. She doesn't want to do any of these things. All she can do is wonder when Phillip will decide to get in touch with her again, what form his touch will take, what he will tell her to do, where they will be... All she can do is wonder if she'll be able to let go of her fears and dance the mysterious *pas de deux* of dominance and submission with him. Only time will tell, and right now every minute feels like an hour she somehow has to get through waiting for him to enter her life again.

Forget work and finances; all she is good for this morning is cleaning her little doll's house from top to bottom while doing all her laundry, including bed sheets, towels, bathroom rugs, everything!

* * *

The doorbell rings at the worst possible moment. In the process of cleaning her doll's house, Mira has made an absolute mess of herself. Her hair is half up and half down (the hazards of a too hasty pin-up) and deep in the midst of mopping her kitchen floor she can't be bothered to do anything except curl it impatiently behind her ears. She is wearing old white socks, and a very a skimpy pair of grey terrycloth shorts that tie closed in front with a delicate white bow adorning the bare skin just

The Fabric of Love

below her navel. And there is lots of skin to be seen, because the only other thing she's wearing is an old violet sport's bra to avoid the slight muscular ache in her chest caused by allowing her breasts to swing freely back and forth as she mops and vacuums. Cleaning is a full-body workout, involving lots of bending and squatting, lifting and folding, reaching and running back and forth, especially if you've decided to cook at the same time. She has allowed herself to be fully possessed by domestic demons today which ground her firmly in the present and keep her from anticipating and worrying about the future... except for in the very back of her mind, which is always filled with thoughts and images of Phillip no matter what she is doing.

The doorbell rings again as Mira stands, mop in hand, paralyzed with horror. It can't be! It just can't be him, not when she's in the middle of two loads of laundry on top of making split pea soup on one burner and Garbanzo and Chorizo stew on the other; not when she looks like something the cats just dragged in.

'Coming!' she cries, propping the mop up against the counter. Wresting the remaining pins from her hair, she shakes it loose over her bare shoulders. 'Please don't let it be him!' she prays beneath her breath. 'Please, please, Lord, don't let it be him!' Yet, naturally, deep down she desperately wants it to be him, so it is a hot and cold slap of mingled relief and disappointment when she opens the front door and sees only the lumpy blue-clad form of a female Federal Express courier standing out on her front porch.

'Package for Mira Rosenthal,' she says with the briefest of glances at the purported recipient; she keeps her eyes fixed on her electronic screen as if avoiding the sight of the half naked beautiful woman she is serving.

'That's me,' Mira claims the feather-light box and dutifully signs her name on the virtual line.

'Have a nice day,' the courier addresses an oak tree as she quickly takes her leave.

'You too,' Mira recites automatically, but in her case she sincerely means it. She is not expecting anything from anyone that she can remember, and it is with a fun, Christmas-like feeling that she takes the box inside and sets it down on the kitchen counter, pulling eagerly on the cardboard tab that slices it conveniently open. The package is so light she wonders what could possibly be inside it – probably a fabric sample she forget she ordered – and her guess appears to be confirmed when she spots the shimmer of blood-red satin... except it is no boring square fragment but instead flows on and on as she pulls it gently out of the box. The piece of cloth is approximately three inches wide and not quite long enough to be a belt. She rifles through the file cabinets of her mental synapses trying to remember when she ordered this. She is already sure she didn't, but she is compelled to try and make sense of this unexpected special delivery. She turns the box over and hastily searches the air bill for a clue, but there is no return address.

Phillip said he would be in touch again soon, and the fabric's coolly sensuous caress is telling her without words that it's from him... and that she knows what it is...

The cat flap rattles, announcing the entrance of one of her non-human roommates, but she scarcely notices, too intent on identifying the origin and purpose of the lovely length of fabric... which suddenly jerks as if alive and begins slipping out of her hand.

'Sekhmet, no!' She rescues the fine cloth from the damagingly curious swipe of her feline's claws. 'This isn't for you, it's for me!' she adds cattily, and Sekhmet walks away indifferently, pretending she was never really interested in it.

Mira has not forgotten what Phillip did with the sash of her robe (she will never forget) but this burgundy-colored cloth is broader and not as long... and soft enough to make an ideal blindfold. She tips the box over and shakes it, hoping something will fall out as if from another dimension in the cardboard invisible to the naked eye that will explain where the suggestive piece of fabric comes from and exactly what she is supposed to do with it. There is no note, nothing except her intuitive certainty the 'gift' is from Phillip and his way of preparing her for what he plans to do to her next.

She has been blindfolded once or twice during sex, but it was always done in a fun, playful way. She knows in her bones that with this man it will be very different, more serious and meaningful, challenging and fulfilling. For the first time in her life, she is sure beyond a shadow of a doubt that the depth of her imagination and the intensity of her desires are not going to be left wanting, not if the erotic appetizer they shared in her treasure-filled garage is any indication.

She folds the sash reverently into the red velvet box in her bedroom, safely away from curious kitties. She then returns to serving the domestic demons she is willingly sacrificing herself to today. It is time to let the finished soups cool before she ladles them into individual portion-sized plastic containers to freeze for easy lunches and dinners in the future. She is in the middle of enough chores to keep her busy until late afternoon, at which point the promise of a shower and a glass of chardonnay beckon her like the Holy Grail hidden beneath a gloriously hot waterfall.

* * *

Mira has just finished lathering herself up with her fluffy lavender sponge and favorite milk soap when her cell phone rings.

She quickly shuts off the water and reaches for her little metal butler where it is lying on top of her towel just within reach of her dripping hand. It crosses her mind that he told her to be ready, yet she seems to have done everything in her power not to be prepared for anything today – a subconscious form of resistance at odds with her excitement. She has only seen this series of numbers once before, but it is already branded into her heart. 'Hello?' she answers as calmly as possible considering her drenched state, both physically and emotionally, for no man has ever inspired such a flood of feelings in her before.

'Did you receive the package?' he asks quietly.

She suffers a thrill of secrecy and danger. 'Yes, I did,' she replies, shivering for more reasons than one.

'I'll teach you the correct response later, Mira, but since you're a virgin to B&D I'm taking it very slowly with you. I noticed the secluded arbor out in your garden. At exactly eight o'clock this evening if you happen to be wearing any clothes you'll take them all off, everything, including your shoes, and you will wait for me there naked, wearing only the contents of the package. You know what to do with it. You will wait for me lying on your back with your arms over your head and your legs spread. You may bring a towel to lie on if you prefer.'

'You want me to lie naked out in my garden blindfolded?' The incredulous question escapes her before she can stop it.

'I won't repeat myself. If you're not there waiting for me exactly as I described, then I'll assume you've changed your mind about us.'

'I'll be there.'

'Then I'll see you then.'

He leaves her to wonder whether or not a pun was intended as the display on her phone once again announces Call Ended.

She scarcely notices the rest of her long-awaited shower. Her property is blessedly private – three full acres of big old trees, flowering bushes and vines, almost all of which are in bloom now and providing a natural protection from neighbor's prying eyes. Nevertheless, she does have neighbors, and it makes her anxious to imagine lying naked outside vulnerably blind. Only the fact that her little arbor is wonderfully private – a horseshoe of bushes over six-feet tall, two of them Rose bushes – assuages her nervousness. Chances are no one will see her, but that of course means there is also the chance someone might, yet because she is probably not in any real danger in the privacy of her yard, how vulnerable she will feel serves to excite her more than frighten her.

CHAPTER SIX

"Don't settle for the one you can live with, wait for the one you can't live without."

Anonymous

Eight o'clock arrives and brings with it those cool, lovely, and sadly evanescent moments just after the sun dips below the horizon when the beauty of the dying day is both softened and intensified – a classic cross-over moment. Mira has a feeling there will be many such moments with Phillip, and her anticipation is so intense it has the power to slow time down to a miserable crawl. The evening seems endless as one glass of chardonnay flows into another. She is sitting with her legs curled up beneath her on the couch wearing her violet robe and gazing at the violet roses left by the man she has agreed to meet naked and blindfolded out in her garden. Part of her feels like a little girl playing a really exciting game with the new boy next door, who at last seems a fit match for her imaginative energies.

'Eat your heart out, Anna,' she murmurs, smugly taking another sip of wine. Her parents are still in touch with Anna's parents, which is why she knows that her ex best friend from long ago married a stock broker and is getting ready to pop her third baby, in Mira's opinion a nightmare scenario if there ever was one. Suddenly she feels sorry for women whose circumstances prohibit them from doing such simple sensual things as lying naked out in a garden waiting for their lover. The blindfold seems symbolically appropriate since she has not been able to truly see anything lately except her thoughts of Phillip.

When the clock on her cable box reads seven-fifty-four, Mira slips out of her robe, picks up a burgundy towel with the red satin blindfold resting ready on top of it, and heads outside wearing nothing but the black hair waving gently down her back.

Being naked out in her yard feels utterly natural to her; she doesn't experience any of the awkward sense of exposure she feared. On the contrary, she feels like a special guest, the center of attention in a wild yet sophisticated celebration serving the heady cocktail of flowers in bloom, each color intoxicatingly lovely in its own way. And even though most of the lively guests are invisible, her naked flesh clearly senses their presence in the prickly grass, in the dark earth, and in the sap-filled barks of old trees. She is surrounded by the cool, shadowy peace of evening... and of life speaking to her through a silence punctuated by the sound of leaves rustling in the breeze...

Dusk, when the sun has set but night has not yet fallen, the ultimate crossover moments when the sky is an indescribable color – a deep, haunting blue that can never be mixed on an artist's palette occasionally deepened by an erratic black streak. The bats are out. She sometimes enjoys sipping her chardonnay out on the porch watching them, twilight's haunting window between night and day the only time they're visible to the human eye... evoking legends of vampires rising from their coffins the instant the sun sets, vulnerable for a few moments before they blend into the darkness to begin wreaking their deadly sensuality...

The red and white roses that will adorn her bower have not yet bloomed, so it is in a deep-green well of darkening foliage that Mira spreads out her towel and kneels naked in the center of it. She has never tied a blindfold over her own eyes before, and she takes great care to get it just right so there aren't any cracks she can cheat and see through. Beneath the slick cloth absolute darkness reigns as she secures it in a firm knot at the back of her head, unable to avoid tangling a few of her hairs in it. Then she lies on her back, bends her arms over her head, and spreads her legs just as he instructed her to do.

For the first minute or so she wonders how long she will have to wait for him like this, but gradually her mind relaxes along with her body, and like the loud, clattering engine of a train slowing down at a major crossroads she stops thinking to just listen. It's true that not being able to see the world magnifies the sounds around her. The soft rustling of leaves seems to grow louder and louder until it becomes a veritable symphony rising in tempo the more she focuses on it. She won't be able to hear Phillip's approach on the soft carpet of grass so well-tended by Ra. Will she be able to sense him? She is glad he gave her permission to spread a towel between her naked skin and all the creepy-crawly creatures living in the dirt, because though she doesn't mind them every now and then accidentally landing on her arms and legs, her pussy is another matter altogether, a sacred shrine off limits to all biological riffraff. And right now her fleshly temple doors are wide open waiting for the man her soul has already dared to identify as the exciting high priest she has been waiting for since she knew how to daydream.

The wind lightly caressing her skin makes her think of the words, 'You know not whence it comes or whence it goes' a metaphor for the spirit as an invisible force that nevertheless has the power to touch us... but not like that... there is something warm and decidedly substantial moving slowly up her legs...

'Phillip?' she whispers, but does not really need to hear him reply. Her body knows those are a man's hands caressing the infinitely sensitive flesh of her inner thighs even as she senses the deepening of the air above her. Suddenly, she longs to rip off the blindfold to see him. Desperate to look at him, to fill all her senses with him, she arches her back beneath the delicious torture of only being able to experience his ghostly touch. She can't even be sure it truly is him. The wild thought crosses her mind that Ramon forgot one of his gardening tools, and that those are actually his hands moving ever so lightly up towards her eagerly waiting breasts, but she immediately dismisses the notion. She doesn't need to see to know that is not her gardener kneeling between her legs; she recognizes the almost palpable magnetic current flowing between Phillip's skin and hers as his fingertips just barely brush her skin. She sighs with pleasure as a cool, warm, firm and moist sensation engulfs one of her nipples, instantly hardening it into a pebble sending ripples of delight into the depths of her sex.

It doesn't take long for a sublime anarchy to reign in her other senses freed from the tyranny of sight. He works on both her nipples with a skill that has her nerve-ends smoldering with a desire that keeps intensifying the wetter her pussy gets. It is too much for her, she has to touch him, she has to feel him, her arms refuse to remain resting passively over her head...

He grasps both her wrists with a swift strength that makes her aware of how delicate her bones are. She moans, knowing she has done wrong, and senses him move away from her as he stretches her arms up over her head again. Tears of frustration and regret that she has failed to submit gracefully to him threaten to dampen the blindfold. She has to bite her lip to keep them in check. The loving way his fingertips caress her open palms soothes and forgives her. Then she senses another welcome disturbance of the air around her and knows he is moving again. Her suspicions are confirmed when she distinctly feels his presence once more concentrated between her legs. The tongue she fantasized about that morning as she touched herself becomes real, and miraculously even more skilled and sensitive to her slightest reaction than she could ever have dared hope.

Small, whimpering sounds of disbelief and gratitude well up from within her, released into the cool evening as he goes down on her with a precision that is almost surgical in its power to cut through her defenses, yet there is nothing cold and passionless about the way he eats her. Her pussy is juicing helplessly, gushing like another small organic fountain added to the three already gracing her garden. The tip of his tongue circling endlessly makes her clitoris feel like a priestess coaxed all the way out of her fleshly temple for the first time by the quality of a devotion at last worthy of her sensitive spirit. In the past so many men simply attacked her clit with all the finesse of farmers trampling on a seed expecting pleasure to just naturally bloom between her thighs as a result; sucking on her body's mysterious seed as though it was a simple sugar-based candy, making it defensively hard and producing the opposite effect of melting her in their mouth. Some of her lovers were a bit more circumspect, but there was not enough passion in the almost mathematical application of licks, sucks, laps and nips they patiently subjected her to, seeking her sexual response like the answer to an almost impossibly complex equation.

As she hoped and suspected would be the case, being orally pleasured by a man feels stunningly different with Phillip. The muscle of his tongue is so firm and thick that when it works its way up between the folds of her labia, opening her up as he savors the nectar of her arousal, her back arches with longing; with the blind need to be penetrated by his cock or his tongue or his fingers, she doesn't care which, she just has to feel a part of him inside her before the she completely loses her mind wanting him. Yet she doesn't dare speak; she doesn't dare beg him to fuck her. Already she has learned enough to suspect pleading with him will only delay her fulfillment, so she submissively endures the divine torment of his features burying themselves in her sex. He uses his whole face to arouse her, not just his tongue, working her pussy up into a drenched frenzy that will suck him down to the very hilt of her incarnation when he finally penetrates her.

Her nipples are so hard that when he reaches up and begins firmly stroking them between this thumb and forefinger a climax blooms between her thighs like a hot house flower, with time-lapse explosiveness, her clit abruptly dissolving between his lips like a drop of dew reflecting all the heat of the sun. Her brain is not prepared for the intensity of the orgasm that takes root in her pelvis and blossoms with devastating beauty in all her nerve-endings and she hears herself cry out as if in pain. The pleasure is so powerful she needed to prepare herself for it, but it's too late as she comes in waves that just keep deepening and deepening rather than ebbing. She has never climaxed like this before without touching herself, with only a man's face buried between her thighs. Her most vital muscles contracting, it takes all the willpower she possesses not to reach down and grab his head, whether to push it away or drive his face deeper into her pussy she cannot say.

'Very good, Mira.' He finally lets her hear his voice.

'Oh, God, Phillip, I've never–'

'Did I give you permission to speak?'

'I'm sorry,' she whispers, and then bites her lip fearing she has further compounded her transgression by speaking again. It feels as much reward as punishment when he abruptly turns her over onto her stomach and spanks her. She has been spanked before, but never like this, and she gasps beneath the impact of a sensation that prepares her for the even more welcome experience of his erection thrusting into her pussy from behind. The soft cotton beneath her is cushioned by lush grass but it does not give way like a bed. The earth beneath her feels rock-solid as he pounds his cock into her slick hole at an angle that leaves nothing to her imagination, his balls slapping her labia as his head violently kisses her cervix. She rests her cheek on the towel and clutches it to brace herself even as the rest of her body rests limp as a beached mermaid beneath his plunging dives. There is nothing passive about her on the inside, however; her pussy is actively, greedily grasping his erection, pulsing open and closed around him like a hungry anemone feasting on his totally fulfilling dimensions. He is so hard she suspects his relentless penetrations would almost hurt if her sex wasn't so wet and relaxed from the orgasm he gave her with his mouth, and when he spreads his body on top of hers it feels like the full, wondrous weight of the universe falling on her as his warm breath caresses her cheek, 'Oh, Mira!'

She moans in response, engrossed in the profound thrill of caressing and squeezing his cock with the most special muscles she possesses. This time he isn't wearing a condom and she is very glad of that, because not being able to see him as well as not truly feeling him inside her would have been unbearable. In her mind's eye she pictures his erection stabbing her and visualizes the walls of her innermost flesh wrapping around it, squeezing his shaft from the base to the head in a continuous rippling motion even as the rest of her flesh remains utterly submissive beneath him. She relishes every second of his beating as he packs the full, rending length of his penis into her pussy with every stroke. She is going to make him come inside her. She will make it impossible for him to pull out of her at the last minute. She is determined to have the impenetrable darkness behind her eyelids illuminated by the exploding stars of his cum surging into her innermost space in an erotic Milky Way. She longs to beg him to come inside her, but he hasn't given her permission to speak. So she begs him silently, with the part of her made especially to coax everything she desires from a man. For years she has been exercising her vaginal muscles in the hope of one day using this sensual skill on her soul-mate, and his breathless groans speak to the effectiveness of her self-training, as does the way his hard-on begins pulsing inside her, further intensifying the pleasure bonding them, until she has to break her silence by crying out as his cock reaches critical mass and he ejaculates deep between her thighs.

Afterwards, they lie still for a few moments. She can tell he is still fully dressed and that he isn't wearing black leather. His shirt is soft against her skin, and before fucking her he pushed his pants down far enough for her to be able to feel his naked hips and scrotum as well as his condom-free dick. She is almost sorry when he lifts his weight off her, and sudden panic prompts her to raise herself up onto her elbows. She is afraid he will walk silently away again while she isn't looking, once again disappearing from her life for an intolerably long time. This nightmare scenario almost makes her speak, but she retrains herself with a monumental effort of will.

'Thank you, Mira,' he says from somewhere above her. 'You may sit up now, which means you may kneel…. no, not like that. We *are* in a temple of sorts, but it's not a Catholic church, so spread your legs more... that's good. Now sit back on your heels and rest the backs of both your hands on your knees... very nice... keep your head lowered... beautiful.'

She is grateful for his firm commands, which offer a civilized contrast to how uncontrollably wet her pussy is. Not being able to see her juices mingled with his sperm trickling down the insides of her thighs causes it to assume embarrassing, almost geographical dimensions in her mind... the tributaries of a river flowing from a temple as old as life... Holding herself perfectly still, she sighs with contentment that her quest for a truly virile man is over at last.

'Did you enjoy that?' he asks, his voice sounding a little closer now and coming from somewhere to her left. 'You have permission to speak.'

'Yes,' she confesses softly.

'The correct response is "Yes, Master".'

Her back stiffens.

'I told you to keep your head down.'

She obeys him tensely, her lips sealed like a tomb behind which all her self-respect is buried as she remains stubbornly silent for a few seconds. 'I refuse to call you what countless other women call you,' she informs him tightly; proudly.

'The women I work with address me as Master Phillip. Did I ask you to call me Master Phillip?'

The beautiful hope and happiness that spark in her heart is fanned by her whispered submission, 'No, Master.'

'I want you to understand, Mira, that only you have the right to call me Master.'

'I hope so...'

'Which means I already care about you, and want you, more than any other woman I've ever met. It means I want you to be my real, one-and-only slave.'

Her joy at his words is compounded by the sensation of him untying her blindfold. She holds her breath, scarcely able to believe she is about to see him again after so long, not to mention after how blindly intimate they just were together. The satiny blackness slips away and is replaced by a slightly less absolute darkness. Night has fallen. All she can see of him at first is his white shirt, lovely and luminous as moonlight. His features are distinguishable only as infinitely intriguing shadows when he kisses her, threading his fingers through her hair and tilting her head back to part her lips so he can tongue her deeply, reminding her of how selfishly his cock used her throat.

'Are you cold?' he asks, crouching before her.

'Not at all... I mean, no Master.'

His smile is a subtle light in the darkness. 'You may rise now,' he says, straightening up and offering her his hand so she can brace herself on it as she obeys him. 'Shall we adjourn to your doll's house?'

'Yes, Master,' she replies happily, and bends over to pick up her towel.

'No, leave it there,' he commands. 'Lots of intense, positive energy was just absorbed by that fabric. I want you to leave it there for at least twenty-four hours to remind you of this special night, Mira.'

'Yes, Master,' she agrees, but makes no move to walk towards her house, afraid he will vanish if she doesn't keep her vision fixed directly on him.

'Come on,' he says gently, and once again his smile hits her retinas as s subtle glow in the darkness. He takes her hand and leads the way to her kitchen door. Somewhere along the way Stormy and Sekhmet join them, doing everything in their power to trip them up as they insist on purring passionately around their ankles.

'I don't know what it is about you, Phillip, but Sekhmet has never reacted to another human being like this before. She adores you!'

'She has profoundly good taste, just like her mistress.'

'Yes, we're both very particular.'

'And I'm grateful for that. You could very well be married and pregnant with your second baby by now.'

'Right!'

He opens the door, intuitively aware she didn't lock it, or rather he commanded her to lie out in her garden wearing nothing but a blindfold so he knew there was no place for her to keep a key.

The doll's house is dark except for a lamp in the living room illuminating the bouquet of violet roses. She automatically switches on the overhead light in the kitchen.

Pressing his body up against hers, he promptly flicks the switch back down. 'Do you have any candles?' he asks in a voice soft enough to be her own imagination, except that his presence is more real than anything she has ever experienced; it makes her heartbeats feel like hammer blows erecting the glorious edifice of their future together in the form of a temple dedicated to love and sex and ancient erotic rituals without end...

'Of course I have candles,' she retorts breathlessly. 'As a matter-of-fact, there are two candles on the fireplace mantle in the living room.'

'Matches?'

She opens the small drawer beside which they're standing and extracts one of her many little boxes of wooden matches.

'Light the candles for us, Mira,' he caresses her hair as he speaks, 'then go find the highest pair of heels you own. Put them on, and walk slowly back into the living room.'

She does not need to clearly see his eyes in the dim light to be hopelessly caught up in the gravity of his regard; nevertheless, the correct reply to his command sticks in her throat, battling decades of feminist indoctrination. 'Yes, Master,' she whispers at last.

He kisses her forehead as if rewarding the supreme mental and emotional effort she just made for him. 'And while you're doing that for me,' he adds, 'I'll open a bottle of wine.'

'How did you know I drink wine?' she asks happily.

'The same way I knew you would let me fuck you ten minutes after we met.'

'Oh...' She escapes into the living room and lights the two candles on the fireplace mantle as he instructed her to do, wondering which high-heeled sandals he would prefer of the many pairs she owns. Then she hears the lamp click off behind her. He is completely banishing the easy comfort of electricity in favor of the warm illumination provided by the two flames flickering in the breeze from an open window, and giving off a surprising amount of light even while deepening the shadows. Her modest wine rack remains in darkness, but he walks straight towards it as though he possesses a built-in honing device for the fruit-of-the-vine. She watches him, mentally thanking her guardian angel for finally coming through. 'Shall I get us two wine glasses?' she asks.

'I told you what to do, Mira.'

She hurries into her bedroom feeling almost literally shoved into its refuge by the tone of his voice, which brooks no argument whatsoever. Almost inevitably, she selects a red pair of sandals from *Victoria's Secret* with stiletto heels and thin straps designed to show off the shapely curves of her feet. Then she cheats and sneaks a quick peak at herself in the bathroom mirror, only to discover there is nothing she can do with her appearance to improve it. Her cheeks are attractively flushed from having her pussy very properly fucked, and her eyes are shining with a happiness she has not seen reflected back at her for as long as she can remember. The slightly humid evening air has given an even fuller wave to her hair, and the contented smile on her lips feels like the new natural setting for her facial muscles. She also takes a moment to clean her excessively moist slit and the insides of her thighs with a tissue. His cum trickling slowly out of her is a distracting sensation, to say the least. Yet suddenly part of her feels guilty about wiping her skin clean of the evidence of his pleasure. She knows she will have to confess doing so to him to find out if he considers it a transgression, and this thought process astonishes her more than anything that has happened between them so far.

She practices a sexy walk from the bathroom to the bedroom door, where she pauses like an actress about to step out on stage for the second act of a performance that, so far, has totally captivated her, and gotten rave reviews from even the most critical parts of her mind. The sight of him sitting casually on her black leather couch, his right ankle resting on his left knee, nearly arrests her progress towards him it has such an impact on her. The white button-down shirt open halfway down his chest and tucked into silky black slacks becomes him just as much as tight black leather, the slightly full sleeves evocative of a prince's romantic garment. Sekhmet is nearly invisible curled up on his lap, obviously well aware of the fact that she has secured the best seat in the house. Stormy is lying on the floor at Phillip's feet, his head resting contentedly on his left foot clad in a polished black shoe. Two half full glasses of red wine wait beside the vase veritably exploding with roses.

The penetrating gravity of his stare draws her to him like an invisible leash, making it hard for her to walk slowly, as though she could possibly be indifferent to how soon she reaches him.

He smiles. 'Mm...'

She proudly tosses her hair back over her shoulders. Her breasts are round and firm, responding to how aroused she is in every fiber of her being.

'A black cat is a very interesting form for Cupid to take,' he remarks.

'Well, you know what they say – dogs think they're humans, cats think they're gods.'

'Come here.' He extends his right hand towards her. She reaches for it with hers, and as their fingertips touch she thinks of the Sistine Chapel's bearded old patriarch in a hospital gown offering the spark of life to a grotesquely muscular young man. Michael Angelo's talent and perseverance notwithstanding, she has never liked that fresco, and she understands why now as electricity literally crackles between her flesh and Phillip's – because the spark of life can only be ignited between a man and a woman no matter what any religions or alternative lifestyles preach. 'Stand right there,' he instructs gently, directing her slightly to one side of him. 'I want to look at you... you have the most beautiful pussy, Mira.' He idly strokes her sleeping feline's sleek fur as he speaks. 'And you know how to use it, too. You pleased me very much out there.'

'Thank you... Master.' Every time she uses this title to address him, Mira feels as though she deliberately shoots up a powerful drug which is making her feel better and better the more she surrenders control of herself. She never realized (although intuitively she suspected) that submitting to the right man could be so intoxicating.

'You may hand us our wine and sit down beside me now.'

She obeys him gracefully.

He chimes his glass against hers. 'To us.'

'To us,' she echoes, and they each take a sip of the Australian Zinfandel.

'Very nice,' he compliments her taste in wine.

'It's okay for the price,' she replies humbly.

'Do you drink wine every night?'

'Yes, with dinner, and usually I have a glass or two of chardonnay before that, to relax.' She knows she sounds defensive, but she can't help thinking of Ian, and shuddering inwardly at the mere possibility of a universe in which she never saw Phillip again and ended up settling for a handsome recovering alcoholic.

'My parents own a vineyard,' he tells her.

She laughs. 'What?'

'A small vineyard in Washington State just big enough for uninhibited personal consumption and to give away cases as gifts every year.'

'That's wonderful!'

'And you're luscious.' He tilts her face up to his and kisses her on the lips, his mouth moving directly against hers as he whispers, 'I think you may be the one...'

'You think?' she breathes, and feels him smile.

He thrusts his tongue into her mouth and wrestle hers into breathless submission for a moment. Then he sits back comfortably and takes another sip of wine. 'I *know* you are,' he adds soberly. 'And to think I had almost given up hope.'

This admission of vulnerability makes him even more stunningly attractive in her eyes.

'But I don't think we should talk about the past tonight, Mira. Tonight is about the present, and everything the future holds for us.'

'Amen,' she whispers, and takes another sip of the young vintage.

'Not that I have any frightening skeletons in my closet,' he teases.

'Except for your job,' she points out quietly, glancing down at her naked breasts.

'You have an amazingly beautiful body, Mira.' He changes the subject.

'Well, I don't exactly have washboard abs,' she observes, patting the little round belly she gets when she sits down.

'And what makes you think fucking a woman with washboard abs appeals to all men? I much prefer a softer cushion. You're toned and yet soft all over. In my eyes you're perfect.'

She smiles. 'My dad used to tease me when I was little because I thought I was more beautiful than Miss Universe.'

'You're the most beautiful woman in my universe, and that's what counts.'

She sighs. 'You say all the right things, Phillip.'

He laughs. 'That's the first time a woman has ever said *that* to me.'

'But how is that possible?' She is genuinely indignant, and has to take another sip of wine to wash away the bad taste of other people's limited perceptions.

'I've never said such things to a woman before, Mira.'

'I believe you...'

'And you trust me.'

'Yes, Master.'

'Then we have all we need to embark on a very exciting life-long journey together.'

'I've been lied to before,' she confesses abruptly, setting her glass down on the table in front of them. 'I'm very trusting.'

'I know.' He places his glass beside hers. 'But you're safe with me now. I'll never lie to you, Mira, and I'll never do anything to hurt you.'

Annoyed by the motion of her warm bed, Sekhmet jumps off his lap.

'Come here.' He slips an arm around her shoulders while his other hand gently urges her cheek down against his chest. 'You believe me when I say that I'll never hurt you, don't you?'

'Yes, Master.' The sound of his heart beating has a profoundly soothing affect on her; a deep, steady rhythm she mysteriously knows she can trust for as long as they live.

'Good, and now I want you to go put on something nice. I'm taking us out to dinner.'

CHAPTER SEVEN

"Do you love me because I am beautiful, or am I beautiful because you love me?"

Charles Perrault, *Cinderella*

The good thing about being self-employed is that no one can force you to work if you don't want to. In some universe that might be considered bad, but not in Mira's. Her office assistants consist of two cats whose only priority (when they aren't napping on her desk or file cabinet) is to sensually enjoy every second they're awake. In the three years she has known them they have had a very positive effect on her disposition. Once again in an alternate universe the effect her felines have had on her might be considered deleterious, but even medical science is on her side now – tests have proved cat owners suffer considerably less stress than non-pet owners. And today she fully shares her pussies' attitude that there is absolutely nothing wrong with the world (except perhaps the inability to refill their own food bowls) and everything exciting about it. She also seems to have adopted their fondness for curling up wherever she happens to find herself in the doll's house just to daydream for a while...

Snippets of the conversation she savored with Phillip over dinner last night keep drifting through her mind. In retrospect, it amazes her how many serious thoughts and feelings he managed to express while all the time maintaining a teasing, light-hearted attitude. For instance, when she described to him how sometimes she is possessed by demons of domesticity, he remarked, 'You can't be possessed by them ever again because you're possessed by me now.' In that other objective universe so many people seem to be trapped in, such a remark might be considered a joke, but it thrilled her like the most serious declaration of commitment. And don't 'they' also say that 'in every joke is a hidden truth'?

Perhaps this morning she is so concerned about what 'they' say because she is defying that 'they' with which she was raised by willingly becoming a man's love slave instead of just calling herself his girl friend, or eventually (hopefully) his fiancé. Frankly, she would let him call her anything he wanted to just for the pleasure of his company. It surprised her (although it shouldn't have) that she enjoyed talking to him as much as she loved being fucked by him. Dinner passed in a dream of fulfillment – excellent food, good wine, and (in her opinion) the best company imaginable. They dined in a French restaurant on Maple, an obscure little culinary jewel hidden away in a strip mall. They both ordered seafood, which presented no conflict with the wine he selected for them, a lovely Italian Frascati.

'Purr...' Stormy jumps onto the sofa beside her. 'Mreow,' he adds, and she understands he wants her to settle down somewhere so he can either curl up on her lap or at her feet and take his morning nap.

'Sorry honey,' she strokes him, 'mommy's very distracted today, but she's also very happy, so very, very happy!'

'Purr... purr... purr!'

She remembers walking into the living room with the intention of changing the water in which her roses are thriving almost obscenely (they could not have bloomed more beautifully if they tried) but then another memory from last night deliciously felled her and she lay back on the sofa to gaze unseeing out the window at the branches of one of her old oak trees. 'Your flesh is bonded to mine now,' he said as they shared a sinfully creamy chocolate mousse for dessert. They did not discuss his work. She made it a point not to bring it up, and he did not volunteer anymore information, but he had said they wouldn't be talking about the past and she was content to let his employment fall into that category for the moment. She learned he was a single child and that his parents were both retired human right's attorneys. Normally, she doesn't much care for lawyers, but there are always exceptions to the rule, and she is willing to give this couple the full benefit of the doubt because they produced her soul-mate. And to think she has Sekhmet to thank for her happiness, a truly humbling thought that leads her to wonder if perhaps she isn't her cat's pet human after all.

She cannot possibly recall everything she and Phillip talked about, all she knows is they were in profound accord over most things, even if they had some superficial differences that only made their growing mental and emotional bond more stimulating. He drove her car to the restaurant. She also discovered that she has his old white-and-gold Jeep Wrangler to thank for putting him on the sidewalk were Sekhmet found him. His one-and-only vehicle is currently in the shop receiving a new engine mount, and as a result he has been taking a cab to work at nights. On impulse the morning they met, he had the driver drop him off a few miles from his house because he felt like walking, Sekhmet found him, and the rest is history. All the little, seemingly unrelated details some people might call coincidence resulted in the most important choreography of her life.

Mira is glad she has some pre-made soup for lunch as a hunger pang tells her it's past noon and she hasn't accomplished anything useful yet; however, that is another erroneous perspective of the alternate universe she doesn't live in. She can't remember a more vitally fulfilling morning, during which she has crossed off her To Do list such things as *Meet a man I can finally respect; Meet a man that really knows how to give oral sex; Meet a man I can enjoy talking to as much as I'm physically attracted to him;* etc. etc. on the top of the list of course being, *Meet my soul-mate.* In this light she has gotten a lot done today, indeed.

A bowl of home-made split pea soup and a cup of Chamomile tea later, Mira feels able to partially concentrate on more mundane tasks. There is no housework to be done, of course, and her computer lures her into her study with the promise of being able to relax on the pretext of getting some work done. She deliberately didn't check her e-mail when she got up this morning, usually the first thing she does as she sips her tea and eats her toast. Phillip was the last person she communicated with, and she wanted to savor that for a while longer. But now with a second cup of tea steeping beside her keyboard, she opens the door on her electronic postman who never rings twice – the sound of her incoming mail is a bird's lovely chirping. She has an efficient junk mail filter, so there's never too much annoying spam crowding her Inbox, making it easy for her to discern at a glance whether she has any important or potentially interesting messages. Today she hits the virtual jackpot.

The name 'Phillip Montaigne' registers in her brain like the notes of a melody heard in a dream. He always manages to get in touch with her in an unexpected way. First, after not hearing from him for three days, he takes the form of a dozen violet roses on her doorstep. Then, during a thunderstorm in the middle of the night, he phones her when she least expects it. Now it's obvious he went to her Interior Design website and obtained her e-mail address. The affect of never knowing just how and when he will communicate with her is both arousing and unsettling, like abruptly feeling him slip his hand up her skirt even though she knows she is alone. Mira opens the e-mail and forgets to breathe as she reads it:

I had a wonderful time. I have to work tonight, but I'll be thinking of you.

Short, sweet and to the point. No mention of when he will call her or when they will see each other again. She clicks on Reply and quickly types:

I'm thinking of you, too... Her fingertips hover over the keyboard a moment before tapping on the appropriate keys to spell, *Master*.

Before she can write, When will I see you again? she quickly hits Send, and sits back in the chair, her heart pounding as though she just launched a guided missile full of desire... and of something else... an emotion that leaves her figuratively reeling, because it's not possible so soon and yet it's true, she already loves this man.

* * *

In a way Mira is glad she knows for sure she won't be seeing Phillip tonight, because the uncertainty and anticipation of not knowing is worse than the sweet ache of missing him and longing to be with him again; however, it also leaves her with entirely too much time on her hands. She can't possibly concentrate on work, there's no more laundry or cleaning to be done, and it's too late to exercise; if she doesn't work-out first thing in the morning she simply can't bring herself to do it. She could conceivably call her parents and invite herself over for dinner, but her restless arousal immediately kills that option. She makes herself comfortable on her sofa and tries to lose herself in Nevada Barr's latest novel, but solving a murder committed in a National Park does not have the power to engross her today despite the heroine's engaging personality.

She tosses the glossy mass market paperback onto the table beside Phillip's roses, and contemplates the sharp silhouettes of thorns partially hidden behind deep-green leaves like the approach to Sleeping Beauty's castle... a nice long cat nap is the only activity that seems to appeal to her at the moment, perhaps because it affords her the possibility of dreaming with Phillip. The only problem is she's not tired, on the contrary; she has never felt so invigorated. This leaves only one other possible option – shopping. Fortunately her refrigerator, vegetable, and fruit bowls are less than half full, justifying a trip to her favorite grocery stores.

A bird chirp's loudly in her study.

She can't help running to her computer even though Mr. Spock would have to calculate the odds the message is from Phillip, which is why she can hardly believe her eyes when she sees his full name written across her screen again in bold black print. She plops down in her chair and once again forgets to breathe as she reads:

I've ordered you some real high-heels along with something else very important I want you to have.

He doesn't sign his name, simply attaches a link to a website. She clicks on it. Thanks to her high-speed internet connection, only two seconds pass before an image appears on her screen of shoes from some wild and impossible dream – black vinyl strap pumps with heels that look at least half-a-mile long, although the description indicates they are actually only six inches high. It seems Phillip was in a shopping mood this afternoon, only he stayed home to do it.

'I can't possibly walk in those!' she declares out loud, addressing the invisible, all-pervasive 'they' her brain has been conditioned to believe in. Another challenge has presented itself that makes a small part of her anxious while exciting the rest of her. 'But I suppose I'll have to learn...' She does not doubt many more challenges are headed her way, and a positive attitude towards them is essential if she is to be a good slave. She has already learned that pleasing this man is totally fulfilling to her in mysterious ways she can't explain, and she doesn't want to; she just wants to keep feeling the way she does, more beautiful, desirable and appreciated on all levels of her being than she has felt in her life.

Mira studies the image of the shoes in morbid fascination. They are strikingly different from anything in her closet. She wonders what else he ordered for her, but apparently he only cared to share the high-heel link with her. The other item is to be a surprise, and if the results of this surprise is anything like it was with the blindfold he shipped her via Federal Express, she can scarcely wait to receive it.

Somewhere in the doll's house her cell phone rings.

She literally leaps out of her chair and runs into the living room, but it's not there. She listens to it ring again, and sprints into the bathroom, but it's not there either. Naturally, she finds it in the last room she looks, lying on her nightstand where she left it all night.

'Hello?' she gasps.

'Do you like the shoes?'

She spreads herself belly-down on the bed loving the way he is coming at her from all angles today. 'Yes, they're stunning, Master, but I've never worn such extremely high-heels before. Can women actually walk in those?'

'Strippers dance in shoes like that every night.

'Well, I wouldn't know, since I've never been to a strip club,' she retorts.

'And why is that?'

'What do you mean? Why should I want to go to a strip club? I'm not gay.'

'Stripping is an art form like any other, Mira. Some strippers are actually very talented dancers. Just because so many bad novels have been written and so many bad movies have been made doesn't mean all books and films are worthless, and just because there are a lot of seedy strip joints doesn't mean there also aren't some classier establishments worth visiting every now and then.'

'I'm sure that's true,' she sits up defensively, 'but I wouldn't enjoy watching a woman dancing naked in front of me, it's not my thing.' She is beginning to despair because he doesn't understand how she feels and because they seem to be having their first major disagreement. It worries her that his world is not one she can actually live in while remaining true to herself.

'How can you say you wouldn't like it if you've never experienced it?' he asks reasonably. 'You don't have to be gay to enjoy the sensuality of the experience. Think of strippers as priestesses of the Goddess, Mira. The power women have over men is not debasing, it's just that, power. A woman worshipping the metaphysical forces expressing themselves through her body is not something you should be ashamed to watch; it's beautiful, and should be empowering to you as a woman, not humiliating.'

'Well, if you put it that way...'

'I'll take you to a very nice place one night when you're ready.'

'I *have* heard of a new aerobic exercise that's all the rage now, pole dancing, or something like that,' she concedes. 'Apparently strippers get a very good workout every night.'

'As will you, so keep your pussy nice and warm and wet for me.'

'It already is...'

'I don't want you to masturbate. Promise you won't touch yourself until I give you permission to do so, Mira.'

'I promise, Master.'

'Say it.'

'I promise I won't touch myself without your permission, Master.'

'What are you planning to do today?'

'I have no idea. So far I haven't done anything useful at all. I already miss you so much…'

'I miss you, too. Are you free tomorrow morning?'

'Yes.' She would cancel an appointment with Jesus Christ Himself.

'Then how about if I come over for breakfast.'

'I would love that!'

'I'm warning you, I don't do low-carb, low-fat or the too-healthy anything so no cottage cheese and fruit, please.'

She laughs. 'I don't do any of those either. How do eggs-over-easy with bacon, whole-grain toast and fully caffeinated coffee with real cream sound?'

'I'm there.'

'What time do you work till?' she dares to ask.

'I'll be there by nine,' he replies.

'Alight.'

'I'll see you then.'

'Okay… have a good night at work.'

He laughs softly. 'Sweet dreams, Mira.'

CHAPTER EIGHT

"I do not wish [women] to have power over men; but over themselves."
Mary Wollstonecraft

She is tempted to have breakfast ready at exactly nine o'clock so she won't have to concentrate on cooking in Phillip's presence, coordinating frying eggs, toasting bread and sautéing bacon while distracted by his penetrating stare. But if for some reason he's late, she'll end up serving him cold, unappetizing food, a risk she cannot take. She settles for having everything ready to go at her fingertips like a cooking show. She will simply have to be careful not to allow how hot she is for him burn everything.

Her small wooden dining table is visible from the open kitchen and looks exceedingly fine set with burgundy place mats, violet cloth napkins and bone-white china. She thought of pulling out her silverware, but it would have required polishing, and she is only preparing breakfast after all; the silver will have to wait for a candle lit dinner.

Sekhmet is either possessed of feline extra-sensory perception and knows the man she set Mira up with is planning to visit this morning, or she is unable to tear herself away from the enticing smell of bacon lying on the kitchen counter. Whatever the reason, she is dangerously haunting her pet human's ankles.

'If you make me trip over you while he's here,' her mistress says sternly, 'I'll never feed you canned Salmon again.'

Stormy has taken an unobtrusive position directly between the kitchen and the dining room, where he is contentedly licking himself, apparently quite loftily indifferent to the smell of raw bacon. Mira knows better, however, for once his sister has procured the prize he will promptly join her in devouring it. For some inherently male reason, he is much more passionate about food that is not officially presented to him on a plate.

For her breakfast date, Mira has chosen an innocent little sundress, the off-white cotton printed with tiny red roses. Spaghetti straps are attached to a bodice-style top, the skirt flaring gently over her hips down to mid-thigh. And on her feet are the red high-heeled sandals she wore for her 'Master' the other night and which match the roses, as do her silver stem-shaped earrings blooming with tiny red ruby blossoms, one of the few expensive gifts she has treated herself to as a financially independent adult; she cannot resist beautifully crafted organic jewelry. Since it is early morning, her make-up is light enough to be non-existent. The blush on her cheeks appears perfectly natural, as does the rose tint of her lips and the dark line of her lashes.

She props the kitchen door open with a brick so she can see her very special guest arriving through the screen door, which he does at three minutes after nine, heralded by Sekhmet's uncannily joyous yowl.

'Please!' Mira chides her cat proudly for daring to express what she herself is feeling but has to politely conceal. Of course, she knew he would still be dressed for work; nevertheless, the sight of his tall body suddenly appearing on her threshold all in black blows her mind as it turns her on in that inexplicable but totally intense way.

He lets himself in without bothering to knock, which would be silly considering the liberties he has already taken with her body. They have known each other hardly any time at all, yet they have long since left such formalities behind. He does not verbally acknowledge Sekhmet's passionate greeting, he simply he picks her up by the scruff of the neck and bangs her forehead gently against his while Mira watches, the pussy between her thighs feeling wonderfully jealous.

'Good morning.' He addresses the two purring cats and the silent woman at the same time, and as he gently drops Sekhmet at his booted feet, his smile draws Mira to him with a magnetism as irresistible as his arms coming around her. Then dimensions are effortlessly crushed and time and space cease to exist except as the warm space of his mouth. Their tongues dance together like pure energy in the arousing process of becoming embodied as he separates his face from hers again.

'Mm,' he smiles, 'that's what I call a good morning kiss.'

'It feels like it's been years since I saw you!' she gasps.

He laughs in that deeply quiet way of his that somehow makes everything amusing and yet beautifully serious at the same time; already she loves the steady, penetrating expression in his eyes more than anything on earth. 'Tell me you haven't made breakfast yet...' His tone somehow manages to make the mundane statement sound sexy.

'No, not yet.'

'Good, because I'd really love to borrow your shower.'

Only then does she notice the small black bag at his feet that Stormy and Sekhmet could not be sniffing more fervently if it contained a batch of fresh catnip. She ignores a stab of disappointment that he will be removing his black leather outfit, yet it might be a good thing since it arouses a very different appetite in her than the kind she can fulfill with bacon and eggs.

'You look absolutely lovely,' he adds, 'so I won't ask you to join me, this time.' He releases her and picks up his bag.

'Let me get you a towel.' She is conscious of every sway of her hips and click of her sandals on the hard-wood floor as he follows her to the linen closet next to her bedroom door.

'Very nice,' he comments.

She is confused as to what he is referring to until she turns and sees him smiling at the neatly folded towels, bed sheets, table cloths, extra curtains and assorted linens stored on the shelves.

'Beautiful, smart, sexy, talented and a domestic goddess as well. You're going to make some lucky man a very nice slave, Mira.'

'*Some* lucky man?'

He laughs. '*This* lucky man.' He takes the towel from her. 'I'm starving. Go start breakfast.'

Without thinking she returns obediently to the kitchen. Soon she hears the shower turn on in her bathroom, and the whole time the water is running and the bacon is sizzling and the coffee pot is gurgling she feels utterly, mindlessly content. She is so happy she doesn't even notice it; she is purely in the sweet, sensual grip of these special moments in which the past is the ground in which they're rooted and the future is the open sky.

When she hears the shower turn off all her senses come to attention because it never seems to take men very long to dry themselves off and dress. His timing is flawless – she has just set the hot plates she had warming in the oven on the table when he appears looking casually resplendent in blue jeans and a forest-green short-sleeved cotton t-shirt. The symmetry of his broad shoulders, narrow hips and long legs strikes an ideal chord inside her. When her DNA was being mysteriously arranged by the Powers-That-Be, she was designed to feel this was the perfect man's body, and she can scarcely believe it's casually sitting down at her table for breakfast.

'This looks wonderful,' he declares, 'and it smells even better.'

She brings the coffee pot over and carefully fills his cup, leaving enough room for the cream she took the trouble to pour into a porcelain pitcher. As usual, she is having Earl Grey tea.

He smiles up at her. 'But you didn't have to go to quite so much trouble.'

'It was my pleasure,' she says truthfully, with a quick glance assuring herself everything they need is on the table.

'Well, next time we can go out for breakfast.' He rises again to pull her chair out for her. 'I don't want my slave working so hard all the time.' His tone is teasing as he resumes his seat, but his smile is in striking contrast to the serious glint in his eyes. 'Not in the kitchen anyway.'

She spreads the violet napkin across her lap, shyly avoiding looking at him.

'Mreoow!'

'Sekhmet, go away,' she says without conviction, for she knows there is no banishing her greedy feline from the smell of cooked bacon and fresh cream.

'I think you've spoiled them just a little bit,' Phillip observes.

Looking up from her plate, Mira is startled to see he has already finished his eggs. 'My God, you eat fast!'

'I was hungry.'

'Another hard night at work?' she asks sourly.

'Very.'

His response paralyzes her – she can't decide whether to hate him for it or to respect him for not indulging her jealousy, which she knows is quite unbecoming considering everything they have said to each other so soon in their relationship. Yet there is no denying her happiness is painfully tempered by fearful suspicions she has to struggle to keep in check. Until she knows exactly what goes on at his 'job' she won't be able to fully relax, and yet she doesn't dare openly ask him about it. She is afraid of what she might find out and that she won't be able to handle it. She is terrified of ruining the feelings growing between them.

He wipes his mouth with the napkin and grasps her left hand where it rests limply on the table. 'What are you thinking?' he asks soberly.

She sips her tea to consider her reply.

He squeezes her hand so hard the slight pain tells her the gesture is a reprimand. 'I asked you a question, Mira.'

Her breath catches and makes it even harder for her to speak. She can't really put her amorphous fears into words. 'I guess…' she clears her throat. 'I guess the thought of you spending three nights a week with other women is just… just a little hard for me to deal with.'

He gently lets go of her hand and spreads some wild blueberry jam across a slice of toast. 'You're deliberately tormenting yourself by putting it that way,' he says quietly. 'I don't spend my nights with these women, they just happen to be there. And did you really think I planned on doing this forever? It's only a temporary gig while I finish my thesis.'

'Your thesis?' she breathes.

'If all goes as planned, I should have my PhD in six months.'

'Your PhD?'

Sekhmet reaches up to plant her front paws on his denim-clad thighs and meows plaintively.

He picks up a piece of bacon. 'May I?'

'Yes, go ahead. What are you getting your PhD in?'

'Guess.'

'I have no idea!'

'That's the nature of guessing.' He picks up his empty coffee cup and gazes down at it for an instant before meeting her eyes again.

She quickly takes it from him, gets up, and pours him another cup.

'Thank you.' He rewards her with the smile that reaches his eyes in that special way that seems to melt her bones and make her grateful there's a chair directly beneath her.

'I can't possibly guess,' she insists.

'Well, then, I'll let you think about it for a while.'

'Phillip!'

'Eat your breakfast, Mira, you need your strength.'

She has no desire to argue with such a promising threat and obeys him, relishing her eggs-over-easy, which she actually fried in Canola oil this morning, throwing fat and calories to the wind. Her first breakfast with her soul-mate is a special occasion immune from her eternal health-conscious diet.

'Do you like to cook?' he asks.

'Yes, I suppose I do. I can't say I love it, but I do insist on enjoying my meals every night, and since I can't afford to eat out all the time, I cook. Also, I could never maintain my weight or my health if I ate out all the time. This way I know exactly what I'm putting into my body.'

'You're in full control.'

'Yes.'

'I'll allow you that control in the kitchen, and in your work, and

The Fabric of Love

in your domestic chores,' he states as casually as if they are merely discussing the weather, 'but when it comes to us, you will surrender that control completely and absolutely without question.'

She takes a breath as if to protest, and then realizes with a shocking thrill that the only words lined up in her head and lodged in her throat ready to emerge are, 'Yes, Master.' Yet she does not allow herself to speak them; she cannot possibly agree to such a thing. She clutches her cup of tea in both hands and stares down into it, but since she uses a tea bag there aren't any leaves on the bottom to be read. 'Yes, Master,' she whispers, divining her future not by any outward signs but by how she feels inside whenever she is with him, or even just thinking about him. She cannot apply normal rules of relationship to this man, and she has no desire to do so, especially considering how unfulfilling she found all her other liaisons before him. Her shipwrecked reason is deep in the sensual jungle following a mysterious path to a dark and ancient realm and there's no turning back now... the Catholic school girl has boarded the pirate ship and is surrounded by the sea of her sexuality and only the sinisterly handsome captain can help her navigate it, her concerned parents no longer visible on the safe, rational shore... there *is* no rational shore when she is looking into his eyes, all that exists is how intensely drawn she is to him.

'You haven't finished your breakfast, Mira.'

'I'm not that hungry right now...'

'Are you finished then?'

'Yes.'

The ensuing silence is so pregnant it only takes a few seconds for the realization to be born inside her (amidst screams of protest from her feminist brain) that she made a mistake he is waiting for her to correct.

'Yes, I'm finished, Master.'

He pushes his chair back and stands up so abruptly her heart takes off in response, but all he does is take her hand. 'Come,' he commands.

He leads her into her bedroom. 'Since you're not hungry for food, I'm going to feed you something else.'

She licks her lips in anticipation of really tasting him for the first time.

He seats himself on the edge of her bed, and with a tilt of his head indicates he wants her to kneel before him. Already he does not need to speak for her to sense what he wants and obey him. 'You're going to spend a lot more time on your knees as a woman than you ever did as a Catholic school girl.' Another sexy threat that thrills her to the subconscious core of her being. 'But trust me, you're going to enjoy it a hell of a lot more.'

They smile at each other for an instant like two kids playing a very exciting game they never want to end. And gloriously enough, it doesn't have to end since 'they' don't exist in this world that magically opened up around her the instant she saw him kneeling in the grass next to her black cat.

He opens his pants – button-fly jeans beneath which he isn't wearing any underwear – and releases his semi-erect penis. Then he reaches in and lifts out his scrotum, those two heavy, luscious balls pushed up at an unnatural angle by the crotch of his tight pants offered up to her as if on a platter. He is as smoothly shaved as she remembers, which makes obeying his next command a pure pleasure. 'Suck my balls, Mira... that's right, don't be afraid, you won't hurt me.'

She takes one of his tender sacks more boldly into her mouth.

'Mm, now the other one... that's good. Now suck my cock.' He grips it at the base and slides it between her lips, pressing its rigid length against her tongue. 'You just had some food, so I won't deep-throat you. I want you to suck my cock however feels good to you. I want to see how skilled you are at pleasing a man with just your moth and hands, and how much it will be my pleasure to have to teach you.'

She hasn't felt this safe and excited and eager to learn since they got to the ancient Egyptians in third grade history class. Then she suspects her oral vocabulary is not as sophisticated as she believed as she is confronted with the intensely eloquent statement of this man's erection. She forms a tight ring around his cock with her lips and twirls her tongue around it, searching for the most sensitive spots on his hard length as she swallows him. He does not react like other men, with grateful groans and helpless pulses that warn her a premature release of sperm is imminent. Phillip reacts not at all to the increasingly fervent ministrations of her mouth, tongue and hands, which she brings energetically into play, pumping him hard with one fist while delicately caressing his balls with her fingertips. She knows she must be pleasing him because he couldn't possibly be harder, yet it's also obvious he is nowhere close to coming and she begins to despair.

'Mm...' he says at last, 'very nice, Mira.'

His praise frees her from purgatory, and she groans with gratitude and pleasure when he grasps the hair at the back of her head. He plunges her face down around his towering erection with a swift, steady rhythm she passionately sustains even after he releases her.

He strokes her hair. 'Would you like me to fuck you?'

With her mouth full of his cock she looks up into his eyes.

'Stand up.'

She obeys him as quickly as she can, her knees a little stiff.

'You look so sweet in that dress, I don't want to muss you up. Bend over the bed and brace yourself on it... no move back a little... that's right.' He lifts her skirt. 'These are very sweet,' he says and she knows he is referring to her white-lace panties as he hooks his thumbs into the elastic, and yanks them roughly down to her knees. 'But your pussy should always be exposed and ready for me. From now on you will have to ask my permission to wear panties. Do you understand?'

Her head spins as a lifetime of being warned about germs ties her tongue. 'Yes, Master.'

'The only exception to this rule is, obviously, when it's that time of the month,' he steps up tightly behind her, 'and when you wear pants. I don't want you chafing this pretty little labia of yours, which you will always keep shaved for me, naturally.'

'Yes, Master!' she gasps as the thick head of his cock lodges itself in her vulva's hungry mouth. She didn't realize how starved her body was for him until the lips of her pussy once again tasted his tender firmness and the promise of so much more of him to come.

'Do you want my cock in your cunt, Mira?'

'Oh, yes, Master...'

'Beg me for it.'

'Oh, God, please, Master... please fuck me...'

His head stops teasingly kissing her sex lips. 'You don't sound like you want it enough.'

'Oh, my God, yes, I do, please... please put your cock in my cunt, Master, please, I want it more than anything!'

'Arch your back,' His hand pressing down on the base of her spine, he penetrates her.

His thrust has the rending effect of a weapon at the angle she is offering her pussy to him. 'Oh, God, Master!' Under the circumstances it feels perfectly natural to be calling him that because at the moment he has complete mastery of her flesh. Even though his erection is only coming into contact with her vaginal walls, it feels as though he is stabbing himself to the very core of her physical being. The intensity of the experience makes up for the slight discomfort; her pussy has never felt so open and so tight at the same time, and she can sense how good her tight slot feels to his hard-on – slick and soft and deep and clinging, the cushion of her cervix kissing his head and welcoming him into a hot, wet harem of sensations as she consciously milks him, tightening and relaxing around him.

'Oh, yes,' he whispers, and a profound triumph deepens her cunt's ability to absorb his relentless strokes as she suddenly (more with the combined power of her senses than her mind) becomes aware of just how much power she actually has over him even in her vulnerable position. Closing her eyes, she clamps her pussy muscles around his erection, squeezing him gently at first and then harder and harder, until it's as if there is no limit to how tightly she can grip him. Her sex is a cosmic black hole sucking him into the ever diminishing singularity of her innermost being, and the bigger and thicker his penis gets, the closer he comes to the event horizon of his pleasure, the more she tightens her hold on him. In her mind's eye she can see the shape and length of his cock wrapped in her hot flesh. No other man has ever inspired her to such visualizations before, much less filled her with the mysterious ability to tighten endlessly around him. She knows when he starts coming because of the quiet, breathless sounds he makes and because he gets so hard she almost can't stand how good his increasingly violent penetrations feel.

'Oh, Mira…'

She cries out in triumph and pleasure as her awareness of everything is momentarily laid waist by the explosion of his pleasure deep in her sex. His throbbing cock fills her almost to bursting as she relishes the sinful baptism of his cum drenching her insides.

Even after he has long since finished climaxing he remains

buried peacefully inside her for a minute, giving vital parts of her time to come back down to earth, which in turn enables her to straighten up with casual dignity as he pulls out of her.

'Did I say you could move, Mira?'

She moans and plants her hands on the bed again, hiding her face behind her hair, half ashamed she is proving to be such a sloppy slave, and half hurt by his reprimand after the transcendent orgasm she just helped him achieve.

Her panties have slipped down to her ankles. He helps her step out of them. 'Okay, now you may get up.'

She turns towards him, and rests her head gratefully on his chest as he takes her in his arms.

'That was amazing,' he whispers into her hair.

'Thank you, Master,' she whispers back, and wonders why human females weren't born with the genes that would enable them to purr, because that's exactly what she feels like doing in those moments. All words are inadequate to how she feels with his arms around her and his heart beating in her ear.

CHAPTER NINE

"The girl answered, 'I do not know where your house is' then he said, 'My house is a long way in the wood'."

Phillip leaves not long afterwards. Mira isn't surprised, she knows he worked all night, and even though she'll miss him, he has left her feeling languidly fulfilled and utterly at peace for a while.

Stormy and Sekhmet materialize from out of nowhere to see him off.

'Is your car still in the shop?' she asks.

'Yes.'

'So you're walking home from here?'

'Yes.'

'May I walk with you?'

'No.' The small black bag containing his leather outfit and boots already in hand, he slips his free arm around her waist and gently kisses her lips. 'I'll talk to you later.'

'But why don't you want me to walk you home, Phillip?'

'No whining, Mira.'

'I'm not whining, I just don't understand why you don't want me to walk you home.'

He opens the screen door, but pauses on the threshold as Sekhmet scents one of his big toes, visible through his leather sandal. 'Do you trust me, Mira?'

'You know I do, Phillip.'

'Then when you ask me a question, you shouldn't question my answer. Just trust me. We'll be walking home together soon enough.'

If he had shoved a piece of rich dark chocolate in her mouth he couldn't have silenced her more effectively or filled her with a sweeter happiness. She says nothing as he kisses her lightly on the lips again, and steps outside.

'Is it all right if I cut through your yard again?' he smiles.

She laughs. 'Yes.' She holds the screen door open so she can watch him disappear around the back of her house. 'Go follow him, Sekhmet!' she whispers, and her black cat races after him as though she truly is Mira's intelligent familiar. 'Oh, God, Sekhmet, come back!' She regrets her impulsive command. 'Oh, well, maybe she'll bring us directions to his house,' she tells Stormy, who remains sitting faithfully at her feet.

She sighs and turns back to face the elegant devastation of her dining room table, and another long day awaiting her. 'I have to get some work done,' she says firmly.

Stormy does not comment on this announcement. He is staring intently out the screen door as though expecting his sister to return at any moment.

Yet how can she possibly concentrate on anything with the distraction of her Master's cum trickling down the insides of her thighs again? She forgot to mention wiping herself clean the other night, and now she postpones doing so because it will eliminate one of the traces of his presence, the same excuse she uses not to clean up the breakfast dishes right away. For a little while longer she wants to savor the knowledge and evidence that he was here with her.

* * *

Everyone knows physical exercise produces endorphins that make you feel really good about life, at least for a little while, and every woman knows the same is true of shopping. It doesn't matter what you're shopping for; there's just something about walking leisurely through stores with countless items theoretically available to make you and your living space more beautiful and desirable, which will (once again theoretically) make you happier. Mira does not hesitate to admit to herself that shopping is the opium of her feminine psyche. The only problem is she does so much of it in her line of work she has built up an annoying tolerance to the soothing consumer endorphins. It's different when you're shopping for someone who isn't intimately related to or involved with you.

She knows she should be thinking about the contents of Ian's condo, but her guardian angels appear to be paying special attention to her these days and have given her a two-week reprieve from her current project. She needn't waste time feeling guilty about wandering around the Ballston Mall, exclusively with an eye to pleasing the other, and only truly important, man in her life – Master Phillip. The extreme high-heels and the other mysterious item he ordered for her on the Internet have not yet arrived, but there's always something she can buy that will make her feel even more desirable than she already does. Lingerie is the icing on the rich sensual cake she suspects will be a part of her daily nourishment from now on, yet even though she owns more baby dolls and sexy satin slips than she knows what to do with, Mira cannot resist a quick tour of *Victoria's Secret*. Their current pink look does not in the least appeal to her, but she is rewarded in the back room with a rack where already radically reduced items are an additional fifty percent off. In her opinion, a woman can never have too many thigh-length short-sleeved cotton shirts to hang around the house in, especially when they're marked down to what is probably their actual cost at six dollars, and there's even one in her size and favorite color – violet. She also buys a white sleeveless T embroidered with a glittering red heart reflecting how big and full hers has felt since Sekhmet brought her soul-mate home instead of a dead mouse.

On her way out of the store she casts a rather forlorn glance at all the tables neatly covered with sexy panties. No other man has ever told her she needed his permission to cover her pubes with cotton or silk or any other material. It is going to take some getting used to; nevertheless, even now she is obeying him and not wearing any panties beneath her innocent sundress, the same outfit she had on this morning when he fucked her from behind, except that she exchanged the red high-heeled sandals for comfortable white socks and sneakers. She loves shopping for high-heels but not shopping *in* high-heels. She respects the health of her spine and likes being comfortable when she's shooting up her relaxing consumer drug.

Mira likes the Ballston Mall because it's small and manageable, not overwhelming like Tyson's Corner, and it is also more suited to buyers who don't want to spend their entire paycheck on one or two items. Fortunately, she has never suffered from the delusion that more expensive means better quality. Her self-esteem has always been deep and rich enough not to need the psychological bandage of designer labels to make her feel she is truly worth something in the mysterious scheme of things. Good thrift stores and consignment shops are still her favorite place to buy things.

She avoids *Hechts* because it takes too much energy and instead makes her way to the comfortably intimate *Rainbow* to see if there are any cotton treasures buried amidst all the cheap polyester. Most of the cute colored T's she wears around the house have come from *Rainbow*, and she can never have too many lounging around outfits since she spends most of her time at home either working or relaxing. She guardedly embraced the trend that swept the nation a few years back that replaced bars with major bookstore chains as a place to find a more fulfilling relationship than the one-night-stand available at eighty-proof watering holes. Yet she never managed to meet a man at *Borders* or *Barnes and Noble*, perhaps because she always became too engrossed in whatever book she wasn't only pretending to be reading and forgot to look up to see if there were any eligible bachelors milling around her. Mira knows her parents are proud of how particular she is about potential suitors and of her financial independence, but she is also aware they keep glancing at her biological clock wondering if she'll ever produce a grandchild for them. She does not have the heart to tell them as a grown woman what she made clear as a child – that she has no desire to have a baby or babies, much less an adolescent or two clipping her sensual and emotional wings. And even though they have not yet discussed it, she suspects Phillip shares her sentiments regarding offspring.

There is no pot of Egyptian cotton gold at the foot of the *Rainbow* this afternoon, so Mira wanders back out into the carpeted mall towards *Parade of Shoes*. Even though she has never seen anything she liked there, they get new stock in all the time and there's always hope.

'Hello.' The sale's girl smiles at her dutifully.

'Hello!' Mira replies cheerfully.

'Is there anything I can help you find today?'

'No, thanks, I'm just looking.'

The usual array of questionably aesthetic and decidedly uncomfortable looking sandals and shoes meet her eyes, but she doesn't know when she'll be seeing Phillip again, so she has all the time in the world to wander around aimlessly. Her cell phone is on and in her purse; he can reach her wherever she is, so there's no need to hurry home to Stormy and Sekhmet.

Mira finds what she didn't even know she was looking for in a pair of black high-heeled sandals with two straps in the front covered with diamond-like rhinestones. The heels are only two inches high, but that makes them ideal for sexy around-the-house shoes, and somehow she knows Phillip will appreciate them. Best of all they're half off – reduced from forty dollars to twenty. She slips off her sneakers and socks, tries them on, walks around in them for half a minute gazing at her sexy legs in the mirrors, takes them off, returns them to the box, slips her socks and shoes back on, and buys them. They are the climax of her shopping day; she knows she won't find anything else she wants or can afford, and suddenly she feels a pressing need to check her e-mail to see if Phillip communicated with her again that way.

* * *

When Mira lets herself into the doll's house, as usual through the kitchen door, Stormy and Sekhmet are nowhere to be seen. She misses their warm purring greeting, but there's still a chance the electronically caged bird of her e-mail will welcome her home with a note from Phillip.

Her Inbox is empty.

Sharply disappointed, she stares at the screen as if the intensity of her desire alone will produce an incoming message, but it doesn't work any better than rubbing a bronze lamp did in ancient Sumeria. She has his number stored in her cell phone, yet like a powerful Gin being released she cannot be sure if it will grant her wish of hearing his voice again, or if her desire will be trapped in a voicemail box, or if a woman will answer instead. She really doesn't believe the latter scenario is a possibility. The real reason she doesn't call him is because she does not wish to disturb him. He is probably still sleeping off his hard night at work, not to mention the very fulfilling breakfast they shared.

Mira knows the social 'they' might categorize her as a bit of a control freak. Her doll's house is always clean and neat; both her hard-copy and electronic files are organized in folders; she has a notebook in the kitchen filled with all her favorite recipes she types out on the computer as she comes across them, then prints out and tapes onto the ruled paper divided into different sections – Sandwiches, Seafood, Chicken, Pasta, etc.; Phillip himself already admired the organized fullness of her linen closet; all her clothes are arranged by season and color; her kitchen invariably looks good enough to be the set of a cooking show; she writes everything she needs to do in her Day Timer; all her bills are paid long before the due date, and she never fails to have stamps on hand for those she can't dispose of online; as a member of *Netflix* she always has DVD's available to entertain her at night; her wine rack never has less than five bottles in it, and there are always two vintages of chardonnay chilling in her refrigerator.

Obviously, she likes to be prepared for things, because in her opinion that's the best way to enjoy them to the fullest. Unlike the infamous Blanche, she has no desire to rely on the kindness of strangers, feeling she can do a better job of most everything herself. She doesn't trust most people to be as intensely discriminating as she is. Mira believes that, in general, people are good, but she is more skeptical about them as individuals she can relate to for a prolonged period of time, hence her marked lack of any close friends. Not since college has she been able to bond with anyone in that way, and the truth is that most days she doesn't miss it. She has Rose to talk to whenever she needs a woman's perspective and sympathy, for she has always valued her mother's innate wisdom. This afternoon, however, with Stormy and Sekhmet gone missing for an unusual amount of time, and Phillip asleep somewhere like a prince in a reversal of the traditional fairytale, she admits it would be nice to have a female friend close to her own age she could confide in about her new exciting yet also intensely challenging relationship. She cannot talk to Rose about Phillip, not yet, and to be honest probably not ever, although obviously she wants her parents to meet him one day, and vice versa. A trip to a private vineyard in Washington State would hardly be painful.

Mira unpacks her small treasures, eager to show her sexy new sandals to Phillip... that's the hard part, not knowing when she'll see him again. It's like floating in the vacuum of space trapped between two worlds – the one behind her when she last saw him, the one before her when she'll next see him. There's nothing for her to control except her impatience and longing, and her growing anxiety the more time passes and she doesn't hear from him. It doesn't matter that only six hours have ticked by since they were together. Every woman knows time can become painfully relative when a man is involved... when you're in love... the speed of light, the speed of love... metal spaceships will never travel through the universe to distant worlds, yet the soul already does so through the vehicle of imagination, and she has already imagined countless ways in which they will meet again and myriads of futures together, lifetimes lived in the few languid blinks of eyes gazing dreamily out at nothing and everything at the same time...

Mira glances at her watch. It's only four-thirty, too early for a glass of chardonnay; she has to wait until at least six o'clock on spring evenings when the days are impossibly long. She opens her refrigerator and stands there for a while pondering dinner, but the big breakfast she prepared this morning has exhausted her culinary self; time to rely on the frozen piece of home-made vegetable lasagna in the freezer. She places it on the counter to defrost and once more finds herself at a loss.

Where are her cats?

CHAPTER TEN

"They came to the wood, and the way grew more and more familiar."

Careful to bring her cell phone with her, she steps outside. The sight of her blooming wisteria vine always pleases her, as do the white stone vases overflowing with violet petunias, and soon her red and white rose bushes will also be in glorious bloom. The towel on which she lay naked and blindfolded while Phillip ate her pussy and then fucked her violently from behind is still lying on the grass, a bittersweet reminder of how pleasurable his company can be that deepens how lonely she already feels without him.

The temperature is ideal, somewhere between sixty-eight and seventy degrees by her estimate, and wandering down one of the curving stone paths of her expansive garden, Mira wonders why she should feel compelled to find something better to do. She pauses beside one of her stone fountains to enjoy the tinkling music of water flowing down from the iron flower growing in its center. Running water and *Feng Shui* are inseparable. For her, the fountain's lovely design justifies the major headache it proves to Ramon at least once a month, because the spout from which the water flows out is so narrow it is constantly clogging up.

Through the branches of a maple tree she can just barely discern the distant outlines of one of her neighbor's homes. Phillip does not live in either of the two houses directly to the north and south of her, she knows that much. To her east is the street, where she assumes Sekhmet found him after his cab dropped him off, and to her west stretches one of the many wooded areas Virginia is still miraculously full of. More than once she has glimpsed a deer grazing on the outskirts of her yard. Perhaps he wasn't just teasing her when he told her he lived over the hill and through the woods... suddenly she's worried Sekhmet took her command to follow him seriously and got lost, and that Stormy went in search of her and got lost himself.

'Stormy! Sekhmet!' She walks westward, looking around for them anxiously. 'Stormy? Sekhmet?' There is not the slightest breeze and the stillness assumes a sinister quality as no reassuring rustling response emanates from the foliage. She begins to worry in earnest. It is close to dinner time, the landmark event of Sekhmet's day she has not once failed to miss. This is the risk people who own outdoor cats take – that one day they might never come back. She lived in a constant state of worry the first year, but lately she has taken it for granted that her felines are smart enough to take care of themselves. She firmly tells herself it is too early to worry even as she keeps heading towards the western border of her property, the direction she assumes Phillip took this morning when he began walking home.

A loud flapping sound to her left makes her cry out, and her heart beats harder than its wings as she watches a goose take flight. It's not the first time she has seen one in her yard, but how abruptly it shattered the stillness is unsettling and contributes to her growing unease. It is only half-past-four, but the sunny, passive afternoon is being overthrown by an aggressive storm front. The sun is suddenly imprisoned behind a wall of grey clouds and the world darkens as though three hours pass in the blink of an eye. She has reached the cross-over place where her well-maintained lawn ends and the untamed woodland begins. This small patch of forest may be surrounded by civilization on all sides, affected by the myriad environmental ills of urban sprawl in ways invisible to her untrained naked eye; nevertheless, in the abrupt gloom the close-growing trees fill her with a series of anxieties programmed into her primordial genes... She slips her cell phone into the pocket of her sundress, no longer clinging to it and to the chance Phillip might call at any moment. A deepening concern for her missing cats is merging with a need to follow the path her lover took away from her this morning. There is no official trail as such that she can see, but like a female egg that can only be penetrated at one specific point by a single sperm, there is a subtly discernable gap in the line of trees a person journeying into the woods would naturally take advantage of. She doesn't think it is her imagination the grass looks slightly more trampled there ... as if by heavy black boots, the kind of boots her Master wears...

She glances up at the sky. The overcast afternoon feels even more oppressively still. There is no warning flash of lightning or grumble of distant thunder, yet every fiber in her civilized being wants to turn back to her doll's house, appalled by the mere thought of getting lost in the woods during a storm. But her purring, loving companions are missing; there is nothing for her at home except a lonely glass of chardonnay, and suddenly a few yards ahead of her amidst the lush chaos of the forest floor she glimpses movement – a patch of sleek grey streaking from behind a tree trunk and vanishing behind some bushes.

'Stormy?' she cries. 'Stormy, come back here!' She starts after him, only now she isn't so sure that was Stormy; it could easily have been a big squirrel or some other form of woodland creature she can't identify. It shames her how ignorant she is of native Virginia wild life. 'Stormy?' Upon receiving no reassuring, rustling response from the foliage, she pauses, preparing to turn back, but just then sunlight finds a gap in the brooding armor of clouds. A big black-and-gold dragonfly takes flight along a luminous runway, while still in shadow a pair of white moths spiral upwards in an ethereally energetic mating dance.

She starts walking again, every few seconds looking down at her feet, not so much to watch her step across the uneven ground as to avoid stepping on anything beautifully alive. Sure enough, a metallic-blue beetle shining like a precious gem is granted a few more minutes, weeks or months of life as she steps aside to avoid casually crushing it. It is vaguely shaped like an Egyptian scarab, yet its color is almost unreal.

'Stormy? Sekhmet?' she calls, but with less concern in her voice as she makes her way between flowering trees. Glancing over her shoulder, Mira makes sure she can still see the reassuring order of her garden and the landmark of one of her stone fountains. It seems impossible to believe that in all the years she has lived here, this is as far as she has ever ventured into the woods flanking her home. What was she afraid of, becoming lost in a patch of forest probably less than a mile square? Is she such a pathetic creature of civilization that she must have a safe, accepted path laid out for her because she dare not venture into the unknown on her own? The six o'clock news with its endless stories of female bodies found buried in the woods doesn't help, nor did her maternal grandmother's stern warning that a little girl wandering alone into the forest would be easy prey for hungry wolves. Granted, she has not exactly been conditioned to be brave, but what she is truly afraid of is modern society and the unusual amount of psychopaths it seems to breed. The only snakes or wolves she might encounter in northern Virginia are of the human variety.

Fortunately, an amazingly big orange butterfly, with a design on its wings that looks freshly drawn by a black magic marker, distracts her from her morbid thoughts and enables her to rest comfortably in her senses again as she keeps walking. The soft, stubborn light makes it appear as if the storm might blow over after all, and a large yellow-and-orange mushroom made of sci-fi suede fascinates her enough to crouch down beside it and contemplate its impressive fungal dimensions. She strokes it tentatively with a fingertip and wonders if the striking looking thing is edible. Then something between a startled laugh and a squeamish shriek escapes her lips as a spider appears between her sneakers. Its eight legs are at least three inches long and as thin as black needles arching out of a heart-shaped orange-and-black body that manages to look sinister despite it miniscule size.

She quickly straightens up again, but now that she has become aware of them, these delicately massive arachnids appear to be everywhere; she has to consciously avoid stepping on them as she moves deeper between the trees. It is not obvious now that someone else (much less a number of people) have walked this way before, and glancing behind her again, Mira's pulse accelerates as she realizes she can no longer see her property.

'Stormy, Sekhmet, I want you both to come home right now!' She strains to make out another mischievous streak of grey or black as her felines play hide-and-seek with her, but what she sees instead is a flash of red hanging from a tree branch. There are no flowers such a deep crimson color, and closer inspection reveals a piece of cloth that appears to have been torn off something even though it is too high to be a fragment of clothing ripped off a hiker by a thorny branch. The piece of red fabric is dangling exactly at her eye level as though deliberately placed there. She reaches up to lightly finger the cloth with the same respectful reverence she caressed the mushroom. Both are mysterious in their own way, except there must obviously be a human, not a divine, hand behind this particular phenomena. The miniature red flag is approximately six inches long and three inches wide and made of a very fine, shining silk. Possibly a woman out for a stroll was wearing a red scarf over her head that got tangled and ripped in the low-lying branches, only the cloth was deliberately impaled on the tree's thing young arm. The length of fabric makes no sense at all except as a rather expensive trail marker, because it is definitely no cheap drugstore ribbon.

The day has darkened ominously again as her friendly light loses its battle with the moody atmosphere, yet Mira tells herself that if it begins to rain the trees will protect her from the full force of the downpour, because another reason to continue her nature trek has presented itself in the form of an enticing gleam of violet a few yards away and slightly to her left. She hurries towards it, forgetting to watch for spiders and other vulnerable forms of life. The fabric riddle continues. Both pieces appear to have been torn from some fantastic multi-hued garment. This second raggedly rectangular piece of cloth is a lovely lavender color and the richest, softest velvet she has ever had the pleasure of touching. It hangs impaled on a branch that pierced it as neatly as a needle, and she stares keenly ahead of her between the trees, no longer searching for her missing felines, who have temporarily wandered out of her mind. Sure enough, another flash of unexpected, if not unnatural, color meets her eye about the same distance away – another few yards ahead and this time slightly to her right. The fabric trail is meandering through the forest in true *Feng Shui* fashion. The third piece of cloth is the same length and irregular rectangular shape as the first two and a bright dandelion, buttercup, yellow that flows soft as satin against her fingertips.

She turns a full three-hundred-and-sixty degrees looking around her, half expecting to glimpse a woodland nymph wearing a multi-colored skirt sewn magically together of autumn leaves beneath a naked torso white as moonlight coalesced into flesh, like an illustration of Daphne from one of her old mythology books... but she appears to be quite alone with the deepening shadows, in which the winding trail of colorful cloth fragments becomes even more intriguingly visible, glowing as if with its own significant light in the gloom. The threat of rain is no longer reason enough to stop her from wandering deeper into the woods, and the next marker on the gradually lengthening trail is silver mesh reminiscent of a spider's web, only the weave is much tighter, and all it has managed to trap in it so far is Mira's imagination.

She is entertaining the wild thought that Phillip left this trail for her, the black overnight bag he was carrying when he left containing more than just his leather outfit and heavy boots. The idea is utterly fanciful, but there has to be an explanation for everything, and these beautiful lengths of fabric have clearly not been exposed to the elements for very long. Why should it strike her as so hard to believe he marked the path between his home and hers? It makes a certain amount of sense. What she's not convinced of is that he did it for himself; this spectrum of colors and textures seems especially designed to lure her deeper and deeper into the woods with the promise of being able to find her way back so she needn't be afraid to explore and enjoy the adventure. If she knows anything so far, it's that her lover is creatively unpredictable, and that everything he does seems orchestrated to evoke an intense emotional as well as physical response from her.

Mira has counted nine lengths of fabric impaled on branches when thunder rumbles a traditional menacing warning overhead. Time for her to listen to reason and turn back and stop behaving like Alice in a wonderland growing increasingly dark and dangerous with threats of lightning – the violent electric union between heaven and earth particularly attracted to the sensually open arms of trees. The woods are not a good place to be during this passionately charged communion between the ground and the atmosphere, yet she cannot resist continuing to follow a trail that somehow feels made for her. It's entirely possible that Stormy and Sekhmet have already found their way home and are waiting for her by their food bowls. It probably *was* just a big squirrel she saw earlier, not her cat's sleek gray back. Stormy would have answered if he had heard her call his name, she is sure of that. She really should turn back...

She can't possibly turn back, not if there's any chance Phillip made this trail for her. It's too expensive, too lovely, too intriguing to be mere coincidence – it's impossible so many different types of fabric were all accidentally ripped off unwary hikers at the exact same height and neatly threaded through each branch. This is the work of one man, or of one person, possibly some anonymous female neighbor who shares Mira's trepidation about becoming lost in the woods. Whoever created the trail, she cannot resist continuing to follow it to its end or until she runs out of markers. Colors have inevitably begun repeating themselves, but they are never exactly the same and their texture is always different. Naturally there are no green strips of cloth, which would be virtually invisible against the leaves. Nor are there black or grey or brown strips; only bright-hued colors tempt her along a gently meandering path. And in her eagerness to follow it, she walks straight through a spider's web. She shrieks in disgust as the sticky threads cling to the bare skin of her arms and legs and tangle with her hair. She is conscious of behaving just like a stereotypical girl as she desperately seeks to caress her flesh free of arachnid secretions, dreading that any little dark bugs the spider might have caught for its dinner are now hopelessly lost in her hair. Thunder rumbles again overhead. If she didn't know better she would say the sun had already set it is so dark beneath the trees. She looks anxiously behind her. The cloth clues she has been following are barely discernable in the premature dusk.

'Oh, my God,' she says out loud, and her voice sounds uncannily loud to her in the pregnant stillness before the storm's water breaks and drenches her like a new-born baby just emerged from the womb. That would be the best case scenario. The worst case scenario would be the umbilical cord of a bolt of lightning seeking to reunite with her. She could very well die less than a mile from her doll's house. In a flash, all her unique memories, hopes and dreams could be reduced to another meaningless statistic on the six o'clock news. Actually, she probably wouldn't make it until the eleven o'clock local broadcast right before Jay Leno, depending on when someone happened to find her body.

She is despairing about what to do – turn back or go forward – when searching for another flash of color she glimpses the mysteriously reassuring geometric lines of a roof and a house beneath it. A moment ago it wasn't there, now she clearly makes out the shape of a house beyond the trees. The cloth trail has led her safely to the other edge of the woods.

CHAPTER ELEVEN

"She wandered about into all nooks and corners, and into all the chambers and parlours, as the fancy took her, till at last she came to an old tower."

Mira emerges from the miniature forest and stands at the fringe of a tree-filled lawn gazing up at a Gothic dream. The structure crowns the top of a hill overgrown with a civilized extension of the woodland she just traversed and which conceals any possible neighbors so completely the house feels utterly isolated. Nathaniel Hawthorne and Edgar Alan Poe come to mind as a flash of lightning illuminates a gabled roof cutting sharply into the sky. She catches a tantalizing glimpse of grey stone overgrown with ivy before the strangely featureless light of a prematurely murdered day descends again. She looks nervously up at the threatening heavens, and a cool raindrop baptizes her forehead. Her brain warns her it is starting to rain, but her heart is so full of other much more exciting perceptions it doesn't care and her pussy knows getting wet never hurt anyone. She has come upon what could very possibly be her Master's house, and there's only one way to find out...

She is about to run in search of the front door when a light suddenly goes on in the tower room. A tall, broad-shouldered silhouette imprints itself on her retinas, and her right hand falls over her heart in an unconscious parody of romantic heroines everywhere as her breath catches watching the slender shadow of her lover undressing. Every cell in her body recognizes him as he pulls his shirt up over his head and tosses it away. A disappointed moan escapes her lips as he walks deeper into the room, out of her line of sight. His silhouette was magically gilded by the light he was standing in front of – a sensual halo that has made her warm all over with the longing to take his already beloved form into her arms.

More wet kisses landing on her chest and arms gently urge her to seek out what she desires. Feeling like Dracula's Mina in her innocent white dress, she runs around the left side of the house in search of the front door, and in the process she discovers that the eccentric structure's square footage is mostly vertical. The wooden front door is almost twice as tall and wide as she is and looks scavenged from a fifteenth-century Portuguese castle. She has to stand on tiptoe to reach the large bronze knocker, which is not shaped like a lion's head... a beautiful pagan face gazes down at her, and what at first appears to be thick, wavy hair is actually bunches of grapes. It is the head of Dionysus. She bangs his thick metal 'necklace' against the dark wood three times, but an almost deafening clap of thunder drowns out her plea for admittance as a bolt of lightning brings the sensual Deities' eyes to life. This is no classical portrait with empty sockets; the visage is more ancient and vivid, and Mira suffers the distinct impression her favorite god is challenging her.

Her emotions are cursed to uncanny synchronicity with the elements, because once again an unnervingly loud explosion of thunder drowns out the sound of bronze striking wood. She cannot be sure if Phillip heard the knocks on his door through the storm, but at least the covered porch is keeping her dry. His property is even more private than hers; behind her no street lined with parked cars is visible… she is beginning to feel as if she traveled decades through a time tunnel disguised as a brief patch of woodland, each colorful strip of fabric a subtle magical shift in dimensions leading her into this unreal realm of Gothic facades, gabled rooftops and pagan accents. The sound of the rain is becoming almost deafening magnified a thousand fold by the leaves of all the trees it is beating against. She has her cell phone and his number stored inside its electronic bowels. She could call him and tell him she is standing on his doorstep like a stray cat desperate for his caress, but that seems a ridiculous course of action when the iron doorknob is already turning in her hand. He forgot to lock the front door behind him. Or perhaps men who think of themselves as Masters aren't afraid of dealing with intruders.

Mira is both relieved and terrified that the door is unlocked and she is stepping unannounced and uninvited into a dark house. What if she is wrong and that wasn't Phillip she saw undressing in the upstairs bedroom? Tall, broad-shouldered men are not all that uncommon after all, yet it's too late now; she's inside and the door closes of its own weight behind her. She tells herself she should call his name and make her presence known to him, the only problem is her voice is cowering in her chest and refuses to cooperate with her good intention. The silence is so deep it would be like trying to yell under water; she can't do it. She is too busy fighting a powerful undertow of fear mixed with the current of excitement washing over her mind and nerve-endings. Then another feeling grips her almost as forcefully as a hand luring her deeper into the house across a darkly polished wooden floor. The front door led her directly into an open hall lost in shadow to her right, but to her left a soft golden light reveals a wondrous fireplace the Interior Designer inside her is covetously drawn towards.

Mira finds herself in the kind of space she has always dreamed of decorating; the kind of space in which all the treasures buried in her garage would come to glorious life again; the kind of space that makes a modern high-rise condo feel like a prison cell to her senses and imagination; the kind of space she could live in until she died peacefully in her sleep of old age with a smile on her lips, her body an almost centuries-old vintage her soul finally finished sipping and enjoying...

She cannot believe it, but her caressing fingertips tell her it's true, the mantel is made entirely of marble – a polished black stone threaded with rosy veins – and the grate is large enough to burn half a small tree a night, at least. The room is not vast as in story book descriptions of mansions and castles, but it is sparsely enough furnished to give the impression of great space. At the same time there is nothing ascetic about the minimal décor. A comfortably large chair sits at an angle to the hearth made of deep-red leather softened by decades of bodies reclining gratefully against it. A lamp with a black wrought iron stand shaped like a slender bark overgrown with a leafy vine sits next to this consummate reading chair, and by its light she is able to make out floor-to-ceiling shelves filled with books...

She would love to explore the rest of the first floor, but her nerves are silently screaming at her like a crowd made hysterical by the paranoid dictator of her brain insisting she really has no idea who the man upstairs is and that she's only imagining it's her lover.

She could very well be trespassing, a criminal offence punishable by arrest, not the sort of bondage she imagines Phillip has in mind for her. Ludicrous as her overly cautious reason seems to a part of her, Mira cannot ignore it. She either has to make her presence known to the owner of this wondrous home, or she has to leave as silently as she arrived.

There is no grand central staircase; an archway opens up onto a narrow stairwell ascending at a steep angle. A dim light in the shape of a candle in its sconce illuminates the landing, but where the steps curve to the left they vanish into darkness.

'Phillip?' Her call possesses less substance than a moth hovering around the light; no one upstairs could possibly have heard it. 'Phillip?' She winces at how loud her voice sounds to her, and she didn't even raise it above a normal conversational level. She has to take a deep breath and muster all her courage to call out as loudly as she possibly can without yelling, 'Phillip?'

The sound of quiet footsteps she imagines being made by bare feet answer her almost immediately, reeking havoc with her heartbeats as whoever she saw up in the tower room begins descending.

'Mira?'

The sound of her name affects her like a blessing descending from above and saving her from all her fears. The warmth in his voice melts her dread just as a figure appears at the curve of the steps – her Master wearing a dark robe tied loosely closed around his waist and exposing most of his chest.

As usual, the sight of him feels like a divine fist hitting her in the womb. 'Phillip!' she breathes.

'I see you found your way to me.' He smiles. 'Come,' he extends his hand, 'I've been waiting for you.'

CHAPTER TWELVE

"She climbed the narrow winding stair…"

Mira feels as full of questions as there are steps leading up to Master Phillip's tower bedroom. 'Did you leave that beautiful trail for me?' she asks breathlessly. She's in very good shape physically, but the stairwell seems to wind up and up endlessly.

'No questions right now.' He leads the way, her hand grasped firmly in his, forcing her to follow at his pace.

'Well, you certainly don't need to go to the gym,' she pants. 'You get a workout at home every day! Who designed this house anyway? It's amazing.'

He stops dead, causing her to collide with his soft cotton back in the ankle-length robe.

'Sorry,' she says quickly, and from that point forward concentrates on expressing her remarks as statements rather than questions. She is aware this might be a slightly deceptive way of obeying him, but thoughts and perceptions keep pouring out of her as freely as the rain beating down on the roof outside sounding louder and louder the higher up they climb. 'I imagine you decorated the downstairs room with the fireplace yourself, Phillip.'

No comment.

'But you couldn't possibly have known I would find that trail...'

Silence, unbroken even by heavy breathing and it annoys her that he is in even better physical shape than she is.

'Some of the treasures I have stored in my garage look made for this place,' she dares this radical observation as they finally reach a landing. 'I found the trail only because I was looking for Stormy and Sekhmet. I was worried about them.'

'I'm sure they're fine.'

She has to bite her lip to refrain from asking, 'How do you know that?' as she steps into the sacred domain of his bedroom.

The masculine décor is just right. Nowhere in evidence, she is pleased to see, is the popular minimalist metal style, nor is his private space taken straight out of a *Pottery Barn* catalogue with its excessive reliance on heavy wooden furniture and its perverse obsession with paisley. A king-size bed with a Shaker-style oakwood headboard is softened by a divinely thick mattress covered with white cotton flannel sheets and an almost feminine profusion of large fluffy pillows. The single nightstand is also en elegant Shaker-style table with a single drawer, its timeless look complimented by a futuristic conical lamp burning a bright red color. She counts three separate Oriental rugs adding warmth and softness to the wooden floor, the darkly vivid colors matching splendidly with a polished black hardwood desk placed beneath one of the windows. The room is a *Feng Shui* master's dream for there are no sharp angles; the walls all curve gently in a cozy egg-shape. And the apparent lack of closet space is more than made up for by a huge antique wardrobe that must have cost a small fortune.

'This is perfect,' she says, thinking out loud.

'Nothing in this world is perfect,' he replies, shedding his robe and standing naked before her as if to deliberately belie the cynical statement, because in her eyes he is absolutely perfect, and the fact that his cock is already almost fully erect is only part of it. 'I very much enjoyed fucking you in that cute little dress, Mira, but now it's time for you to take it off.'

She reaches behind her to unzip it, and careful of the weight of her cell phone in one of the pockets, she slips the dress down her hips and steps gracefully out of it.

'Very good...' He is gazing at her naked pussy lips. 'I was afraid I might have to punish you for wearing panties when I expressly forbid you to do so without my permission.'

'I would never disobey you, Master.'

He smiles. 'Perhaps not consciously, but you will, and often, and I'll deal with it. You'll get better with time.'

She is hurt by how little faith he seems to have in her.

'It has nothing to do with you personally.' He reads her petulant look. 'This is just a new world to you, and you'll inevitably stumble as you learn the rules.'

'But you're supposed to teach me the rules...'

'I will, but some things cannot be taught; some things you have to discover on your own.'

She very much wants to ask him what he means by that and to give her an example, but she expects the ban on asking questions is still in place.

'Take off the rest of your clothes.'

She quickly removes her sneakers and socks.

'I suppose I can't expect you to go trekking through the woods in high-heels,' he remarks wistfully. 'Oh, well.' He smiles again, this time playfully, and surprises her by drawing her into his arms and holding her close, her cheek pressed against his chest.

'I really am worried about Stormy and Sekhmet,' she confesses.

'I told you, Mira, they're all right.'

'You can't know that for sure.'

'I sense they are.'

She is careful to avoid a questioning inflection, 'So you believe in what is traditionally known as woman's intuition.'

'Of course, women possess qualities any intelligent man would rely on to enhance his own abilities.'

She laughs because his answer is so perfect it makes her feel strangely giddy.

'It's a gut feeling I have that Stormy and Sekhmet are fine, although the gut has nothing to do with it. Just because intuition is a form of knowledge that transcends the physical senses doesn't mean it isn't a very real perception, and that it won't continue developing in human beings just as walking upright was latent in our ancestors.'

'I hope you give me permission to ask questions soon, Master, because there's so much I'd like to know about you and this house.'

'It was left to me by my great grandfather. I couldn't possibly afford it on my Master's salary.'

She pulls away from him to look up at his face. 'That's funny,' she says, reflecting his smile, 'because this house was made for a Master. I thought your family lived in Washington State.'

'They're originally from Virginia. They worked in D.C. for years until they could finally afford to buy their vineyard and get the hell out of here.'

'I suppose you have a cleaning lady,' she remarks cattily.

'Nope, can't afford one, not yet.'

'Oh, so is that why you want a slave, because she'll cook and clean for free?'

The glint in his eye tells her she has fallen into the trap despite all her careful effort and asked a question. He grabs her hand and pulls her over to the bed. He sits down on its edge, and instructs her to kneel. 'No, not in front of me, like this... that's it, I want you over my lap.' His legs are breathtakingly hard against her belly as he drapes her across them. She whines, bracing herself against the floor with her bare toes on one end and with her fingertips on the other. 'Regular discipline is a very important part of a slave's life,' he informs her, 'but right now I'm not going to spank you as punishment; this is purely for pleasure, my pleasure and yours.'

'But how can pain be pleasure?' The words have barely escaped her lips before a sharp, hot blow to her ass cheeks makes her cry out indignantly. 'I'm sorry!' she gasps.

'That's all right; any excuse to spank you is a good one. You have the most beautiful ass.' His amazingly hard palm lands across it again with a loud smacking sound.

Mira moans, and continues to moan as he spanks her, yet after a while she is no longer sure the sounds she is making are actually ones of protest, because beneath her hotly outraged nether cheeks her pussy is getting so hot and wet her perception of what is pain and what is pleasure is flowing together into one intensely indistinguishable sensation. She was never spanked as a child, and apart from a few playful slaps on the ass delivered by a handful of former boyfriends who didn't last, her buttocks have never been the subject of so much passionate attention.

'Are you enjoying this, Mira?'

'No, Master! I mean... I don't know...'

He strokes her burning cheeks, and then squeezes them each appreciatively. 'Mm,' he insinuates the tips of two fingertips between her labial lips, 'I think you are enjoying it.'

The teasing dip of his digits makes her aware of how wet she is. Her pussy's traitorous response to the humiliation of being spanked is a smoldering need totally at odds with her reason. She is both disappointed and relieved when he urges her gently off his lap and onto her knees on the rug before him. He opens his legs, and she braces her hands on his inner thighs as she bends her head and slides his erection between her lips. She loves how tender his skin remains over his rock-like hardness beneath it, and his semen tastes wonderful to her. She twirls her tongue around his head, gripping the base of his shaft with her left hand while her right hand gently cradles his balls.

'Oh, yes,' he whispers, encouraging the swift bobbing of her head up and down his cock. Blowing him is a totally engrossing experience, a way of wordlessly praising how thick and hard and long his penis is; a way of worshipping his erection while also claiming it as hers. She is pleasantly possessed by a feeling of timelessness, of an endless, sensual continuum as the scepter containing all the power of his pleasure slides in and out of her mouth... into darkness and back out into light... into warm, wet, sucking depths and back out into cool, caressing air... she can almost taste intoxicating secrets of life and creation as she sucks her Master's cock forgetting everything else in the world, all her senses and attention concentrated on his beautiful hard-on.

'Oh, yes...' he says again so softly she barely hears him over the lusty slurps of her tongue as she savors him even more fervently. The more she swallows of his sweet pre-cum the more mysteriously hungry she gets for more of him. She has no idea, nor does she care, how much time has passed before he says, 'I'm going to fuck you now.' He moves farther up on the mattress and spreads himself out on his back, watching as she crawls onto the bed with him.

'Oh, my God, this is a feather mattress,' she exclaims as she molds herself to his side, her cheek resting between his shoulder and his chest as she caresses the sparse black hairs providing a pleasant contrast in texture to his tender skin. 'You have wonderful skin,' she tells him.

'So do you. I love everything about you, Mira.'

It is the first time she has ever heard him say the word 'love'. As far as she can remember she has never heard him casually say he loved anything. He enjoys. He likes. He appreciates. He does not *love*. 'I love everything about you too, Phillip... except your job,' she is honest enough to add, and is rewarded by the gentle vibration of his chest as he laughs beneath his breath.

'I told you not to worry about that.'

'I know.' This is also the first time they have just lain peacefully in each other's arms. They are silent for a few minutes, during which she feels absolutely no need to invite any words into the room.

'I love listening to the rain,' he murmurs.

'Me too... sometimes I think it sounds like a huge cat curled around the house purring.'

'Mm, I like that.'

'I'm falling in love with you, Phillip,' she whispers.

His silence seems to extend beyond the edges of the known universe. She is beginning to drift off into a numbing despair when his voice finally rescues her from a hopeless void, 'Part of me keeps thinking it's too soon, but it's true... I love you, too, Mira.'

She closes her eyes and sighs as deeply as if she's been holding her breath all her life.

He rolls on top of her, thrusting a knee between her thighs, and she gladly spreads her legs for him. He pins her hands up over her head, raises his hips, and enters her.

She cries out beneath the wonderful shock of his abrupt penetration. She loves the feel of being pinned down by him – by his weight, by his hands, by his stabbing cock, and by his tongue plunging into her mouth. She responds to his savage kiss submissively, raising her legs around him, opening them as wide as she can to offer her pussy to him at the most deeply inviting angle, loving the experience of his hard-on plunging into the ultimate depths of her flesh. He buries his face in the side of her neck, and bites her, groaning.

'Oh, yes, yes!' she whispers, loving the experience of being absolutely possessed by him; of her body offering no resistance to his driving, biting, sucking, thrusting energy. Her clit quivers with pleasure as he bangs her, but how good it all feels has little to do with her body's temperamental seed. She has heard of the mythical G-spot, like the X on a treasure map that's only a fantasy, or at least it was… this evening her cervix feels full of subtly priceless sensations she never knew it was capable of, so much so that a clitoral climax seems almost superficial by comparison. She must be in love because the missionary position never felt so good. She is purely the vessel of his pleasure lying utterly pliant and submissive beneath him, until he starts coming, then her pussy begins deliberately milking him, her innermost flesh contracting and relaxing and deliberately prolonging his ejaculation. No military general could ever have felt more triumphant than she does as he collapses against her, his penis pulsing deep between the slender borders of her thighs. She lightly caresses his back with her fingernails, moving both her hands up from the base of his spine to the back of his neck slowly and gently, directing the energy concentrated in his groin back up to his consciousness.

After a few minutes he rolls onto his back beside her and she snuggles beneath his arm, her cheek resting contentedly against his chest and shoulder again.

He announces quietly, 'I think I'm going to call in sick tonight.'

She raises her head to look up at his face. 'Really?'

'Really.'

'You don't have to…'

'I know I don't *have* to do anything.' The Master is back in his eyes.

'Of course not, that's not what I meant…'

'I know,' he relents, gently forcing her head back down against his chest. 'I *want* to.'

'You still haven't told me what you're getting your PhD in, Phillip.'

'You still haven't guessed.'

Suddenly she remembers her concern for Stormy and Sekhmet.

'What's wrong?' He senses her body tense against him.

'I'm sorry, but I'm still worried about my cats.'

'Well, then, we'll just have to walk over there and make sure they're all right.'

'Could we?'

'We can do anything we want to, Mira.'

CHAPTER THIRTEEN

"That which thou hast promised in thy time of necessity, must thou now perform."

Now that Phillip has promised her they will soon be leaving to check on Stormy and Sekhmet, Mira relaxes enough to inadvertently fall asleep in his arms...

When she wakes, she has no idea how much time has passed, and except for the increasingly vague anxiety about her cats – who have always been able to take care of themselves – she really doesn't care how many hours, weeks or centuries have elapsed. Phillip's eyes are closed, and the deep, even rhythm of his breathing beneath her cheek tells her he too has fallen asleep, which for some reason makes her inordinately happy. She gazes up at his face, and as though sensing her dreamy gaze, he opens his eyes and smiles at her.

'Sorry, I must have drifted off,' he murmurs.

'So did I.'

'It was nice.'

'Yes.' Curiosity and excitement have completely replaced the anxiety that drove her out of the doll's house and into the small forest between their homes. She can't wait to see the rest of his place.

The downpour outside has spent itself and it has either stopped raining completely or there is a gentle, silent drizzle falling. They get out of bed and dress as companionably as if they have been living together for years. It feels pleasantly natural to be slipping back into her dress as she watches him pull on a pair of black jeans, and then slip a simple short-sleeved cotton shirt over his head. Its neutral faded burgundy color goes strikingly well with his black goatee and hair, but then she seems to feel that way about everything he wears.

'Are you going to show me your castle now, Master?'

'I think you probably saw most of it.' He smiles up at her from where he's sitting on the edge of the bed slipping on his brown leather sandals. 'It's not as big as it seems. It extends higher into the sky and deeper into the earth than it actually takes up space on the ground.'

She sits down next to him, pressing one of her arms against his to absorb his strong warmth, which already she hates being separated from. 'Don't tell me you have your own private wine cellar.'

'All right, I won't tell you, but I do.'

'Oh, my God.' She lets her face fall into her hands as if her skull suddenly weighs too much for her to hold up, but it's really all the doubts and frustrations other man have forced it to contain she is letting go of now.

'But that's not all I keep down in my basement.'

She looks up and opens her eyes again as she feels him get up off the bed.

'Come.' His eyes and mouth are hard again in that way that helplessly arouses her, but she discerns the ghost of a smile buried in the deep dimples on either side of his firm lips.

'I'm not sure I'm ready for this,' she admits even as she lets him take her hand.

Trent Reznor and *The Downward Spiral* come to mind as they descend the tower staircase. 'Whoever designed this place was either a sadist or a masochist or both,' she remarks.

'You think so?' he replies neutrally.

Even in her sneakers and walking down she has to make an effort to match his pace until they reach level ground. 'I love your living room,' she declares. 'Have you really read all those books?'

'I inherited some, the rest are mine. I'm working on it. The kitchen is on the other side.'

'Oh, may I see it?'

'Not tonight.'

She follows him to a narrow door hidden in shadow, and does not need to ask to know it leads down into the cellar. Suddenly, all her nerves stand on end like a cat's back arching, and she hesitates. He opens the door and switches on an electric bulb no brighter than moonlight diffused through heavy cloud cover, but at least he doesn't expect her to descend into the terrifying unknown in total darkness. It's not much of a relief, however, and she continues to hesitate, afraid of seeing something down there she won't be able to live with. 'You don't have a torture room down there, do you?' she asks tightly, forgetting all about the ban on questions.

He turns towards her. 'No, Mira,' he answers gently, stroking the length of her bare arms lightly with his fingertips, a gesture that has a deeply soothing effect on her taut nerves, 'I have a play room. There's a big difference. You should know there can be a world of difference between S&M and B&D.'

'You mean between sadomasochism and bondage and domination?' she asks urgently, feeling as if she missed a vital course in college.

'Precisely. When you think of extreme pain and distasteful activities, those are the most radical manifestation of S&M, while normal vanilla couples playing at blindfolding and tying up is the mildest form of B&D, and there's a whole spectrum in between. Sometimes the two merge, but never anymore than you want them to. Do you understand?'

'So... experiencing severe pain all the time is not part of being a sex slave?'

'Not at all.'

She sighs, 'Well that's a relief!'

'Did it hurt when I spanked you?'

'Yes.'

'Would you say it was painful?'

'In a way, yes, and no...'

'Did you enjoy it?'

She suddenly appreciates the expression 'cat got your tongue?' when she finds herself unable to respond. The truth might incriminate her and get her into a world, a lifetime, of trouble.

Fortunately, her silence appears to be answer enough for him, because once again he says, 'Come' in that quiet but inexorable way that has her feet obeying him before her mind has given them permission. She finds herself walking down the stairs in front of him as though she is not at all concerned about what she will find at the bottom.

This time the descent is relatively brief, and with the flick of his wrist he reveals the wine cellar of her dreams. 'Oh, my God, look at all this wine!'

'A lot of it is accumulated Christmas, birthday and Thanks

Giving gifts from mommy and daddy,' he explains. 'It's not as varied and exciting a collection as it might seem, but I haven't really started working on it yet. I have to pay off my student loan first.'

Perhaps it is the fact that her soul is somewhat intoxicated by the sight of so much wine – so many bottles full of sunshine and rain, earth and air and fruit ripening beneath the full moon, growing older and wiser, more intoxicating to the palate and the psyche – but she suddenly feels so relaxed that she boldly sweeps aside the black velvet curtain herself.

The same switch that revealed the wine cellar apparently also illuminates the play room, after all, you have to be able to see what (and who) you're doing to truly enjoy all the subtleties of the experience. She appreciates the archaic touch of electric candles in their sconces lining the traditional gray stone walls, and she discovers the lighting can be dimmed or brightened as Phillip turns a circular knob all the way to the right, making the forbidding space as bright as possible. He is flooding her visual cortexes with light, as if this will help clear the spider webs of negative preconceptions out of her brain while she takes in all the arcane furniture and equipment.

Almost inevitably, the first object that captures her Catholic school girl's attention is a wooden cross shaped like a large X placed against the back wall. What appear to be black leather straps are attached to the four corners… her vivid imagination immediately pictures herself naked and spread-eagled against it while he fucks her from behind for as long and as hard as he wants to without her being able to resist him, as if she would want to.

There is what could pass for an innocent black leather weight bench except for all the miscellaneous straps and chains dangling from it, and a red leather chair that looks as though it was stolen from a Victorian gynecologist's office. But what really interests her is the adult 'swing set' – an iron frame with what looks very much like a black cloth swing hanging from its center.

'That's used for suspension,' he tells her, following her eyes, a smile on his lips as he reads her expressions.

She is relieved not to see any iron maidens, or racks on which people are stretched until they look like refugees from an El Greco painting. And even though there is an entire wall devoted to such items even her inexperienced eye recognizes as whips and riding crops, there is nothing that looks as if it would inflict permanent damage – no needles, no nails, no clamps, no evil-looking vices, nothing that causes her flesh to shudder and cringe.

'So these are your toys?' she speaks at last.

'Yes, I guess you could call him that. Not very frightening, are they?'

'No, not at all, they're very intriguing, actually.'

His smile deepens. 'Come on. Let's go find your missing pussies.'

* * *

Left to herself, Mira would have taken a cab home, but she has no qualms about crossing a dark patch of woodland with Phillip along. With him – and a flashlight big and heavy enough to double as a weapon – to help guide her way, what would be a frightening prospect turns into an exciting adventure as they find their way back to her doll's house through the toy forest. She preserves the sense of mystery by not asking him again if he left the fabric trail for her. This man is teaching her to put into practice on a daily basis what she already understood conceptually – that she does not need to give her mind one-hundred percent evidence of something to know in her heart and soul that it's true.

It has stopped raining but all the leaves are wet and cool, and moist drops kiss her bare shoulders whenever she brushes against a damp branch in the darkness. She is content to let Phillip lead the way while she walks right behind him and slightly to the right, following his silhouette and the beam of the flashlight. It comforts her that he seems to know exactly where he's going, and it further lifts her spirits whenever she catches a glimpse of cloth – little beacons of color lighting their way.

'I've always been a coward,' she muses out loud, thinking of a line from an old Kate Bush song.

He stops dead in his tracks as if she stabbed him in the back. 'How's that?' He turns to face her, holding the flashlight down so the light pools at their feet – a tiny yellow sphere with no true power to stave off the night.

'It means I'm scared to be out here at night even though there's nothing around that can actually hurt me. It's a primal fear of the dark, I guess, and of forests.'

'You're right, there's nothing out here that can hurt you,' he agrees mildly.

'The fear isn't rational,' she defends herself.

'Is any fear rational?'

'Well, yes... I mean it's perfectly natural to fear you'll be hit by a car if you step out into the middle of traffic. It's perfectly reasonable to be afraid of cancer, or something.'

'Why stop there? The list goes on forever, doesn't it? If you give into one fear you inevitably fall victim to them all. It's common sense not to walk out into traffic. It's a death sentence not to overcome the paralysis of fear.'

It's disturbing not being able to see his face or his eyes as he speaks, and she wishes they would keep walking. The pool of light revealing a patch of ground at their feet is making her feel strangely claustrophobic, as if her awareness is being forced to take refuge inside it – a small constricting cell of visibility protecting her from the amorphously threatening darkness surrounding them. 'But there's a place for fear just like there's a place for pain,' she insists half-heartedly. 'Pain is the body's way of telling you something's wrong. Fear is the way to realize you're in danger and vulnerable so you need to protect yourself.'

'Yes, but that's different than being afraid even when you're not immediately threatened by anything.'

'Yes, okay, I get it, can we keep going now?'

'Why, are you still afraid?'

'No, not with you here, Phillip.'

'But if your fears are insubstantial how can I possibly protect you from them?'

She laughs. 'You have a point there,' she admits, and the sound of her laughter somehow lessens the oppressive weight of the darkness. Because she can't see the individual trees, they have become a single essence weighing on her psyche with their almost depressingly patient and indifferent presence. Laughter feels like a charm holding all evil forces at bay, and it also seems to satisfy Phillip because he starts walking again. The random way the flashlight beam picks out branches and trunks and roots and the ground covered with a soft carpet of dead leaves is at once hypnotic and slightly dizzying. When the light at last flows across smoothly mowed grass, and then spotlights one of her white stone vases so it glows bright as a chunk of the moon fallen into her yard, Mira almost feels as if they journey millenniums in the seconds it takes them to step out from between the trees onto her lawn.

It is dark in her garden, but Phillips switches off the flashlight as they walk hand-in-hand towards the doll's house. She didn't leave any lights on or even lock the kitchen door behind her, yet much to her parents' chagrin she has never much worried about intruders, for up until now hers has proven to be a safe neighborhood.

The sound of the cat flap rattling is music to her ears.

'Stormy!' she exclaims as his sleek, purring body wraps around her ankles. She scoops him up into her arms. 'Where have you been you silly, stupid pussy?' She is glad Phillip refrains from laughing at the silly sing-song tone of her voice, which she has allowed few other human beings to hear. Sekhmet is already proudly perched on his forearm, her lean black body resting across it as though it is a pedestal made especially for her, one paw curled up on his palm while her other front leg hangs elegantly straight. And thus encumbered with purring cat fur, Mira and Phillip enter the doll's house.

Despite how much she enjoyed her Gothic adventure this evening, she is glad he doesn't turn the light off in the kitchen after she switches it on. Part of her needs the steady passionless glow of electricity; candle light is sensually demanding.

'Would you like a glass of chardonnay?' she asks, seriously craving one herself and eager to share.

'I would love one, but first I'll need to use your phone.'

'To call in sick?'

'Yep.'

She gladly fishes the phone out of her dress pocket for him.

He carries it over to her couch, where he seats himself with his left ankle resting on his right knee. Apparently, there is a limit to Sekhmet's devotion to Master Phillip – the sound of the electric can opener. While he makes his phone call, Mira busies herself feeding her pets. She scoops the gourmet food into Sekhmet's bowl first, and then feeds the more patient Stormy before rinsing two wine glasses and filling them generously with one of her favorite California chardonnays, *Chateau St Jean*. Phillip's voice is so soft it is impossible for her to make out what he is saying, and by the time she carries the wine into the living room, he has finished his conversation. Now her electronic butler has the number to his job stored in its memory, not that she'll ever dare dial it.

'Thanks,' he says, accepting the glass from her.

'My pleasure.' She sits down right beside him on the comfortable black leather cushion.

'The roses are still looking good,' he observes.

'Yes, they're beautiful!'

He spots the remote control on the side table beside him, picks it up and turns on the television without asking her permission she observes with a secret smile as she sips her chardonnay. He begins flipping through the channels in traditionally annoying male fashion, never really pausing long enough on one scene to determine what is happening or if it might be interesting.

'I have over two-hundred channels,' she warns, wanting to save herself from becoming aggravated with her beautiful Master.

'And how many of them do you actually watch?'

'Less than ten, I think, but that's cable companies for you, they make you choose packages; you can't just pick individual channels.'

'Hey, the sci-fi channel!'

'One of my favorites. Don't you have cable?'

'Nope, can't afford it. I spent too much on my toys.' He winks at her. 'Here's to real-life entertainment.'

'I'll drink to that.'

For lack of anything better to watch, he leaves *Stargate-SG1* playing on low volume, sets the remote down, and slides a little lower on the cushion, making himself comfortable. The digital clock shows half-past-nine. 'So, where would you like to have dinner tonight, my lovely slave?'

'You're taking me out to dinner?'

'Didn't I just ask you where you wanted to go for dinner?'

'Well, as long as you let it be my treat this time...'

'Mira,' he grasps her free hand with his, 'I'm only teasing you a little about my financial straits; I'm okay, and I can't think of anything I'd rather spend my money on than us.'

CHAPTER FOURTEEN

"Beauty is eternity gazing at itself in a mirror."

Kahlil Gibran

Mira regrets having taken Ian McFarland on as a client, not because she has anything in particular against him; she simply cannot concentrate on work. Her sample books are figuratively gathering cobwebs like ponderous stones from an abandoned temple. The only fabric swatches that interest her are the ones hanging from trees in the patch of woodland behind her doll's house. Ever since she left the big interior decorating firm and struck out on her own she has not taken what can be considered a real vacation – two or three continuous weeks of work-free relaxation. The time seems to have come to draw a red line through at least seven blank white plots on her calendar, preferably more. When Ian gets back into town and calls her, she'll tell him some white lie about a minor family emergency. She doesn't doubt he'll give her all the time she needs to straighten out her personal problems. The red pen she fishes out of her desk drawer takes on all the properties of a sword in the constant battle to make money as it spills its blood in a straight line across two whole weeks, and gains that much neutral ground for her where she can relax away from the financial fray.

'There!' she says to Stormy where he sits perched on her desk next to the calendar watching the progress of the thin red thread with great interest. 'Mommy's taking her first real vacation ever!' She smiles at him, and he bangs his forehead approvingly against hers. She feels like applying the principals of *Feng Shui* to her own life for a change. She feels like meandering lazily and contentedly through each day instead of cutting a straight path from one professional or domestic goal to the next. Without realizing it, her need to be in complete control of her life has had a negative effect on her ability to truly relax and simply enjoy who she is and how far she has come and how far she can go. Ever since she met Phillip, his actions have seem designed to eliminate this *shar-like* patch in her emotional being. It is daunting to realize just how many fears from her subconscious basement were cluttering the otherwise lovely and luminous space of her psyche like ugly Victorian knick-knacks she should have consciously rid herself of years ago.

'I've lived a very sheltered life,' she tells Stormy, who is now reclining on his side directly over the red line she drew across the calendar whilst cleaning his whiskers. 'Apparently you don't think that's a problem, but then you have a lot more adventures than I ever do. God only knows what trouble you and Sekhmet get into when you vanish into your jungle bushes.' He pauses in his ablutions to look straight into her eyes for a long, disturbingly intelligent moment which is abruptly destroyed when he furiously attacks an itch in his buttocks with his teeth. She laughs. 'Come on,' she commands, and he leaps off the desk to follow her out of the office.

* * *

One of Phillip's presents arrives. This time it comes via U.P.S., delivered by a handsome young man dressed all in brown and full of such good cheer it makes her happy to know he apparently loves his job. After she dutifully signs for the box on the virtual line, he deposits it in her arms with a smile that promises she will love its contents even as it renders them unimportant in comparison with the free and priceless gift of his positive energy.

'Have a great day!' he says, literally leaping off her front step and running jauntily to his waiting truck.

'You too!' she calls after him.

Still smiling, she sets the box – which does not weigh very much – on the table in front of her couch, where it is instantly joined by Stormy. Then Sekhmet appears out of nowhere to inspect what in her opinion is obviously *her* package and she is simply allowing Mira to open it for her. The haughty tilt of her chin clearly says, 'I have people for that!' as she waits for the cardboard portals to open and admit her.

Mira fetches a knife from the kitchen. 'Get back,' she says firmly, not wanting to accidentally cut one of her cats as she slices through the tape, and she is also careful to put the knife away again before dealing with the utterly annoying Styrofoam eggs concealing the box's contents. Sekhmet and Stormy are not so patient. Already they are batting a few of the environmentally evil little balls across the coffee table and playing their own version of feline soccer. 'God, I hate this stuff,' Mira mumbles, struggling not to let anymore of the filling spill out as she reaches into the depths of a material that will survive until the sun goes nova. She finds another smaller box within the bigger box, and manages to extract it without getting kitty soccer balls all over the living room. She then takes the time to toss the box and its contents in the trashcan outside, safely away from covetous cats, deliberately prolonging the suspense... or deliberately postponing the moment when she will have to face the mythical shoes her Master expects her to walk through the real world in.

The high-heels are terrifyingly beautiful. The black vinyl shines in the sunlight pouring in through the window like some space-age material, a 'normal' curved shoe with a closed toe and a buckle strap perched on a platform three inches high to accommodate a slender six-inch heel that tapers open slightly at the end. Mira has no idea how she will ever be able to balance her weight on them, much less walk, but she quickly kicks off her black leather flip flops and prepares to make the attempt. Her Master accurately guessed her shoe-size, for the supernatural heels fit like a glove. She finishes strapping them on, and tentatively pushes herself up off the couch.

'Wow...' She towers over all the familiar objects in her living room which suddenly appear made for very short people. It dawns on her that this is the lofty angle from which a tall man like Phillip perceives everything. She puts one foot in front of the other, and is amazed when she manages to sustain her center of gravity and take another mincing baby step into her new life as a sex slave.

Mira makes it all the way to the full-length mirror in her bedroom, where she promptly pulls off her little cotton housedress and stares at herself in the mirror.

'Wow...' she says again, and understands. What the astronomical heels do for her legs is unbelievable. Their shapely curves are breathtakingly lengthened, and the shoes have an equally appealing effect on her upper body, pushing her ass out and curving her back so her breasts jut forward, enhancing her natural desire to have them kissed and caressed and fondled. The extreme heels perform a subtle but stunning magic with her figure, the way her legs 'go on forever' also making her curvaceous torso appear more slender, which in turn makes her breasts look fuller. Wearing only the long black hair flowing down her back and the black 'stripper' heels, Mira gazes at herself in the mirror in awe of her beauty. She has never looked as good as she does now, and she never will. This is the ultimate 'outfit'... although something tells her there's something missing...

There is a loud, urgent knocking on her front door.

'Oh, Jesus!' she gasps. She is too high up off the floor to just casually bend over and pick up her dress. 'Just a minute!' she cries, and bending straight from the waist makes use of her years of stretching and exercising to brush her fingertips against the cloth and snatch it up. 'I'm coming!' she yells as she slips the dress back on over her head. There's no time to take off the shoes. She walks as quickly as possible across her hardwood floor, and opens the door.

'Sorry miss, there were actually two packages for you.' The U.P.S. guy is back, his smile apologetic now. 'It was so small I didn't see it.' He hands her the light little package, caressing her legs with his eyes. 'Nice shoes!'

She smiles. 'They were in the other box you brought me.'

He grins. 'I wonder what's in this one,' he says, but doesn't stay to find out, nor does he redundantly wish her a great day again since obviously, in his opinion, she is having a very good day, indeed.

The second mystery gift from Master Phillip is a black leather collar about two inches thick set with tiny faux ruby hearts.

'Mreow!' Sekhmet is clearly of the opinion that this second delivery is also meant for her.

'Your neck is much too small for it,' Mira snaps, her emotions in turmoil. If she were to show her parents the first three presents from her lover, only the violet roses would fail to raise their blood pressure. How could they ever condone their precious daughter being collared like a cat; like just another mindless sensual pussy? Obviously, they can never know about it.

She carries the collar into her bedroom. Already she feels quite comfortable walking in impossibly high-heels, but all her life she suspected she was never normal, and now at last she feels as though she's entering a realm where she can truly be herself.

Standing before her full-length mirror again she slips on the collar, adjusting it so it fits snugly but still lets her breathe and swallow freely. She then twists the buckle to the back, and once again gazes at her reflection. There is absolutely nothing missing now.

'Mirror mirror on the wall, who's the fairest slave of all?'

'Mira-ow!' the glass replies as Stormy steps out from behind the wooden frame and fervently begins scenting her new shoes.

Her phone rings on the nightstand.

She teeters sexily over to answer it, but when she sees 'Caller Unknown' written across the display, her elation ebbs. 'Hello?' she answers in her sexiest voice.

'Mira?'

'Yes?'

'This is Anna, Anna Bianco, remember me?'

'Oh, my God, Anna?'

'Hi.'

'My God, it's been.... forever!'

A baby wails in the background. 'Just a minute, Mira, duty calls, but I'll be right back, don't hang up.'

She is sorely tempted to do just that, yet part of her is thrilled to hear from her old best friend again, frustrating as their relationship was. It did not survive the sheltered confines of Catholic school; once they hit Fairfax High they drifted apart almost at once.

'Okay, I'm back. I asked my mom to get your number from Rose. I hope you don't mind.'

'Of course I don't mind,' she lies blithely. 'It's great to hear from you. I heard you were pregnant…' She bites back the word 'again'.

'Eight months.'

'My God.' Her vocabulary has seriously degenerated. It's very odd talking to her childhood friend wearing nothing but six-inch heels and a black leather collar, especially knowing the woman on the other end of the line would not be able to wear such an 'outfit' at the moment and look, much less feel, desirable. 'How many children do you have?' she asks carefully, having discarded less flattering nouns such as 'kids' and 'brats'.

'Two at the moment, can you believe it?'

'No!' It's the most honest thing she has said so far. 'How do you do it, Anna?'

'Some days I really don't know.'

"Do you have… help?'

'Oh, yeah, mom and dad are great. When I can't take it anymore, it's off to grandma's house they go.'

Mira suffers a queasy sense of déjà vu.

'So what's up with you?' Anna interrogates cheerfully. 'I hear you're running your own company.'

'Yes,' she laughs, 'my one woman and two cat company.'

'You're an Interior Designer?'

'Yep.'

'That must be exciting work.'

'It can be. Sometimes it's just work.'

'You don't sound too thrilled with your successful career, Mira.'

'Oh, I am, it's just that I'm on vacation right now and I don't really feel like thinking about work.'

'Vacation, really, where are you going?'

'Nowhere.' She winces at how lame that sounds. 'You see, I just met someone...'

'Oh, that's great.'

'And I really can't concentrate on work right now, if you know what I mean.'

'Well, how would you feel about getting together one afternoon and catching up on things? Evenings are for hubby and the kids, but I can get away during the day.'

She thinks fast, but can't come up with a gracious way to extricate herself from this completely unexpected invitation. 'That would be great.' She is somewhat morbidly curious to see Anna again, whom she suspects could never understand why Mira is standing in the middle of her bedroom wearing nothing but shiny black vinyl heels even their Barbie's would have hesitated to slip on, and a black leather collar marking her as a man's slave.

'How about tomorrow? I know mom can take the kids then.'

'Sure. Okay.'

'This place is a mess. Would you mind if I drove over to your house?'

'No, I'd love you to see my doll's house. Would you like to come by for a light lunch and some tea?' They giggle as the formal tone of her voice suddenly transports them into the past.

'Oh, I would simply love to come over for some tea, darling!' Anna declares in her best British accent.

Phillip is working again tonight and tomorrow night, and for once she knows exactly when she will see him again – not for forty-eight hours. She invited him over for dinner but he declined the invitation, saying he would rather take her out afterwards. He did not clarify on this 'afterwards' nor did she bother asking what he has planned; she is coming to enjoy the mystery.

CHAPTER FIFTEEN

"If you want a drink, you may get it yourself; I am not going to be your slave."

'Anna!' she exclaims, schooling her voice so it doesn't sound like the gasp of shock it is; her old friend is obviously indulging the infamous food cravings pregnant women suffer from.

'Sorry, Mira, mom wasn't feeling well enough to take care of both Lizzie and the baby this afternoon, so I just left her with Brad junior and brought his sister along. I hope you don't mind.'

'Of course I don't mind, come in.' She refrains from offering Anna help in crossing the threshold lest the gesture insult her. 'Hi Lizzie.' She grins stiffly, eyeing the little girl like an explosive with legs walking into her neat little home. Through the corner of her eye she sees Stormy and Sekhmet dash into the kitchen, and a second later the cat flap rattles as they quickly make their escape.

The Fabric of Love

Smart cats, she thinks. *I'll get you for abandoning me!* It seems to her that time thickens and slows down as Anna makes her way over to the couch. Lizzie clings to one of her mother's hands and never takes her eyes off Mira, an ominous calculating expression in her huge blue-green eyes. When Anna finally makes it to the couch and gingerly seats herself, Mira sinks with sympathetic relief into the chair across from her.

'Twins,' Anna says proudly, patting her planet-sized belly.

'Twins? Oh, my God, congratulations!'

'Brad's happy too, although at first we were a bit overwhelmed. We weren't planning on four kids, you know.'

'I can imagine.' Mira can see the girl who was once her surly playmate haunting the pudgy features, and the light-brown hair she always envied so (because it was perfectly straight, never curling wildly out of control like hers always did) is still the same, only shorter now, neatly cropped around her face. She knows next to nothing about being pregnant, but clearly water retention is an issue. 'What's it like?' she asks curiously. 'Being pregnant, I mean? Oh, but I'm sorry,' she leaps to her feet, 'I should offer you something to drink.'

Lizzie is perched on the edge of the cushion right next to her mother, her hands clasped primly in her lap, her disturbingly conscious gaze never once leaving their hostess' face.

'Would you like something to drink, Lizzie?' she asks, addressing her as an adult because her silly cat voice doesn't feel appropriate; she really has no idea how to relate to children.

'Mira asked you a question, honey.'

'Honey' is wearing a pink little dress with pink little socks and Dorothy's ruby-red slippers Mira belatedly envies. *She* would have liked a pair of ruby-red slippers. She also would have liked a video of all her favorite Disney cartoons, but no, she had to settle for picture books.

Lizzie tosses her head back as if arrogantly aware of how superior her wish-fulfillment capabilities are compared to what Mira's and her mother's once were. 'I would like a coke please, madam.'

Mira bristles inwardly at the 'madam'.

'In a glass with ice not in the can.'

'I'll have the same.' Anna smiles proudly at her offspring.

'Oh, I'm sorry, I don't have any coke in the house,' Mira announces in a falsely apologetic tone.

Mother and daughter glance at each other.

'I don't drink soda.' She is compelled to explain her lack of sugary and nutritiously empty liquids. 'All I have is water and tea, wine and beer.'

'We'll both have some ice water then,' Anna says quickly as Lizzie's eyes narrow threateningly.

At least the little demon appears to be well behaved, Mira thinks.

Two hours later she has cause to regret the fact that she forgot to knock on wood.

'Sorry,' Anna apologizes for the umpteenth time. 'I should have brought her toy piano or computer with us. I don't know what I was thinking.'

'It's okay,' Mira lies, also for the umpteenth time. 'I don't mind her playing with my lap top.' She grits her teeth and smiles. 'How old is she again anyway?'

'Four-and-a-half.' Anna sounds disgustingly proud of the little devil she spawned.

'Four-and-a-half... computers didn't even exist when we were that age, did they?'

Anna laughs from where she is progressively sinking deeper and deeper into Mira's couch looking as if it will take a crane to lift her off it. 'Yes, they existed, we just didn't know about them, much less know how to use them.'

'I guess it's true what they say that kids grow up a lot faster these days.'

'So, tell me more about this man you're seeing now. All I know is his name is Phillip and that he's strikingly handsome and that his parents own a vineyard and that apparently he's the boy next door.'

Mira has to laugh. 'There's not much else to tell, really,' she says evasively, wishing she hadn't finally been forced to throw out the violet roses that looked so beautiful for an almost supernaturally long time. 'He's like no man I've ever met.'

Anna's delicate mouth looks even smaller in her puffy face as she gives Mira another one of her pregnant Mona Lisa smiles. 'It's always that way in the beginning,' she states with smug cynicism.

Mira keeps an eye on Lizzie where she's sprawled out on her stomach gazing intently at the lap top screen while manipulating the mouse across the Oriental rug and looking for all the world as though she's completing one of Einstein's unsolved equations. 'She seems like a very smart little girl,' she observes, trying to change the subject. She doesn't have to worry about her young guest stumbling upon any rape and torture scenes because she's not connected to the Internet; she's playing in *Adobe Photoshop*, a program that took Mira months to master. She remembers when crayons were all the rage, in fact, she still has to suppress the desire to buy a box whenever she sees one. She almost surrendered to the impulse recently when *Michael's* was having a sale of sixty-four colors for ninety-nine cents.

'Have you introduced Phillip to your parents yet?'

She tries to determine whether her friend's innocence is genuine, and generously concludes that Anna is simply clueless. Two babies, and two more on the way, is bound to wreak havoc with a woman's sense of subtlety. 'No, not yet, it's too soon. We only just met.' She wants to ask her old friend all sorts of improper questions such as, 'Is your vagina as tight as it used to be?' But maybe Anna had C-sections, which appear to be all the rage these days, and maybe a small scar is preferable to a distended pussy. Unfortunately, everything she wants to know is inappropriate for polite conversation. At least lunch was an entertaining and tasty affair of grilled cheese with tomato sandwiches accompanied by reduced fat Cape Cod potato chips and iced tea. But what she enjoyed most about it was being able to chew and sip and refrain from trying to make conversation with someone who was essentially a total stranger to her.

'Is there some reason you don't want to talk about him, Mira?'

She remembers clearly now (how could she have forgotten?) the infuriatingly superior way her friend could sometimes behave, and now, ensconced in her couch like a female Java the Hut, she is making Mira squirm like Princess Leia dressed in a skimpy slave outfit. The subconscious weight of 'they' is embodied in Anna's matronly virtue; she rules supreme in the middle of a beautiful single woman's living room. Mira's life may be clean and orderly and hedonistically pleasurable, yet Anna's timelessly fecund presence makes it seem to be lacking in something vital.

'Why don't you tell me about Brad,' she counters. 'All I know about him is that he's a stock broker with excellent sperm.'

Anna has the good grace to laugh.

Fifteen minutes later, Mira is figuratively squirming in her chair regretting how successfully she managed to shift the conversation from her Master and soul-mate to Anna's financially successful husband.

'Look, mommy!' Lizzie scrambles to her feet lap-top in hand, and Mira holds her breath as she totters across the living room with the thousand-dollar notebook held proudly out in front of her.

'It's lovely, dear,' Anna coos, 'now go show Mira.'

Lizzie gladly complies with this request.

'Wow!' Mira exclaims. 'That's *very* good.' She has seen a lot worse on museum walls.

Satisfied with the praise, Lizzie resumes her belly-down position to begin creating another masterpiece.

'I remember you said you never wanted children,' Anna comments, stepping energetically back on memory lane since she doesn't have to physically move to do so. Her tone implies she's waiting to hear that Mira has changed her mind.

'That's right, and I still feel that way. I'm just too selfish. Two cats and a man are my idea of paradise.'

Anna's complacent little smile stiffens almost imperceptibly. 'For now, anyway.'

'Forever.' She clearly remembers now what was blessedly forgotten – the dead-end arguments they used to get into to the tune of 'Is so!' 'Is not!' 'Is so!' until one of them just gave up in exasperation. *Where the hell is Stormy?* she wonders. She could really use a warm, purring body on her lap to soothe her bored tension. It is unpleasantly dawning on her that her old friend is trying to use her to feel good about her conventionally fertile life by getting Mira to admit she is dissatisfied and lonely, that she's missing something. Anna appears to be getting increasingly (although always politely) miffed that her single female specimen is refusing to be poked and prodded into confessing that what she secretly wants deep down is a house and children and a husband, necessarily in that order. She wants her ex best friend to admit that this career girl thing and living on her own is not what her heart and soul truly crave.

'Phillip is a Master,' Mira hears herself announce happily. 'He dominates women for a living.'

'Excuse me?'

'You should see him when he's dressed all in black leather.

Sometimes he beats women, and they love it.'

Both of Anna's hands come to rest on her belly as though to shield her unborn babies' ears. 'Mira, what are you talking about? Did you just say your new boyfriend beats women for a living?'

Mira smiles; she can almost see the smoke emanating from her old friend's traditionally programmed brain. She is deliberately setting out to short-circuit it, but the way she sees it, Anna has only her own insufferable smugness to blame. 'Well, sometimes, usually he just dominates them with his intensely sexy will power.' She has no idea exactly what Phillip does on those three mysterious nights a week, and right now she doesn't care; Anna's expression is just too entertaining. 'You see, he's my Master and I'm his slave. I'll show you.' She exits into the bedroom, and returns carrying her new black leather collar in one hand and her six-inch black heels in the other. 'He bought these for me,' she says proudly.

'Jesus Christ, those aren't real shoes, are they?'

'Oh, yes they are, very real, and you can't believe what they do for my legs.' She glances down at Anna's swollen extremities. 'Would you like to see.'

'Um, no, thank you... mom wasn't feeling well, I really should get going.' She struggles to stand up as quickly as possible.

Mira sets her treasures down and walks over to help her. 'Are you sure you can't stay a little longer?

'I'm sure. Lizzie, honey, let's go.'

'But mommy, I was just-'

'I said let's go!'

Mira suppresses a grin as she escorts them to the door. 'This was fun, Anna. We really should do it again soon. Good luck with the twins.'

Anna mumbles a polite inanity, but it's obvious she can't get out of there fast enough.

The minute Mira closes the front door behind her guests – cutting off the sound of Lizzie shrilly complaining about the loss of her latest masterpiece – the cat flap rattles, announcing the return of her cowardly felines.

'You two suck!' she says fondly. 'I can't believe you made me go through that all by myself.'

Sekhmet inspects her food bowl even though she knows perfectly well it's not dinnertime yet. Only Stormy has the good grace to purr around her ankles by way of apology.

CHAPTER SIXTEEN

" 'Oh dear!' said the princess. And the three drops of blood heard her, and said, 'If your mother knew of this, it would break her heart'."

Mira should have foreseen the consequences of her impulsive honesty, but she didn't, and it's too late to take it all back now. Rose is at the other end of the virtual line demanding to know what Anna's mother was raving about.

'She said you told her daughter you were a man's *slave?*'

Mira is tempted to exclaim, 'I did not!' but the fact is she did, and now she somehow has to make the sensually exciting world of BDSM palatable to her sedately conventional mother.

'Mira, talk to me honey, what exactly did you say to Anna?'

At least Rose is giving her the benefit of the doubt, undoubtedly remembering all the times Mira came home disappointed by her friend's lack of imagination. Yet the opposite seems to be the case now and Anna is guilty of an overactive imagination, hopefully as a result of hormones gone out of control in her pregnant brain.

'Mommy, I'm in love.'

'Oh, my... I see... well, that's wonderful, dear, but...'

'I have no idea what Anna told her parents, but I'm sure she exaggerated, or at least tried to make it sound negative. She hasn't changed a bit. I really got the feeling she was trying to make me feel bad about my life; trying to get me to admit I couldn't possibly be happy if I wasn't married and pregnant. It really pissed me off.'

'But it's-'

'The man I'm seeing is much more interesting than her stupid stockbroker husband, Brad, will ever dream of being!'

'I'm sure he is, dear.' Rose's voice is placating, the audio equivalent of a hand smoothing ruffled feathers; it is how she has always dealt with Mira's intense and sometimes bristling temperament. 'But why hadn't you mentioned him before?'

'I wasn't ready yet. I'm sorry you had to find out about him this way, but trust me, you'll love him. He's a wonderful person.'

'What's his name?'

That's a safe place to start at least. 'Phillip.'

'Well, that's a very nice name!' Rose declares inanely, but she is genuine enough for it to come out sounding charming.

'Yes it is, a very nice name, but he's even nicer.' Mira laughs wondering how long her mother will allow her to continue skirting the issue of whatever it was Anna said to her parents. 'So, what exactly *did* Anna say to her parents?' She grabs the bull by the horns.

'Well, it made absolutely no sense to me, some nonsense about indecent shoes and dog collars and sex slaves...'

'She was referring to the high-heels Phillip bought for me, and to the black leather... um, necklace.' She is allowed some poetic license. It's rather like trying to feed meat to a vegetarian by calling the chopped bacon in the stew diced tomatoes. 'Remember how I used to love to play fantasy games when I was little, mommy? Well, Phillip and I are sort of playing a game together; playing at being Master and slave, and it's really a lot of fun for us. But just because we choose different terms for our relationship doesn't mean our feelings for each other aren't as loving and as caring as Anna's are for Brad, and vice versa.'

'Mira, you're a grown woman,' her mother reminds her sternly, 'life isn't a game.'

'That's not what I mean! You shouldn't take me literally, mommy. I said its *like* a game, but that doesn't mean it's not serious. What I mean is that it's fun and healthy, not negative and scary like I'm sure Anna tried to make it seem because that's the way she perceives it. She's even more intolerably dull now than when we were kids.'

'You sound very defensive dear, as though you're trying to prove something to yourself.'

'I don't need to prove anything to myself, I'm just trying to get you to understand, but there's really no point in continuing to talk about this over the phone. You just have to meet Phillip, that's all, and see for yourself.'

'Your father and I would love to meet him. What does he do for a living?'

'He's getting his PhD.'

'So he'll be a doctor...' A note of approval softens her concerned tone. 'A doctor of what?'

'Viniculture.' Mira finally takes her guess. If she's wrong, Phillip will simply have to be getting two PhD's.

'Viniculture...' Rose searches her mental files, but clearly she has never met such a doctor.

'A doctor of winemaking.'

'Winemaking?' Clearly it never crossed Rose's mind that something as culturally rich and healthy as wine ever required the services of a doctor.

'His parents own a vineyard in Washington State.'

'An entire vineyard?'

'Yes! And he has a wine cellar in his basement.' Absolute honesty is as impossible as zero gravity beneath the complex layers of the earth's atmosphere – her parents can never know what else Phillip has in his basement.

'And how did you meet this wine doctor?'

'Sekhmet brought him home, can you believe it.'

'Sekhmet? Your cat?'

'Yes... mom, I have to go, I have another call coming in.'

'Phillip?'

'Yes, I love you. I'll call you later.'

'Mira-?'

'Don't worry, mommy. Forget whatever Anna said, the truth is much more complex, and wonderful, trust me.' She disconnects her mother and quickly lets Phillip in through the virtual portal. 'Hello?'

'Hello. Were you on the other line?'

'Yes, how did you know?'

'It took you a while to answer, and you sound a little breathless, as if I interrupted something.'

'Not really, I was just talking to my mom.'

'About?'

'About you, actually.'

'I see.'

'Are you getting your PhD in viniculture?'

'Very good, Mira. You finally guessed it.'

'I don't believe it! You are, really?'
'Really. What else did you tell your mom?'
'I told her I was in love with you...'
'That's nice.'
'You see, my ex childhood pregnant friend was here today and she annoyed me so much I sort of felt like shocking her, so I showed her the shoes and the collar you sent me and told her the truth – that you're my Master and I'm your slave.'
'Very good, Mira, I'm pleased.'
'Only problem is, she told her parents, and her parents called my mother, and you get the picture.'
'I see,' he says again.
'I tried to make her realize that terminologies are irrelevant and that what matters is the depth of feeling between two people in a relationship. She knows I've always been rather unusually intense, and I tried to let her know, if not in so many words, that I'd finally met a man who could handle that. But, of course, all you have in your basement is wine.'
'Of course.'
'You don't have a problem with meeting my parents soon, do you?'
'Why would I have problem with that, Mira? Call your mom back and tell her we can all have dinner together soon, but not tomorrow. Tomorrow you're coming over to my house for a slumber party so we can play with all my toys.'
'*All* your toys?'
'Well two or three of them, at least.'
'Ok.'
'Ok?'
'Yes, Master.'
'Your lack of discipline has just introduced a new toy into my

planned play, Mira. I've been very lenient with you, but the more time passes, the less excuse you'll have to be so sloppy.'

She closes her eyes. 'Yes, Master.'

'I'm proud of you for being honest with your mother, and I'm happy you trust me enough not to feel you have to keep our relationship a dirty little secret. We're just at the beginning of our journey, but over time your parents will see that no other man could love you as I do, or will, because it'll only get better.'

'I believe you, Master.'

'You have my permission to touch yourself this evening. It sounds like you've have a hard day.'

'Oh, yes, Master, thank you, I have... but, God, I'm sorry, I forgot to thank you for your gifts!'

'You showed them off to another woman and proudly told her you were my slave. That's thanks enough.'

'No it's not. I really love them, thank you.'

'And I'll bet you love how great you look in them, too?'

'Yes...'

'When you touch yourself this evening you will be wearing your collar and your new heels and nothing else. Understand?'

'Yes, Master.'

'What will you be thinking of as you touch yourself, Mira?'

'I'll be thinking of you, Master.'

'And what else?'

'I'll be wondering which of your toys you're planning to play with tomorrow.'

'Yes, you will.'

* * *

Mira has an entertaining, if also somewhat nerve-racking, evening cruising some of the most tasteful kinky sites on the Internet. She learns there is a very powerful fashion element to BDSM she was only vaguely aware of. Black leather is hardly the only fabric of choice, in fact, vinyl and rubber and latex seem to be even more popular – extremely shiny black latex, or candy-apple-red latex, and even purple latex a slightly darker shade than her favorite color. She lingers longest at a web site devoted to kinky couture. Her metaphysical side is immediately captivated by images of beautiful women clad in skintight reflective black latex wearing high heels even more extreme than the ones Phillip gave her... heels in which it would be impossible to do anything except lean against the stone balcony of an old mansion overgrown with ivy... and certainly a woman wearing such shoes could only crawl across the grass towards an old tombstone growing amidst the trees... crawling like a cat is definitely the best way to get around in nine-inch stiletto heels. And yet it seems to Mira that the women in these photographs are more than sex objects. Power and vulnerability are combined in them in a totally stimulating way. The high-heels they are wearing are not meant to get around in any normal sense, they are for taking mysterious root in while being violently fucked, for holding erotic sway in. When a woman wears shoes with heels as sharp as knives she is offering herself up as a sacrifice, and yet they are also the weapons she wields to conquer the man whose erection sinks into the hole in her shiny black latex as if into the haunting heart of the universe itself...

Mira is fascinated by the shiny black latex fabric that reflects the whole world off a woman's figure. She loves the juxtaposition of innocently lush nature with this unnatural material clinging to a woman's curves like a second, magical skin. Some of the photographed latex suits cover an entire woman's body except for her face and her feet; even her hands and fingers are sheathed in built-in gloves, with a zipper strategically placed over her ass and crotch so it isn't necessary for her to strip to be fucked. All a man has to do is skin the cool black peel away from her pink pussy and thrust into the warm and tender depths within. Mira feels that to wear such an outfit would be to assume the profound power of the energy-filled darkness of space containing the sensuality of all the worlds and of life itself. Shining black latex is a fabric she would definitely like to explore, and the artistic quality of the photographs she admires reassure her. They offer a necessary antidote to all the crude amateur images the Internet virtually bombards her with that are, at best, good for masturbation only.

Stormy leaps onto her desk and stares at the computer screen while she is studying images of naked women in bondage. Perhaps it is all the string-like rope that appeals to him, but she suspects it is her aura of intense concentration that attracted him into exploring the source of her focused attention. She doesn't want to admit it, but there is something perversely stimulating about pictures of helpless naked women, especially ones involving suspension, where despite how bound and immobile a girl is, all her orifices are still available for use. Mira is not entirely sure how she would feel finding herself in such a position, but she suspects she will find out soon enough. She also suspects that if she asks her Master to get her a shiny black latex bodysuit for her birthday that he will be happy to comply with her request. At least she already has the opposite end of the kinky spectrum covered, because she is the genuine item – a Catholic school girl. It is also flattering to note that Egyptian-style bangs and long black hair like hers possesses a timeless appeal transcending the traditional blonde bimbo.

'What do you think, Stormy, would you like to see your mommy dressed as a black cat?'

He quickly licks his right paw, ignoring the question as utterly ridiculous.

'I'll bet Sekhmet wouldn't like it.'

Windows keep popping up on her screen seeking to lure her into virtual worlds all promising to be the most extreme, graphic, shocking, etc. etc. for a small membership fee. Phillip's toast of the other night comes to mind, 'Here's to real-life entertainment.' When only the visual cortex is engaged, all the other senses are left out, which in Mira's opinion creates a dangerous imbalance, because real life is so much more than just what you can see. She can't taste, touch, smell, or otherwise interact with any of the men and women virtually crowding her study, much less have any affect on them either physically or emotionally.

'I don't know how far I can go in this world, Stormy. I guess I just have to trust Phillip to know, and especially I have to trust the fact that as far as I desire to go is how far he desires to go, too.'

Stormy finishes cleaning his right paw and begins industriously working on his left one.

'Come on.' She pushes her chair back and gets up. 'Let's go have some dinner.' She has had her fill of kinky images for one evening. In school she never used to get nervous before a major test, but she is nervous tonight because her whole body will be involved in the test tomorrow, not just her mind. And if she doesn't pass, she will, more likely than not, lose the love of her life...

She needs some wine.

CHAPTER SEVENTEEN

"That is an art that pleases me well; if thy daughter is as clever as you say, bring her to my castle tomorrow, that I may put her to the proof."

She arrives at her Master's house at exactly six o'clock as he commanded her to. She does not knock; he indicated the front door would be unlocked. She is carrying a black bag with two changes of outfit – one for playing in, the other for dining out in later. Per her Master's instructions, she walks straight to the door leading down into the basement. The light illuminating the steps is already on and she quickly descends. In the wine cellar she sets down her bag, and proceeds stripping off the sneakers, socks, shorts and tank top she wore to follow the colorful fabric trail through the forest. Beneath them she is wearing thigh-high black stockings that don't require a garter belt to stay up, and her new black leather collar with the faux rubies is already around her throat. All she needs to do now is slip into her extreme high-heels. The knowledge that her Master is waiting for her behind the black velvet curtain sends a warming rush of adrenaline through her naked body in the chilly basement, and the wine bottles around her seem to offer their mysterious support as she walks carefully across the stone floor. She is carrying nothing now except her pride and her beauty and her love for the man she is confident is about to use her as she was made to be used.

Outside it is still daylight, but inside the earth it always feels like night. Perched on the erotic pedestals of her extreme high-heels, completely naked except for the stockings and her Master's collar, it seems to Mira that her senses are coming fully alive like never before; her fingertips have never felt anything so luxuriously soft as the black velvet cloth she parts to reveal the scene from a nightmare, or a dream... definitely a dream. Along with the three dimensions all her perceptions, both physical and conceptual, seem to orbit the figure standing there to greet her. Phillip is dressed entirely in black again, but with a breathtaking difference – his shoulders and arms are bare, his torso hugged by a tight black latex T-shirt reflecting the artificial candlelight. On a normal day, she would do anything he wanted her to, but when he looks like this, heaven and hell are the limit. For the space of a few accelerated heartbeats they simply stare at each other. Mira is not sure how to proceed now and waits for his direction.

He approaches her, the sound of his boots eloquently taking the place of words. 'Good evening, my beautiful slave,' he says formally, but a subtle smile shines in his eyes.

'Good evening, Master.'

'You look absolutely beautiful in your slave uniform, Mira.' He lifts the weight of her hair with the backs of his hands and tosses it over her shoulders to fully expose her breasts.

His physical proximity makes her weak; in the towering heels it's as if she weighs less than normal. She will do anything for him. Her body was made for him. This is not a figure of speech or a metaphor; as he takes her arm and leads her deeper into the room it feels like the literal truth. The pages of the haunting exam she must take to graduate into her new life as a sex slave are opening up and she is facing her first challenge. It is no normal black leather weight bench, but it looks comfortable enough sitting in the heart of a minimalist metal structure from which hang four chains and buckled straps.

'Lie down on your back, Mira.'

She obeys him as gracefully as she can, her backside making rather swifter contact with the cushy leather than she intended; she is still getting used to her new center of gravity in the extreme shoes. It feels very nice to stretch out on the comfortable platform, and she is only vaguely wondering what he has in mind, content to savor the mystery like a rare vintage. There is also a little bit of 'ignorance is bliss' in her current submissive attitude, although she knows that will change soon enough; soon she will know whether or not she can remain so pliant, whether or not her flesh can pass all he has in mind for it. And there's no way she can cheat because the only way she can pass is to truly enjoy the challenge.

'Are you frightened, Mira?'

'No, Master, I'm not.'

'Good, because there's no reason you should be.'

The 'bench' is just the right height to put her hips on a level with his. 'Raise your legs and spread them,' he commands.

She obeys him naturally, her pussy lips parting as if in wonder, and the slick sound her labial lips make as they open speaks loudly of unconfessed hungers. Suddenly, Mira realizes he is going to force the truth out of her, and that she won't be able to lie to herself or to the world anymore about the dark depths hibernating in her libido. She has never had her legs spread and suspended like this. The gynecologist's office was just a terrible tease that did not even hint at how gloriously vulnerable this position would make her feel. Her arms suffer the same fate as her legs, spread open over her head with her wrists resting in what feel like fur-lined straps he buckles just tightly enough that she can't wriggle her hands free. The final touch comes as a surprise. She gasps when her head is thrown back as he bends over to release a lever beneath the cushion. Immediately she worries that if he forces her to sustain this pose for too long the blood will rush to her head and she won't be able to bear it.

'Master...' she says, a tremor of uncertainty in her voice.

Darkness fills her vision as he comes and stands directly over her prone face. The universe is divided in half in his gleaming black thighs, and it feels like the hand of God descending over her features to gently caress her cheek and part her lips with the tip of his strong, demanding thumb.

'Mira, the first and the last and the most important lesson a slave has to learn is to trust her Master. You're worried I'll leave you like this for too long?'

'Yes, Master,' she admits, intensely grateful for his perceptive understanding.

'Very good, you were honest with me about it. But you came here of your own free will, Mira, which means you trust me. Yet clearly that trust still has its limits, and these limits are the only things in the room that are going to cause you pain and discomfort. There can be no limits to how much you trust me. The trust must be absolute and include the largest and smallest of your fears and anxieties.'

'Yes Master, I understand.' Her world is literally upside down. Pleasing him is all that matters to her now, and yet she knows that in doing so she will also mysteriously be fulfilling herself. This is the dance he mentioned, the beginning of the death spiral – the death of the doubts and fears limiting her experiences. She is in absolutely no physical danger, she knows this, yet being completely bound and helpless for the first time in her life is still an unnerving experience. Part of her is desperate to feel anxious. Another part of her is so excited she has to close her eyes as he cradles her head in both his hands and lifts it, stopping the flow of blood to her skull. He massages her scalp with his fingertips, and for an instant she can almost imagine she is at the beauty salon getting her hair washed, her head tilted back into the sink.

'Would you like to suck my cock?'

'Oh, yes, Master.'

He gently lets go of her head again, and she opens her eyes to try and get a glimpse of his penis as he unzips his tight pants. She needn't have worried. Soon his erection is all she can see, taste, smell and feel. He sinks to his knees and begins fucking her face. His hands caress her throat on the outside while the engorged head of his cock strokes it from the inside. Her wrists and ankles jerk in their straps in sympathy with her gag reflex, but whether she likes it or not the slender shaft of her neck remains completely open to him. The cool pillows of his balls press against her features in breathless contrast to his hard-on filling her mouth and throat like porous stone stiffening and swelling against her wet tongue. Dimly colorful lights flash behind her closed eyelids as the intoxicating smell and taste of him act like a powerful drug lessening her discomfort. Her pussy cries hotly at being so left out of the action; at feeling so empty compared to her mouth, which technically wasn't even made for his penis the way her cunt was. Her nose smothered in his scrotum, Mira breathes in the scent of his skin like an elixir. She swallows his erection's tender sword, and the point metaphorically pierces her heart – the excruciating experience is thrilling because she truly loves him.

When his penis slides out of her mouth she gasps to fill her lungs with air, surprised and rather awed by her ability to swallow him whole without choking. He slips out of her slowly, allowing her time to savor the full length of his cock caressing parts of her no man has ever reached before. She sees him stand up, but before she can begin to feel abandoned, he adjusts the lever beneath the cushion and raises her head level with her body again. Her cheeks are flushed, and her awareness of everything feels relaxed and open in an arousing way. It seems right that her hands and arms are raised as if in supplication or worship or both, because she just worshiped him and now a part of her is silently pleading with him to reward her efforts. Her pussy is open and aching for him. Her cunt's juicy feast is offered up for his cock to begin carving her up and serving them both the pleasure she can't get enough of. On the other hand, she suspects it is too soon in the test for him to reward her by making a hot little red star of her clitoris. He has moved out of her line of sight, and she is just beginning to seriously miss him when he appears again, but only for an instant.

'Oh, no,' she moans as a blindfold falls over her eyes.

'Oh, yes.'

As always the caress of his deep, quiet voice assuages her ruffled emotions. If he says 'oh, yes,' then 'oh, yes' it is. Another small eternity seems to pass as she lies there in her supplicating pose, and the position turns her on so much she feels as if she is begging all the angels above to follow Lucifer down and fuck her one by one...

As if in response to her sacrilegious fantasy a flaming kiss suddenly lands on her skin over her heart. She cries out in confusion, not sure if what she just felt was pain or intense pleasure. Then it's as if she is surrounded by falling angels planting hellishly hot kisses on her naked breasts. Crying out again she arches her back in an effort to throw off their demonic attention, but all she succeeds in doing is offering one of her hard nipples to the concentrated attention of a burning tongue.

'Oh, my God, Master, Master!'

'I'm here, Mira.'

'What *is* that?'

'What does it feel like?'

'Hot wax! Is it wax, Master?'

'Yes, it is. How does it feel?'

'It feels like beautiful demons kissing and licking me, Master!'

He laughs. 'I like the way you think, Mira.' Then he ceases to speak as the wax rains swift hot kisses along her body down to her navel. She emits a little shriek as the tiny crater in her flesh fills with molten liquid, making her vividly aware of the fact that it's the center of her body as a sweetly debilitating warmth radiates up into her breasts and down into her sex.

'Oh, no, no, please...' The painfully hot pecks are making their slow way down to her pudenda as everywhere the flame shed its burning tears her skin is tightening beneath a stiffening armor of wax. Her sensitive clitoris cannot possibly handle such an ardent kiss, she couldn't possibly bear it, and yet she holds her breath anticipating the terrifyingly intense sensation. She does not know whether to be disappointed or relieved it when it never comes. Instead she suffers the sweet, deep relief of his cock suddenly sliding into her pussy. She moans in gratitude, and then again in frustration desperately wishing she could see him. She could never have foreseen what an exciting new dimension would be added to the pleasure of his penetrations by the straps and chains holding her legs wide open. She cannot defend herself from his thrusts; she cannot control the angle or depth of his penetrations; her hole is forced to absolutely accept his relentless strokes, and the sensation is devastating. She is vaguely aware of her hands fluttering like wings as her cries rise eloquently around them, letting him know how much she loves being violently stabbed by his erection, and especially how much she loves the excruciating fact that she cannot defend herself from it. Once again relief and disappointment define the nature of her heartbeats as he pulls out of her almost immediately, letting her know there is much more to come and that her first major test as a sex slave has only just begun.

Mira makes a mental note to add more inner thigh exercises to her workout as he releases the straps around her ankles and she has to very gingerly close and lower her legs after their long suspension. Her arms, strengthened by weightlifting, are not as affected. She is hopeful the blindfold will come off next. She should have known it was too much of a reprieve to expect so soon as he grasps both her hands and helps her sit up, keeping her blind and vulnerable while he urges her gently to her feet. He lets go of her hands, and she resists the temptation to cling to his arm as she relocates her center of gravity on the six-inch black pedestals. She has a vivid picture in her mind of the other 'toys' in his play room, and wonders where he will lead her next. Then a strangely sharp, clinging sensation beneath her chin makes her tilt her head back proudly.

'This way, my slave.'

'But I can't see...'

'That's right, you have to trust me. Follow the directions of the riding crop and don't be afraid, just concentrate on its touch.'

This command would not be half as daunting if she was barefoot or wearing normal shoes, and if she was more familiar with her surroundings, but she supposes that's the whole point – to intensify how vulnerable she feels as anxiety and arousal battle each other in the core of her being, which he so effortlessly reaches with his penis when he fucks her. It is much harder for her to access this haunting sensual core of herself merely with her willpower; she wouldn't be able to do it if the desire to trust him, and to show him that she trusts him, wasn't intricately woven into the exercise. She hesitates as the tip of the crop snakes out from beneath her chin, and a moment passes before she feels it again at the base of her spine. She moves tentatively forward, pausing in confusion when she feels the tip of the riding crop press against her left thigh.

'Turn a little to the right, Mira.'

She obeys her Master's voice, blindly following his lead. She can't be sure, but she suspects the wooden cross in the back of the room is their destination. Naturally, she knows better than to ask. She hesitates again as the crop comes to rest directly behind her knees. A few seconds later, a fiery lick across her ass cheeks comes as a shock. She gasps, and tears spring into her eyes beneath the blindfold.

'You're not listening with your body, Mira. Stop thinking and start feeling.'

'Yes, Master, I'm sorry!' The flesh of her buttocks is burning in silent in sympathy with horses everywhere. She takes great care to keep her skin soft and supple using all the latest fruit-based products, but she never realized just how incredibly sensitive her glove-like organ can be.

'Stop right there,' he commands.

She gladly plants her towering heels together and stands with her arms relaxed at her sides, her breasts and ass thrusting out into the chill air of the cellar, her nipples straining for his attention.

'Spread your legs.'

It seems a simple enough command, but when she slipped on the extreme high-heels she stepped into another dimension where gravity became more severe. She manages to shift her feet apart, having no desire to feel the hot snaky reprimand of the crop across her buttocks again. His warm hands grasp her wrists to lift her arms over her head, and then he presses the full length of his body against hers so she has no choice but to fall forward into the void.

'Master!' she cries, but already her cheek is resting safely against cool, smooth wood as once again he secures her wrists over her head, and then firmly manacles her ankles to keep her legs spread.

She has been fantasizing about this position and this cross ever since she saw it; however, she couldn't have imagined the intense gratification of his hands parting her ass cheeks so he could thrust his tongue up into her pussy from behind. His skilled oral devotion comes as a blessing to her overwrought senses. She is deliciously aware of her lush labial lips as he takes them in his mouth, alternately sucking and feasting on the sweet and tender crack in her flesh. Tendrils of pleasure indistinguishable from pure, hot energy are slowly unraveling deep in her pelvis, snaking down to meet the tip of his licking, flicking, thrusting tongue, and the subtle, exquisite conflagration is concentrated in her swelling clitoris. Everything is so hard – his fingers digging into her nether cheeks, the wood pressing against her nipples and belly, the stiff leather cuffing her wrists and ankles – and she is so soft and yielding and helpless.

'Oh, Master, please, please…'

He shoves his face into her vulva with a ravenous growl.

'Oh, God, please fuck me, Master, please!'

His features cease to imprint themselves on the haunting clay of her hotly juicing sex. 'I suppose I could do that,' he says. And he does.

Being nailed to the cross takes on a whole different meaning to the Catholic school girl inside Mira. Her breasts are no longer crushed against the wood because they're in his hands, his fingers pressing cruelly into her tender mounds. He braces himself on their soft fullness as his cock surges into her cunt over and over again in a tight, pounding rhythm. It seems to Mira that her whole life was leading up to these moments when absolute fulfillment pushes all the thoughts out of her head. She is at peace as she never has been before and not despite the violence trapped between her thighs but precisely because of it. No man has ever fucked her so selfishly. No man has ever banged her from behind when she was bound and helpless to defend herself. No man has ever driven his erection so deep into her pussy. He stabs her with increasing force in between pausing to circle his hips and grind against her ass cheeks, forcing her to savor the sensation of his hard-on packed into her hole; intensifying her awareness of his cock remorselessly rammed up into her body as he stirs her juices up with spiraling motions, making a hot cauldron of her cunt. The darkness behind her blindfold is black magic – a staggeringly powerful spell is being worked by the controlled confines of her limbs and senses and transforming her into the pure, unresisting vessel of his pleasure. Her sex, her breasts, her legs, her ass, her neck, all of her was designed with his lust in mind. Ground into the palms of his hands, her nipples are hard as diamonds refracting pricelessly sharp sensations through her flesh as his penis seems to drive deeper and deeper into her pelvis. He flings her hair over one shoulder and bites her neck with such vicious abandon that she grows limp as prey in a predator's jaws, allowing herself to be absolutely possessed and loving it even as she marvels at the paradox that his giving no thought to her comfort and pleasure pleases her more than anything.

He comes inside her with a vengeance, as if drowning all evidence of any man who has been there before him. Afterwards, he remains buried inside her, the weight of his body pressing her against the cross, and she is so stunned and fulfilled she is glad of its support. Surely this was the climax of her first test as a sex slave. She hopes it was because her senses and emotions are completely spent for the moment, as spent as his penis, also only for the moment, thank the Lord.

'Mm,' he says at last, his voice vibrating deliciously down her spine. Then he steps back, and yanks her blindfold off.

She opens her eyes but all she can see is her left arm bound above her and a portion of stone wall.

'I'm tempted to leave you like this for a while, Mira. You're such a lovely sight.'

'My ankles, Master...' she whispers.

'I know, they hurt, but you're doing very well in your new shoes, my beautiful slave.'

She is afraid he really intends to leave her there for awhile and her feet literally couldn't stand it. She is very glad when he begins freeing her ankles.

'You did very well, Mira. Did you enjoy yourself?'

'Oh, yes, Master!'

'I want you to share everything you felt with me over a bottle of wine. How does that sound?'

'That sounds divine, Master.'

* * *

Mira is very glad to sit down on a padded black leather surface as she slips off her black magic heels. She feels as beautiful and timeless as a priestess who just performed a sensual ritual deep in the heart of a temple with the high priest who watches her now as she divests herself of ritual attire.

'I've never felt so happy and so relaxed, Phillip,' she says even as she groans with relief to be standing up on her bare feet.

'You'd better get used to it, my slave.' He smiles and allows her to slip her arms around his neck.

'My God, you're so tall,' she exclaims. When she was wearing the heels her face was nearly on a level with his, now she has to look up at him again.

'You're so small.' He kisses the tip of her nose.

She giggles. The evening has been full of unexpected sensations so intense they nearly defy her ability to rationally remember them. 'I brought a change of clothes as you instructed, Master.'

'That's nice, but for now you're remaining naked.'

Before they leave the room she turns and looks at all the arcane objects it contains, and the space fills her with a sense of reverence mixed with gratitude that her guardian angels at last led her to this dark church, and to this man with whom she can worship her sensuality as never before.

In the wine cellar, Phillip picks up the black bag with her change of costume in it, and she follows him up the stairs.

CHAPTER EIGHTEEN

"We don't see things as they are, we see them as we are."
                                                    Anaïs Nin

Mira cannot seem to get enough of Phillip or his cellar. What she once almost dreaded she now looks forward to with a thrill of anxious anticipation she likens to an athlete struggling to reach the top of her form. During her demanding sensual encounters with her Master she is obviously not trying to set any kind of record, and there are no invisible judges to give her a perfect 10 as a sex slave, more and more what she fervently desires to do is transcend her limits, emotional, mental and even physical. She has come to appreciate her threefold nature as never before. She is more aware than ever that often what excites her feelings makes her brain anxious, and her body is caught in the middle. It was much more difficult for her to have an orgasm before she met Phillip. Her sensual wiring is not as moody and difficult to turn on as she had believed it was with other men. Every time she says 'Yes, Master' a switch is thrown inside her between the tense career woman in full control of her life, and between the sensually submissive slave in love surrendering all doubts and fears into the hands of her love and lord. And it is almost as if Sekhmet has noticed the changes in Mira because lately she behaves a bit more respectfully (if not affectionately) towards her pet human. Of course this change in her cat could simply be Mira's imagination, but who is to say how many aspects of the world aren't as well; therefore, she chooses to believe that she and Sekhmet are growing closer as she achieves a mysteriously higher status in her feline's mind as a pussy with a Master whose lap they both love resting on (although Sekhmet clearly considers herself superior for being able to curl her entire body up on his thighs whereas Mira can only rest her stupidly heavy human head on them.)

Phillip at last gave her a tour of the rest of his miniature castle. The square footage is indeed primarily vertical; nevertheless, there is more than enough space for a single man, and for a loving couple. The kitchen left Mira speechless. 'Food and wine go hand in hand,' he said, and she nodded in stunned agreement. Apparently he really was teasing her about his financial straits because no expense was spared on his kitchen that she can see. Black granite counters speckled with white like a starry night as seen now only from remote places on earth free of light pollution, and stainless steel appliances, were offset by polished oak cabinets, many of which were graced with stained-glass doors through which she could see an assortment of stemware worthy of a man who would one day inherit a vineyard.

'But you said you hate to cook, Master,' she reminded him.

'Yes, I don't much care for it, I'll admit, but my slave happens to be an excellent cook, and she deserves the best tools, and the nicest atmosphere to work in.'

She didn't point out that he designed this dream kitchen long before they met because she suspects that the foundations of his entire home have much to do with belief in Choreography as opposed to coincidence, and with his aggressively positive nature. He mentioned when they first met that he had begun losing hope that he would ever meet the right woman, but he had set the stage as though he never doubted it. There are a myriad of things she loves about him, especially the way his intelligence and his imagination work together, and how he can make what to her appears to be a mountainous obstacle feel like a challenge she can easily conquer with the right attitude. He is actively reinforcing her life-long belief that how you perceive things, and how you structure and illuminate your thoughts makes all the difference in the world. If you're climbing a mountain and deliberately choose cheap, poorly made equipment you can get yourself killed; you should always bring the best attitude along no matter what it costs you in courage.

Mira loves everything about Phillip's home, but his back porch holds a special place in her heart. In nice weather it is a haven of ivy-covered trellises surrounded by flowering plants and flanked by big beautiful old trees. There is an outdoor fireplace, and of course a hot tub that will make it a cozy and stimulating place to be even on cold winter nights. Black wrought iron chairs surrounding a table with a glass top, and an abundance of gas lamps, also make his porch a beautiful place to dine. It was where they enjoyed the first dinner she prepared for them, and for which he opened a special bottle from his cellar – a thirty-five year-old vintage from Portugal his parents had given him for his birthday five years ago.

Mira should not have been surprised that Phillip effortlessly charmed her own parents. To see the three of them conversing pleasantly, and generally getting along splendidly, was such a relief she had to excuse herself and savor a moment alone in her old bathroom. They had stopped by her childhood home for a social drink before going out to dinner, by themselves; she had felt it was too much to ask of her lover that he dine with Rose and John so soon in their relationship. Her mother clearly felt there was nothing wrong with having a doctor in the family, even if all he did was preside over healthy grapes and the bottles convalescing in his cellar, and Mira's good-natured father had grown even mellower with age; it would not even occur to him to pass negative judgment on a man his daughter so thoroughly approved of, for he had always trusted her demanding taste in everything, men included. Once again Phillip reduced the mountain in Mira's psyche to a pleasant little hill they soon got over together. Before she knew it, Rose and John were standing in the front door smiling and waving goodbye as she and her Master drove off in a cloud of love given a silver lining by her parents' blessing.

'The Catholic school I went to is just two blocks away down Old Lee Highway,' she informed him.

'A genuine Catholic school girl...' He shook his head as if he couldn't believe his luck, yet whether it was good or bad luck she couldn't tell by his grin, which always made his goatee look even darker and more sinisterly arousing. 'I'd like to see the church where you used to kneel and pray wearing your little plaid uniform.'

'Are you serious?'

'Why not, it'll be fun.'

'If you say so, Master.'

St. Leo's had not changed a bit. The church was as ugly on the outside as she remembered it, plain and modern in a completely uninspired way. This late on a weekday there were few cars in the parking lot; school had long since let out and apparently no mass-es were scheduled. Phillip's jeep had successfully survived its engine transplant, but they still preferred getting around town in her Camaro (which boasted the luxury of air-conditioning) and his driving skills (like many of his other skills) took her breath away as he pulled into a spot directly in front of the church with effortlessly controlled speed.

'We'll have to come back here after I buy you a new uniform,' he said.

Laughing, she let herself out of the car, not sure if he was serious or not.

'Mm, I'm getting hard just thinking about you in a little plaid skirt and white socks.' He gripped her ass with one hand and squeezed it so hard she cried out in protest.

'Are you really sure you want to go in there, Master? There's nothing to see except an ugly old church.'

'Yes, I'm sure.' He grasped her hand, and the firmness of his grip told her there was no arguing with his decision.

It had been years since Mira was inside a church, and she was surprised by all the emotions that swept over her as she stepped into the stone-paved foyer. She would never forget standing there as a little girl craning her neck to see inside the church. She had been part of a crowd of people bundled up in dark winter coats attending candlelight Mass on Christmas Eve, snow falling like a blessing behind them in the night – like infinite fragments of the Virgin's pure veil – while inside the church hundreds of phallic candles burned and the flames reflected off the handsome priest's gilded vestments. Cold darkness behind her, warmth and light before her, and all around her a comforting mass of humanity made special by her parents' beloved faces, and by the distant, rather bored profile of a boy she thought she was passionately in love with...

Memories brushed her like invisible wings as Phillip pulled open the door leading into the church itself, and waited for her to precede him into the empty silence. The time when churches offered a peaceful, compassionate refuge to people living in the brutal chaos of the Dark Ages had long since passed, but Mira's psyche could still sense the relief of finding sanctuary in a way that made her seriously wonder whether the concept of racial memory wasn't more fact than fiction. As if with a life of its own her hand reached up so she could dip her fingertips into the well of holy water and make the sign of the cross. Phillip wasn't watching her; he had his eyes fixed on the pristine white altar, and then he was studying the narrow booths in which Mira had confessed to a hidden priest about yelling at her mother and lying to her grandmother – the extent of her sins at so young an age. It was also where she had smoked her first cigarette with a group of the school's more daring girls who, for some reason, had welcomed her into their exclusive fold one day. She had done her best afterwards to hide how much she had hated the smell of chemically processed tobacco and the nauseous experience of nicotine contaminating her bloodstream.

The church was completely empty. Not a single soul knelt in the pews silently praying to God or the saints or whatever.

'Come here,' Phillip whispered, and took her hand again even more firmly.

She was not surprised that he led her directly to one of the confessionals. At least there was no one around to see when he opened the narrow wooden door, and shoved her gently into the dark interior. Then he joined her, and she didn't care about anything except the feel of his body pressed hard against hers and the sensation of his teeth biting into the side of her neck as his swelling erection dug into her womb.

'Oh, my God!' she breathed as he sucked on her flesh with the fierce hunger of a blood-thirsty vampire. He had given her a hickey before, but he had never used his teeth quite like he did in the house of God that evening, as though he truly meant to tear open her skin and drink her blood. 'Oh, Master...' There it was again, her brain being afraid while the rest of her was so turned on she never wanted him to stop; she longed for him to truly possess her body and soul. Images of vampires sleeping in a crypt beneath the church flashed on the screen of her closed eyelids as he reached down and yanked her dress up around her waist, never once loosing his vicious grip on her neck. He was going to fuck her in a confessional, and her pussy felt as deep and dark and wet as the crypt in her imagination. All she desired was the stake of his cock plunging deep into her body. She clung to his shoulders when he thrust his hand between their bodies to unzip his slacks. The angle was wrong so she lifted one of her high-heels onto the padded bench where she had once sat as a little girl confessing her innocent sins. She couldn't remain silent as he stabbed her with his erection and she was afraid her cry could be heard throughout the whole church, yet it didn't matter; nothing mattered now except the fact that she was going to die from the dark joy of being his willing victim. His confidence and intelligence, his masterful personality, had hypnotized her into absolute submission, and the more she gave him, the more selfishly he used her, the more she longed to give him and the more she surrendered all resistance and grew absolutely languid against him.

Her brain forced her to gasp, 'What if someone comes?!' but the most important parts of her weren't at all concerned, and soon how violently he brought himself to a climax banging her and sucking on her seemed to blow her mind so she was aware only of their mutual fulfillment.

Unbelievably, their violent love making was not sensed by any of the priests or nuns living in the residences adjoining the church.

The Fabric of Love

Mira's knees were literally week as she stepped out of the booth where she had just confessed her deepest, darkest desires with her whole body. She didn't need a mirror to know he had marked her, and even though she was proud, she was also glad of her long hair which would hide the evidence of his vicious lust during dinner in a restaurant. She smiled to herself. At least she would never hear him quote Dracula and say, 'I don't drink... *wine.*' She did not cross herself leaving the church. Her pussy was so warm and wet that immersing her fingertips in the cool holy water would have felt like the ultimate hypocrisy.

Back in the comforting confines of the Camaro, she rested her head against the seat and gazed at her Master's handsome profile as he started the engine and sped out of the church parking lot.

'I... I really liked that,' she confessed.

'I know you did. We'll be exploring more of that in the future.'

She chose not to ask him what he meant, content to savor the frightening, thrilling promise.

CHAPTER NINETEEN

"Time spent with cats is never wasted."

Collette

Because they live so close, just a quick walk through the woods, Sekhmet and Mira both have to wait for the special treat of Phillip spending an entire night in their home. Mira has yet stay at his place from sunset to sunrise because she doesn't want to leave her cats alone all night, although if the truth be told she would probably miss them more than they would her. Phillip is a very tall man, nevertheless, she is astonished and dismayed that his feet hang off the end of her queen-size mattress. Her bed, which always felt so big and luxurious to her when she was sleeping in it alone, suddenly seems very small. Her Master is a slender man but his shoulders are broad, and even when he rolls over onto his side his powerful body dominates most of the mattress. She is willing to give up a good night's sleep for the pleasure and emotional comfort of his presence, but come morning she has reconciled herself to the fact that she will have to detach herself from her felines somewhat so that she and her Master can enjoy the luxury of his king-size feather bed.

'We should bring them over to my place,' Phillip says over breakfast as they are discussing Stormy and Sekhmet.

'I'd have to put them in their carrier and drive them over.'

'Then I suggest you do so.' He pours himself another cup of coffee. 'They need to begin getting used to my house and to their new territory.'

They're sitting in the *Pan Am Family Restaurant*, which as far as Mira can tell is actually family owned. Blue plastic booths and white walls covered with sketchy uninspired paintings of Greece somehow manage not to offend her aesthetic sense, perhaps because of all the dark-brown wicker baskets hanging from the ceiling overflowing with healthy plants. The service is so pleasant and efficient, and the diner-style food so abundant and delicious within it's traditional unhealthy parameters, that she and Phillip have taken to having either breakfast or lunch their on Saturdays. She has lost count of how many cups of coffee her Master has already had this morning. She is still slowly sipping her second cup of Earl Grey tea (she appreciates a management that doesn't mind her bringing her own gourmet blend) but what she is truly savoring are the last words her sexy, commanding, tender, intelligent, funny, infinitely wonderful companion just said. He just let her know, with a sweet subtlety wafting over her soul like an angel's perfume, that they will be living together soon. The slight hangover she was suffering from this morning vanishes in a rush of euphoria. Ever since she met her Master the endorphin count in her blood has skyrocketed, and these very special endorphins don't just vanish thirty minutes to an hour after their sensual workouts but remain as a deepening contentment in her emotional system.

'Well, you let me know when would be a good night for you, Master, and I'll bring them over.'

'Tonight would be good.'

'Okay.' And the matter is settled with the relaxed ease she is growing more and more accustomed to the more time she spends with him. If she wasn't so happy she might be a bit disturbed by how much energy she once wasted worrying about both big and little things without even realizing how tense she allowed things to make her. That's not to say that everything is perfect now, after all they're still living in the real world. For instance, they occasionally tend to indulge their love of good food and wine a little too much, hence the slight fog in her skull this morning. Yet other than that there are no flaws in their relationship that she can see – it is a beautifully cut diamond that demands much from both their mental and emotional synapses, but in her opinion this is a good thing.

'So, what would you like to do today, my beautiful slave?'

'A trip to a grocery store would be nice,' she replies, and as usual feels guilty about dragging him shopping with her, an activity he has made it clear is not on the top of his favorite's list. Yet he always seems to enjoy himself (thanks in part to how well his willpower and his positive attitude work together) especially when they visit *Super H-Mart* which is like teleporting to a huge fish and farmer's market in Hong Kong for an hour. 'We really have to stop eating out to all the time,' she adds, striving to justify her love of food buying.

'And why is that? Don't you enjoy our dinners out?'

'Of course I do, Master, but it's very expensive; just one meal at a decent restaurant with a bottle of wine costs my entire grocery bill for a week.'

'That's true,' he agrees, pouring himself yet another cup of coffee.

'We're also going to gain weight if I don't start watching our fat and calorie intake.'

'Now we wouldn't want that, would we? I hereby command you, my slave, not to let that happen.'

She laughs. 'Yes, Master, it will be my pleasure.'

'Where exactly do you need to go?'

'Super H-Mart and Trader Joe's.'

'Okay. And then what?'

'Whatever Master desires.'

'Very good, Mira, but I think we'll have a quiet evening with the pussies tonight. We opened one too many bottles of wine last night, but of course it's your fault for making such a delicious meal.'

'Of course.' She smiles, and even though she does her best to hide it, she is relieved that another intensely demanding sojourn in the cellar is not on the agenda for this evening. Being fucked by her Master is a serious workout, and while she enjoys it like nothing else on earth – while the feel of his cock thrusting into her pussy mysteriously fulfills her on all levels of her being – the truth is her pussy sometimes needs a day or two to recover, as do other parts of her body if she has been in even mild bondage for a prolonged period of time. The more she gets to know her Master, the more she loves all the subtleties of his personality. She is surprised and grateful for the sense of humor she had not expected from the stranger dressed entirely in black who commanded her to take off her robe for him.

* * *

Stormy and Sekhmet refuse to cooperate. Mira has locked the cat flap so they can't escape the house, but that doesn't make the task of getting them into the carrier any easier. Fortunately, Phillip is there to assist her; Sekhmet is much more likely to respond to his cajoling voice than to Mira's impatient, and increasingly frustrated, commands. When it concerns being imprisoned in a moving plastic cage is the only time Stormy ceases to be his usual compliant and amiable self. He hides so far under the bed there's no way she can pull him out, and she doesn't entirely trust him not to scratch her to defend himself from incarceration. If they can just get Sekhmet into the carrier she knows Stormy will slink out from beneath the bed in response to his sister's yowls of protest, and she can catch him then.

'Sekhmet, come here sweetheart.' Phillip is kneeling in front of Mira's desk, beneath which Sekhmet has taken refuge. 'Come on sweetie, I've got a very special treat waiting for you at my place. Come on... that's a good girl, you won't be sorry.'

Mira watches in wonder as he straightens up holding Sekhmet by the scruff of the neck like a black rag that just cleaned two resentful yellow eyes up off the floor. 'I can't believe she listened to you!'

'Of course she did. She's a good little pussy. Aren't you sweetheart?'

Sekhmet may have yielded to his persuasion against her better judgment, but she is not about to purr now as she usually does in response to his voice. He urges her gently into the carrier, and quickly closes the metal door on her little black backside. Mira waits for howls of protest to ensue, but a miraculous silence reigns in the study. And apparently Stormy finds the stillness more disconcerting than his sister's screams because he peers out from beneath the bed.

'Got ya!' Mira snatches him up into her arms, but then holds him tenderly against her breasts. 'It's okay, baby, we're just going for a little ride.'

Phillip is crouched beside the carrier and effortlessly soothing Sekhmet by letting her smell and lick his fingertips through the bars. 'Ready?' he asks.

'Ready.'

He opens the carrier door.

Mira gently shoves Stormy inside next to his sister.

He quickly closes the door again before Sekhmet can escape.

'Wow, that was easier than ever.' She tosses her hair away from her face and steps into his arms as he straightens up. 'You have no idea what I go through every time I have to take them to the vet. This is the quickest I've ever gotten them both in there, thank you, Master.'

'You don't have to do everything alone anymore, Mira,' he says soberly.

'I know,' she sighs, and slips her arms around his neck so she can rest her cheek against him. 'I still can't quite believe it...'

'Mreow!'

'Merr!'

'I think we'd best be going,' he suggests.

'Yes, I think that would be a good idea,' she agrees.

He carries the passionately protesting felines out to the car while she does a quick check of the doll's house to make sure everything is turned off. Then she grabs her overnight bag and locks the kitchen door behind her. They did indeed go grocery shopping earlier in the afternoon; the trunk of her car is full of plastic bags. She insisted on paying for the groceries, but they decided to keep them all in Phillip's kitchen since they seem to be spending more and more time at his place.

'I'm glad were not driving to Florida with those two in the backseat,' he remarks as she slips into the car.

'I think they must have some Siamese blood in them.'

'No doubt!'

Even though it is a blessedly short drive, by the time they reach his house Mira's nerves feels as frayed as a delicate cloth subjected to a cat's sharpening claws for a month.

'Okay guys,' Phillips declares as he sets the carrier down in his entrance hall, 'time to explore.'

'And to shut up!'

The second he opens the cage Sekhmet shoots out like a fur-covered bullet, moving fast enough to prove all the supernatural tales of black cats appearing and disappearing as if at will. In contrast Stormy steps out of the plastic cell with painstaking slowness, one tentative paw emerging at a time, all his whiskers extended to their full, quivering reach sensing the atmosphere of a whole new world surrounding him. Sekhmet has vanished into the living room and Mira can only pray she won't do anything damaging by way of revenge.

'I'll start bringing the stuff in,' he says.

'I'll help you.'

'I'll get the bags. You set up the litter box, please.'

'Okay... I mean, yes, Master.'

They smile at each other.

CHAPTER TWENTY

"Surely something resides in this heart that is not perishable – and life is more than a dream."

Mary Wollstonecraft

A few hours later Stormy and Sekhmet have explored Phillip's house from top to bottom several times, not including the cellar, from which they are forever banned. The evening is unnaturally cool for early August in Virginia, and it is all the excuse Phillip and Mira need to strip naked and step into the hot tub where they sit across from each other. A filet mignon roast and too large Idaho potatoes are cooking in the oven, and the cold white wine flowing onto her tongue is a delicious contrast to the embracing heat of the water. The sun has sunk below the horizon but it isn't dark yet, and the sight of her Master's handsome face framed by the beauty of his yard at twilight is all she can possibly ask of life as she takes another inspiring sip of chardonnay. Every relaxing moment she spends with him is promisingly pregnant with all the sensual feasts they will share in every sense.

'I'm so glad you're here,' he tells her quietly. 'You make me very happy, Mira.'

The deep, penetrating look in his eyes is the very heart of the universe for her; everything lives in and for him. His awareness, his soul is the reason she was born and took form and developed a visual cortex so her being could gaze into his like this. Together they are the reason for everything mysteriously delivered in an envelope of flesh, and the closer they become, the more they open up to each other, the more every day and every night feels like a love letter written in blood from the heart of the cosmos. 'Do you believe in the soul, Phillip?'

'You know I do, Mira.'

'I just can't imagine dying and never seeing you again...'

'Then don't imagine it.'

She smiles, sadness and happiness battling in her pulse. 'Yes, Master.'

'I've had certain... experiences that can only be explained by the possibility that I've lived before,' he confesses.

'Really? Such as?'

'I'll tell you about them some other time, not tonight. Suffice it to say that I definitely believe there's such a thing as a soul that survives the death of the body.'

As if in response to his assertion of immortality two black streaks soar erratically over their heads. 'Oh, look, bats!' she exclaims happily. It is much darker now; the leaves of the trees are almost indistinguishable from the sky, and soon only the porch's halo of light will reveal individual flowers and bushes. Mira took it upon herself to light all the gas lamps so the night would not swallow them up as they sat in the hot tub. A powerful jet of water is massaging her lower back, and she lifts her right foot in search of some aquatic reflexology, all the time holding her glass of chardonnay above the frothing water. 'Mm…' The hard bubbles beating against the sole of her foot somehow help relax her entire body. 'I understand now why Chinese concubines were treated to foot rubs with little circular mallets,' she muses out loud, 'but only on the night their lord had chosen to spend with them as a reward for being in his favor.'

'Tell me more.' He sounds intrigued.

'I don't know much more really, I've never particularly cared for the Chinese culture; I much prefer the Japanese and the Hindus.'

'Oh, yes, Tantric sex… that's something else we should explore in the future, not anytime soon, though; we're not ready for that yet.'

'It's wonderful having things to look forward to, isn't it?' She sets her glass down on the tub's wooden platform in favor of sinking even lower into the hot foam and subjecting her other foot to a jet's teasingly inconsistent massage. 'I could never be just another concubine,' she continues thinking out loud, something she can do with her Master she was never really able to do with anyone else. 'I could never share your love and attention with other women, but then love has had very little to do with marriage throughout most of history.' She glances at him uncertainly, regretting her use of the word 'marriage' afraid he might take it personally. They have known each other less than three months; it is definitely too soon to even discuss such a possibility.

'I understand you couldn't share my love with other women,' he says, and pauses to drain his glass, 'but what about occasionally sharing my body?'

'That's different,' she replies, too busy riding a wave of relief that he didn't even blink at her Freudian slip to think about it. 'In ancient Egypt there was only one wife and all the other women in the household were either servants or concubines... not that I would like that either; I wouldn't want other women around all the time.'

'That's perfectly understandable, and there never will be, but I'm very proud of you for grasping the difference between loving someone and fucking them.'

'When we first met, I was very jealous of the women you dominate, but I'm not anymore, not like I used to be, anyway. I know they don't mean anything to you, not like I do.' She sits up and reaches for her wine again. 'But are you saying that sex and love have nothing to do with each other?' The darkness around them suddenly feels threatening rather than promising.

'Not at all, when you have sex with the person you love, you're making love, not just fucking.'

'Then why was the Chief Wife in ancient Egypt not allowed the same sexual freedom as her husband?' she demands, centuries of oppression fueling her retort.

'Because he had to make sure those were his babies she was breeding, not some other man's. It had everything to do with preserving the bloodline and the political power that went with it. In the ancient Egypt of the future, things will be different.'

She laughs. 'I like that, an ancient Egypt of the future... it would be a wonderful place to live.'

'And we've already begun laying the foundations for such a sensually enlightened society, my beautiful slave.'

'But it would also have to be an intensely spiritual society,' she points out, shying away from the glorification of superficial hedonism. 'And I'm not talking institutionalized religion here.'

'Mira,' he sets his empty glass down on the tub's wooden lip, 'to be enlightened implies a certain depth of mind and spirit. When I say "sensually enlightened" I'm not talking about the

Playboy castle, I'm talking about integrating all aspects of our being, which is a sacred art and the only true pleasure to be had in life as we know it.'

She carefully discards her own glass again, and wades across the waves into his arms. 'You are the smartest, wisest man I have ever met, Master.' She plants her lips against his. They taste better to her everyday as a result of all the fascinating thoughts and concepts he expresses with them, and tonight they're slick from being kissed by hot foam as well as tartly sweet from the chardonnay. She loses herself in his mouth for timeless moments, playing contentedly with his tongue, and then wrestling with it more urgently as she feels his penis hardening between her thighs.

She pulls back. 'Do you love me, Master?'

'You know I do, Mira.' Beneath the water his hands wrap her legs fully around his hips. 'I love you more than anything,' he adds intently, positioning the swollen head of his cock at the entrance to her flesh. 'You're the most important thing in the world to me, never forget it.'

'But what about when I'm old and ugly?' she asks breathlessly as his hard-on slips into her cunt and fills her up as only he can.

'You'll never be ugly!' he says through his teeth, jamming his cock even deeper into her pussy and leaving no room inside her for doubts.

'But I'll be old,' she insists, 'and how can I be a beautiful sex slave when I'm old?' She knows she is being perversely needy and begging for his reassurance, but she doesn't care; she needs him more than anything and she is afraid her growing happiness will be cruelly cut down one day for some reason or other.

'We'll both be old,' he points out, 'and you'll be even more beautiful in my eyes than ever, and I'll still be your Master and the love of your life, won't I.' His fingers gripping her ass are silent, indelible statements she has no desire to argue with as he holds her down around his erection and thrusts urgently up beneath her. 'For a deep and intelligent woman, you can be very silly sometimes, Mira. How can you possibly think that our love will dim with time?'

'I didn't say that,' she moans as his hands now clutch her hips and force her pussy up and down his rigid length.

'Yes, you did say that.'

'Oh, God, no, I didn't!' she cries, holding on to his slick shoulders. She resents the rushing heat of the water that does not allow her to fully feel him, and the chemically-treated foam is competing with her vagina's natural juices and winning. Their genitals are completely underwater yet his greedy shaft has to ram past her dry opening into the moist interior.

'Are you arguing with your Master?' he demands.

'No, Master, I'm sorry...'

'What's wrong?' He studies her face. 'Don't you like having my cock inside you?'

'I love your cock inside me, Master, but... it doesn't feel as good in here.'

He slides her tight hole off his dick. 'Come on.' He takes her hand, and side-by-side they climb the steps out of the hot tub.

The porch is a dry golden haven of gas lamps and candle light and a large wicker couch covered with water-proof cushions. He seats himself, and she knows he wants her to keep riding him, but she isn't yet wet enough on the inside.

'May I touch myself, Master?' she asks, standing before him.

'Yes, you may,' he replies.

She shivers. The night feels even colder than it really is to her flushed skin, but the tremor that courses down her spine has much more to do with the look in his eyes and with the sight of his hands cradling his generous balls and stroking his ideal erection as he looks at her. She doesn't feel at all shy tonight. With her hair half dry and half wet, black tendrils clinging snake-like to her taut breasts, light-jeweled drops of water caressing her body all the slow way down her belly and legs, the candle light gilding her smooth skin to a flawless, ageless perfection, she feels timelessly beautiful as she crushes her clit beneath her fingertips and firmly coaxes her pussy into juicing. Her clit is another wick coming to warm life on the porch and igniting that sweet, greedy tension in her pelvis which can so easily lead to the devastating conflagration of a climax. In a matter of seconds, she is ready for him. She straddles him, her knees sinking into the cushions on either side of him, and takes possession of his erection to guide it slowly inside her. She wants to savor the experience of his hard-on's demanding dimensions opening her up, and she also wants him to watch his cock parting the folds of her labia and slowly disappearing into her warm, embracing slot. Only when his penis is packed inside her to the hilt does she brace herself on his shoulders – as straight and broad as any pharaoh's – and begin massaging his cock with her pussy muscles as she rides him, working her cunt swiftly up and down around him.

'Keep touching yourself,' he commands.

She moans, only interested in pleasing him at the moment.

'I told you to touch yourself, Mira.'

She obeys of course, and forgets her reluctance, wondering why she ever felt it in the first place as her fingertips work her clitoris like the magic button of her sensual wiring. Her hips selfishly orbit the climax building inside her, his rampant penis the motionless center of the beautiful storm in her nerve-endings.

'That's it, make yourself come,' he urges quietly, caressing her breasts and gently pinching her nipples.

Up until that moment she was concentrating on the pulsing wick of a candle burning in a bronze lamp hanging from the ceiling, but now she looks down into his eyes, and ecstasy mysteriously unravels her from the inside out as she sees all the flames reflected back at her in his penetratingly dark irises.

'Mm,' he says after she finally descends from the blindingly beautiful realm of her orgasm. 'Get up.'

She is literally weak in the knees, the warm glow in her sex relaxing all her other muscles so that it takes her longer than it normally would to lift herself off him, stand up, and then position herself on her hands and knees on the cushions. He kneels behind her, and she tosses her head as he penetrates her, flinging her hair across her back so he can grab its mane as he swiftly rides her to his own pounding climax.

'Mreow!' Sekhmet materializes from the shadows. She assumes the statuesque pose of her namesake and stares up at the two naked human bodies pretending to be cats with eyes the same burning yellow of the flames illuminating her like a sacred icon.

Mira returns her stare, not sure if her feline's eyes are blazing with jealousy or cold with contempt or if her regard is, somehow, fiercely approving. She sits down beside her Master on the couch and rests her head on his chest, cuddling up against him for warmth as they both gaze back at the cat.

'Well, Sekhmet,' he says, 'do you and your brother approve of your soon-to-be new territory?'

She turns her head.

Stormy slinks out from the cover of another shadow and rubs his purring body up against his sister's.

She hisses and swats him with her paw, but her claws are sheathed, betraying her secret fondness for him.

He removes himself to a safer distance and begins licking his penis, his hind leg thrust comically straight up into the air.

'They love it,' Mira translates. 'I'm getting cold. May we go inside, Master?'

'Yes, we may.'

'I'll get the wine glasses.'

'No, just leave them. I have plenty more, and there's still some wine left in yours that will serve as an offering.'

'As an offering to what?' she asks, intrigued.

He shrugs as they get up. 'Whatever's out there... there are unseen forces all around us, Mira, best to keep them on our side.'

'Yes!' she agrees, and walks gratefully into the warmer embrace of the house as he opens the screen door for her. 'Dinner should be ready soon. May I put something on to serve, Master?'

'Yes, I suppose you may. It's getting chilly and I'd like to eat outside, if that's all right with you. We'll be cooped up inside long enough during the winter.'

'I love eating outside.'

'Mm... and I love eating you.' He pulls her into his arms and kisses her. 'But I suppose that will have to wait until later.' He lets go of her just as abruptly. 'I don't want you burning our dinner.'

She follows him upstairs. The climb to his tower bedroom never fails to leave her a bit winded, and she wonders if she'll ever get used to it. He heads for the shower to rinse off, but she contents herself with the soft hug of a large Egyptian cotton towel before slipping into a pair of black cotton house pants, and a violet shirt with long sleeves that end in tulip-like ruffles that cover her upper hands Medieval-style. And because he has given her permission to wear clothing, it means she does not have to wear high-heels while moving about in the kitchen and carrying a heavy tray out onto the porch. Soft black 'ballet' slippers are just what her feet need to hurry back down the tower stairs, at the bottom of which Stormy and Sekhmet both greet her vociferously.

'Yes, yes, I know, it's past your dinner time,' she apologizes happily. 'But don't worry, I brought your bowls and your favorite canned tuna.' Her devoted (hungry) entourage follows her into the kitchen, which still takes her breath away with its utterly efficient beauty. She knows where everything is already, and has not quite gotten over marveling at a straight man with such excellent taste in plates and stemware. The stainless steel side-by-side refrigerator was going sadly to waste before she came along, but now its clean white plastic bowls are at least modestly filled with food. Once she and her Master live together, and she is not dividing groceries between their two homes, this dream refrigerator will be bursting with cheeses and condiments and fruits and vegetables and meats and everything else needed for a sensually enlightened existence, which naturally includes regular orgasms of the taste buds by way of excellent nutrition.

She takes the roast out of the oven, and thrusts the metal tip of an electronic meat thermometer into the thickest part of the filet, watching anxiously as the temperature on the display escalates. She sincerely hopes she did not overdo it, but sometimes it's hard balancing gourmet cooking with great sex, a demanding task she is more than happy to live with.

'Meow! Meow! Meow!' Sekhmet is letting her know *she* is always supposed to come first.

'I'm coming!' The temperature of the roast is perfect. She tents it loosely beneath tinfoil so it will finish cooking while releasing more of its delicious internal juices. 'Okay.' She quickly opens two cans of tuna, and quickly dishes the feast out into two separate bowls. 'See, it's just like we're at home,' she says, and as she straightens up from feeding her cats, Mira realizes it's true, they are at home, in her Master's castle, and as long as they live she'll never feel that cold, paralyzing loneliness in her soul again. 'You have no idea how lucky we are, babies,' she says, but her words fall on ears deafened by the greedy smacking of the jaws beneath them.

She has just finished loading the large wicker tray with plates, napkins, glasses, forks and steak knives when her Master enters the kitchen, as usual looking intensely sexy even though he's very casually dressed in black slippers, black sweat pants and a black sweatshirt. He steps up behind her and slips his arms around her waist as she lifts the foil off the filet mignon.

'Mm!' He buries his face in her damp hair. 'That looks fabulous.'

'Thank you, Master, but timing is critical here; I really need to serve this right away.'

'Which means I'd better hurry down to the cellar for a bottle of wine.'

'Yes, and please hurry, Master. I'll meet you out on the porch.'

'Want to just have one of mom and dad's bottles tonight?'

'Sure, that would be great. I love your parents' wine.'

'And they'll love you, my slave. I've already told them I'm getting married.'

She nearly drops the tray.

'Not any time soon, mind you, I want to get my PhD first, and continue your training before we take that conventional step, but it *will* happen Mira, you know that, and when the time comes, I'll ask you properly.'

They both stand perfectly still gazing at each other while she holds the tray up between them like an offering, and the longer they just stand there lost in each other's eyes, the more the silver and the crystal and the fine fabric placemats and napkins begin to feel like symbols of everything they can possibly desire together. There are only two words she needs to speak, only two words she needs to utter to express everything she has always believed deep in her soul and everything she is daring to feel, only two words which say it all and which no one can prove untrue in the universe that is all theirs, 'Yes, Master.'

EPILOGUE

"...So they divided the apple of life, and ate it together; and their hearts were filled with love, and they lived in undisturbed happiness to a great age..."

Mira steps out of the elevator and walks slowly down the carpeted corridor. She reads the numbers on the walls as she walks and soon comes upon the door she is looking for. The sign reads *The Teal Center For Therapeutic Bodywork, Ltd.* She steps into the elegantly appointed, expensively hushed office. A handful of wooden chairs with comfortable flower-embroidered white cushions are mostly empty, except for one occupied by a tired-looking older woman who glances listlessly up at Mira as she enters. Another quick overview reveals an astonishing assortment of health-related magazines, from New Age aura therapy to the latest in mostly incomprehensible medical journals. The nicest thing about the suite is all the live healthy plants that are somehow thriving despite the absolute lack of sunshine; there are no windows to the outside world in the waiting room.

Mira walks over to the reception desk and gazes sedately down at the young man sitting behind it. 'I have a two-thirty appointment with Heather,' she says.

He checks a roster. 'Mira Rosemond?'

'That's me.'

'Have a seat, please. Oh, wait, is this your first time here?'

'Yes, it is.'

'Then you'll have to fill out these forms, please.' He hands are a clipboard with several sheets of paper trapped beneath it.

Mira reluctantly accepts them, and seats herself beside a lily plant in bloom. It is a pleasant exercise to be able to check 'No' in all the boxes pertaining to problems with her health. It is also somewhat depressing to realize just how much can go wrong with the human body. Fortunately, despite all the demands upon her flesh lately, she appears to be the picture of health. Finally, she comes to the bottom of the forms and the question, *What is the reason for your visit?* She glances at the bored young man behind the desk, and decides to be honest, imagining the truth will light a fire beneath his complacent ass. A secret little smile on her lips, she begins writing, cramming as much as she can into the limited space provided:

Six months ago I met a man who introduced me to the world of BDSM, and since then I've had more passionate sex than I ever thought a human being could handle without doing internal damage. We have sex at least once, sometimes two, three (and on occasion four) times in twenty-four hours, and I'm very often bound in intensely pleasurable but also severely demanding positions. I'm using all my muscles like never before, and sometimes, especially after a long suspension, I'm a bit stiff in places for days. I mentioned this to my Master, and he agreed to regularly pay for me to have a fully body massage as a reward for all my hard sensual work.

Farther up on the page, where she was asked what type of massage she desired, Mira opted for a deep penetrating massage during the first hour of the session, followed by a spa-like, relaxing massage and a bit of Reflexology during the last thirty minutes.

Satisfied with her responses, she returns the clipboard to the young man with a smile. Then she sits down again and begins flipping through one of the expensive glossy magazines, searching for any valuable information on how she can take better care of herself physically. She is confident that she has the emotional, sexual, spiritual, creative, relaxing, etc. etc. sides of her life pretty well covered thanks to Master Phillip. It annoys her how old, commonsense truths have been rehashed to sound like cutting-edge revelations, for example, *Broccoli is good for you* takes up an entire page. It seems a bit too much information for readers who, as a general rule, can't do the simplest of equations – a low-carb diet + a high fat diet = a low fiber diet, and yet a diet high in fiber is absolutely essential to maintaining health and longevity. Apparently, many people believe looking good for a brief period of time is more important than feeling good for a long time. And yet being lazy and simple-minded inevitably backfires, because unless you're healthy and feel good you can't look good, not for long. Despite all the beauty secrets and health tips promised in the table of contents, Mira learns absolutely nothing new; there are no revelations in this magazine owned by a disembodied corporation.

'Mira?'

She looks up into the face of a pretty, smiling young woman.

'That's me.' She smiles back.

'Please come this way.'

Mira gladly discards the glossy magazine in favor of following the surprisingly petite massage therapist to her 'office'. Heather closes the door behind them and stands with her back to it as Mira takes in the small, dimly lit room dominated by a very comfortable looking bench covered with a clean white sheet and a crisp, thick outer blanket. A CD player in the corner is playing soft New Age music at an almost subliminal volume, and on the opposite wall a large poster of the human muscular system dominates the very deliberately soothing space. Heather is reading her new client's chart. Mira seats herself in the only available chair and waits, doing her best not to regret her rather boastful honesty.

Heather is a true professional; she could not have appeared less affected by her client's grocery list. They are soon agreed as to the type of massage Mira desires, and she is left alone in the room to strip off all her clothing except for her panties, which she had to ask her Master permission to wear today. She must admit, she has not been a very good slave when it comes to asking him for permission to cover her labial lips when she is going out alone in public. Perhaps because punishment for this small transgression (which is still a major flow in her character because it involves disobeying him) is so enjoyable she does not feel compelled to be more disciplined concerning her obedience of this particular rule. She has taken to being spanked like a fish to water. Six months seems to be a long time, but the beautiful and utterly compliant sex slave inside her is obviously still in the early stages of gestation.

She makes herself comfortable on the small bed-table as instructed, spreading herself out on her belly with the soft, heavy sheets covering her back. Heather returns soon afterwards, and for a full ninety minutes is silently efficient. Mira is grateful conversation is not expected from her. How such a delicate-boned woman can have such strong hands and powerful arms is beyond her; nevertheless, she is grateful she did not have to go to a man to get penetrating muscular therapy, because one of the best things about the experience is the fact that there's nothing sexual about it, enabling her to fully relax. In retrospect, the only complaint she has is that her much abused ass was left out of the excruciatingly pleasurable experience. Other than that, she is blissfully happy with her ninety minutes of sex slave maintenance. Ever since she met her Master, her body seems to be populated with many more muscles than she ever knew were there. More than once she squirms against the cushion in delicious agony as the other woman's rigid fingers grind one of her sore muscles into her bone, remorselessly working the tension out of it. Mira loves suspension – she loves being both helpless and weightless as her Master fucks her from what ever direction he desires, lunging up into her cunt with all the force of his lust – but she didn't realize what a workout the latex straps are on her inner thighs until Heather's fingertips began expertly kneading the muscles all around her pussy, and they wordlessly let her know just how well used they've been lately.

An hour-and-a-half sounds like a long time, but in reality it is much too soon when Heather gently sets down the foot through which she was transporting Mira into paradise, covers it with the cool sheets, and says, 'Come out whenever you're ready.'

Mira has no desire to move, but she knows that 'Come out whenever you're ready' means 'Get dressed, pay, and leave because I have another client waiting' so she does what is expected of her and gets up. She dresses slowly; no one can force her to rush. Phillip has expanded her horizons as she had scarcely imagined possible in large and small ways that all have a profoundly positive effect on her well-being. She has dreamed of a full body massage like this for years, yet she could never justify the expense on what the infamous 'they' inside her brain deemed an unnecessary luxury. Phillip did not see it that way at all when she brought it up. In his remarkable mind, pleasure is a necessity; a very important part of caring for her and making her as happy as she makes him with her beauty in every sense. And the beauty of her body and soul belongs completely to him, its mysterious purpose being his pleasure and fulfillment, which brings her full circle back to the massage she just enjoyed so much, and to a feeling of contentment within the envelope of her flesh that deepens with every passing day.

Heather meets her out in the waiting room and offers her a small paper cup of cold bottled water. 'How do you feel?' she asks, as if she didn't know.

'Are you kidding? That was wonderful, thank you. I'll be seeing you again very soon, I hope.'

Mira feels as though her bones have been replaced by a bird's more ethereal skeleton as she walks down Fairfax Drive towards the Metro. Her feelings are light as feathers cushioning her thoughts and her imagination is ready to take off in countless wondrous directions. She scarcely notices the train ride, and then her car greets her in the parking lot like an old friend embracing her blissfully relaxed muscles as she slips inside.

It is after five o'clock when she walks through the kitchen door. Stormy and Sekhmet are waiting for her next to their food bowls. The gray cat immediately leaps up to greet Mira, but even though she remains were she is, regally sprawled across the tile floor, Sekhmet at least refrains from yowling peremptorily for her dinner. She has mellowed considerably since Master Phillip became a regular visitor, and Mira jokes that he is training two pussies at once.

Since she was given a special treat this afternoon her furry babies deserve one too. She opens a can of lump crab meat to Sekhmet's vocal ecstasy and Stormy's silent appreciation. She is so relaxed after her full body massage that even the sight of all the boxes stacked around her doll's house fails to depress her. Ramon and some of his friends (relatives?) will be here first thing in the morning tomorrow to help her move. Unfortunately, they can't just cut through the forest but have to drive around the long way to Phillip's house. She is not letting herself think about how much she will miss her doll's house and her garden; it would be as ridiculous as a butterfly missing the cocoon where it waited safely for its transformation into a fulfilled creature after so long spent dreaming of the life it was meant to embody. Ramon has already moved her stone vases filled with violet petunias to her new, and even bigger, garden, which he will be tending from now on. She will miss the individual trees she has grown personally fond of, but since she was fortunate enough to be able to sell her doll's house to a botanist and horticulturalist she is not worried about the fate of her oaks and maples. Her belief in Choreography versus coincidence has gone from an intimate *pas de deux* to a veritable chorus line of events. All the complex steps of coming together as one are working out so smoothly for her and her Master that the odds of it all being pure chance defy reason. She could never have known the tapestry which had been figuratively gathering dust in her environmentally controlled garage would fit perfectly on the wall over his bed. All her beloved possessions have found the stage on which they can come alive again through the powerful drama of her intense and unconditional love for the leading man who at last, miraculously, walked into her life. The black-haired doll whose red lips he caressed with his thumb the morning they met also has a place of honor in their bedchamber, and whenever Mira looks at her, time ceases to exist... She is back in her garage with a stranger dressed all in black walking towards her and giving her a command that changed her life forever, because she obeyed him.

FOOTNOTE:

Unless otherwise indicated, all the quotes at the beginning of each chapter are from *Grimm's Fairy Tales*.